The Book of Kindly Deaths

Eldritch Black

**SPENCER HILL
MIDDLE GRADE**

Spencer Hill Middle Grade

Contact: Spencer Hill Press, PO Box 247, Contoocook, NH 03229, USA

Please visit our website at
www.spencerhillmiddlegrade.com

First Edition: September 2014
Black, Eldritch
The Book Of Kindly Deaths : a novel / by Eldritch Black - 1st ed.
p. cm.

Summary: Upon discovering a mysterious book holding her family's dark secrets, a twelve-year-old girl is forced from the modern world into a land of shadowy nightmares.

The author acknowledges the copyrighted or trademarked status and trademark owners of the following wordmarks mentioned in this fiction: Mary Poppins, Zippo

Cover design by Lisa Amowitz
Interior layout by Jennifer Carson

ISBN: 978-1-939392-95-4 paperback
ISBN: 978-1-939392-96-1 e-book

Printed in the United States of America

For Lora, Mum, Gaye, and Nanna for your support,
belief, and guidance, with much love.

CHAPTER ONE

Awakening

On a desk in the room with the stained glass window sat a book.

It was a thick volume with a worn and cracked black cover showing a gold symbol, a rectangle within two circles that sparkled and flickered as if teased by ghostly fingers. Voices whispered from inside the book, growing in volume, a few human, a few not. As their distant howls and cries grew, the book rocked with such force that it flew into the air and hovered.

When it thumped back onto the desk, the thick fountain pen next to it leapt into the air like a small brass salmon. As it clattered down upon the desk, a spark shot from the pen's nib, playing over the book and sending its pages flying open.

One by one, the pages flipped, faster and faster, an animated blur of neat blue writing seeming to jump with the book as its dusty pages turned.

Beyond the room with the book and the stained glass window, the room that had no business being there, the dark, sprawling house was silent.

Like a cat, tensed and still and waiting for its prey to make a move.

The man in the old-fashioned suit awoke. He took a deep breath and filled his lungs, his eyes wide with the exertion.

The man stood, muttering at the dull ache in his borrowed joints. He had no idea how long he'd lain on the cave floor. How many days and nights had passed in that black and dreamless sleep? He glanced down at his clothes, fussily wiping spots of mildew from his cuff with long, thin fingers.

All he knew, as he scrubbed, was that he felt a terrible yearning for the book. And that it had fallen from his grasp many, many moons ago.

The man began to walk, taking large strides, stretching the ache from his long legs as he went. At the cave's entrance, the remains of its original occupant stared lifelessly, its large, curved teeth yellowed in its broken skull.

He kicked the bones as he passed. Whatever creature they'd belonged to hadn't dared confront him, not even in his deep, dreamless sleep.

Beyond the cave, a small graveyard. More bones.

One of the graves stood empty, a smashed coffin lid beside a dark hole. The grave where he'd found his new body. The man's flesh was still weaving itself together as he raised his mottled hand, shielding his eyes from the soft, insipid daylight.

The man climbed the hill above the cave, and the farther he got, the more treacherous the ground became. He began to slide and slip, throwing out his hands and grasping at tufts of brown grass. He splayed his fingers, remembering how strong his previous incarnation had been, allowing the memory to give him the strength he needed to continue.

Eventually, he made it to the summit and looked out over a body of cloud-gray water. Far in the distance, a string of twinkling lights strewn across the horizon drew his eye to the mainland.

He shook his head, fighting to control his voice. It was a struggle to speak and would be until the body he'd dug up was fully his to occupy. "When...I?" he asked, the words ragged and guttural. He tried to swallow. "When... am...I?" He pointed a pale white finger toward the coast. "Whenever...am. I...been tricked."

Eliza Winter stood in her grandfather's garden for the first time in six years.

Flowers towered above her, the few petals left on their stems curled, dead and withered. She stamped her feet against the chilly January day while her parents fussed around the car, removing bedding, blankets, and backpacks.

Eliza would have offered to help, but as she spotted the agitation on her mother's face, she thought better of it. She gazed along the path, at the tufts of grass glittering with frost, remembering how her grandparents, Tom and Susan, had always kept the garden so pristinely tidy. Eliza wondered what they'd make of it if they could see its state now.

She glanced up at the wide, sullen sky with sadness as she thought of the people who had lived here. The people she'd barely known.

The house reared before her, taller and darker than the other houses on the street. As her eyes fell upon the small tower jutting from the side of its sloping roof, Eliza recalled standing in its room as sunbeams filtered through all four windows. A stark contrast to this drab and bitter winter's day.

Eliza looked past the tower to the chimneys, tall stacks of dark-red bricks, wondering when smoke had last risen from them.

Three months? Three years?

Her mum had only told Eliza of her grandfather's disappearance a few days ago. And while no one knew exactly how long Tom had been missing, Eliza got the feeling her parents weren't expecting to see him again.

"Miss Winter!" She jumped at her father's voice. He grinned, balancing a large bag on his head and swaying across the pavement like a clown. Behind him, her mother threw worried glances at the neighbors' windows.

"Miss Winter," her father repeated as he tossed her a ring of keys. "Open up, would you? And get the kettle on. Before we die of thirst and hypothermia."

Eliza forced a smile and walked through the garden. As she neared the house, she glanced at its windows and was relieved to find them empty.

The man in the well-tailored suit hiked down the hill, a grim sense of purpose in his crane-like strides. His eyes were set on those distant lights, an unpleasant sneer playing over his thin, cracked lips.

A cliff yawned below him, and again he let the memory of his old body fill this new, borrowed vessel. It may have been a worn old thing, he thought as he looked at the bones he'd stitched together, but it would suit this world. He slithered over the edge of the cliff and wove his way down the rocks like a spider, his gnarled fingers grasping the crevices and cracks. Eventually he stood on a shore, the sea breaking over the dark-green pebbles and rocks at his feet.

The man in the old-fashioned suit took a deep breath, fixed his eyes on the coast across the sea, and stepped into the icy waters.

Eliza walked up the steps leading to the tall, red front door; as it loomed before her, she did her best to ignore the knocker.

It was just as she remembered it. Just as ugly and just as strange. A vile brass gargoyle with a malevolent grin. Eliza tutted, glancing into its mocking eyes. "It's just a door knocker."

But still her hands trembled as she lifted the key.

"Come on, you're twelve years old, not six!" she chided herself.

The phantom of a forgotten memory crossed her mind. A ghost of an event that had occurred the last time she was at this house. Although the recollection was fleeting, she still felt an icy sting of dread.

In the distance, her parents' voices jarred her, her mother's irritation slicing through Eliza's thoughts, lending her the strength and certainty to reach up and unlock the door.

The book on the desk leaped and flipped, and the stained glass window above the desk shuddered as a strange, pungent breeze wafted through the tiny cracks in its ancient glass.

Far below, in the house, beyond the hidden room, a lock turned.

As the front door opened, the book crashed back down upon the desk, its cover shut, its pages silent.

CHAPTER TWO

The Collector Calls

*D*espite being in her grandfather's house for two days, Eliza had explored very little of it. The place made her feel restless and uncomfortable. It was strange and utterly creepy, unlike her own home with its bright magnolia walls and the tang of bleach and order. Where everything was in its right place.

But as dark, cold, and dusty as Tom's house was, at least it felt *lived* in.

As Eliza browsed through the bookshelves she recalled her mother's specific instructions. *"Leave the books alone, they're just twaddle and silly imaginings. There's nothing here for normal people."*

Eliza didn't question her mother's advice; she'd learned well over the years that curiosity and questioning led to punishment. And the punishment, more often than not, was a lengthy spell indoors. Which was pretty much the last place Eliza wanted to be.

But as she peered at the bookshelves while her parents worked outside, Eliza felt a temptation to pick up one of the books, to find out exactly what it was that her grandfather read and collected. Instead, she sat once more before the roaring fire her father had made and picked up the book her mother had approved for her.

From outside came the sound of her father shouting. Eliza smirked as she pictured her parents cataloguing the garden shed, their fear of clutter matched only by their terror of spiders. She imagined a great furry beast running up her father's arm and up into his hair and smiled. She slumped back into the sprawling chair, which was as old-fashioned as everything else in the house, another relic from a bygone age.

An empty seat sat next to Eliza's, and she pictured her grandparents occupying them, wondering what they might have spoken about in the evenings as they sat before the fire. Two strange people in their strange house, cut off from their family.

A painting sprawled above the fireplace, and there was something about it that left Eliza feeling quite unsettled, although she couldn't say exactly what it was. It showed a large black tower looming above a city, a sea of distant rooftops below. And although there was nothing remarkable about the tower or the houses, something about the buildings didn't feel right. It was as if they existed somewhere, but not in this world. Which was, of course, utterly ridiculous, and yet a part of her was sure it was true.

Eliza looked away, taking her focus back to the fire and away from the dark city.

Moments later, she jolted in her seat as two loud knocks filled the house. Eliza stood and glanced through the window into the garden, but her parents were out of sight and presumably still in the shed. Two more knocks cracked the air, and now Eliza could see an image of that repulsive brass gargoyle crashing against the door.

"Who in their right mind would touch that thing?" she whispered. As she reached the front door, Eliza gazed at her hands, wondering why they were trembling so badly.

The first thing she noticed about the man at the door was his height. He seemed almost too tall. This consideration was followed by a series of other observations that struck her like blows. *He's a locust*, she thought. *A human locust in a suit.*

She stepped back as a powerfully irrational fear swept over her, that at any moment he would leap at her like a grasshopper and devour her until all was darkness.

Eliza looked up at the top hat crowning the strands of white hair that bisected his long, narrow face. Why was he wearing a top hat? Was it a costume? Was he a charity collector?

No, he was no collector for charities. There was no warmth in those narrow, bloodshot eyes. They were so red she couldn't tell their color within the weave of broken blood vessels. His eyes were set into an elongated, yellow-white face, his paper-thin flesh stretched tautly over his skull like an old drum skin.

He grinned, revealing a mouth full of monstrous yellow teeth, and coughed into his gloved hand, looking as if he might be about to say something but had accidentally swallowed his words.

"Can I help you?" Eliza asked, despite her better instincts, which were screaming at her to slam the door in his face. She could smell the sea, salty water, rotten fish, and seaweed. Perhaps it was coming from his dark, moldy suit.

The man nodded briskly, tottering forward, and coughed out his reply. "Mr. Eustace…Fallow. Book Collector."

"Oh," Eliza replied. His name didn't seem as if it could be real. "Look, *we're* really busy today."

"I…look for the book." Mr. Fallow extended his hand for her to shake, his gloved fingers as thin as pencils. He reached forward with surprising speed and snatched her hand, shaking it furiously as he gave an awkward bow. "You fetch the book now. Yes."

Eliza tore her hand free, stepping back into the house. "There aren't any books here. Look, I have to go."

He shuffled after her, his glove splayed on the doorframe like a spider. "Just one book. Black cover, gold symbol…a closed door inside two circles. Make you rich." He delved into his jacket pocket and produced a pouch, which he shook. It sounded like it contained pebbles as he promised, "Full of coins."

"Look," Eliza tried to close the door, "there's nothing for sale here. Go next door."

He pushed back on the door, his foot edging towards the threshold but shying away. "Need book. Then go."

"No. You're going now. And don't come back. Please." Eliza slammed the door with all her might, closing her eyes, expecting to hear the sound of snapping fingers.

But no sound came.

She opened her eyes.

The door stood where it should and beyond, an uneasy silence. Eliza bolted it and ducked into the next room, running towards the curtains, desperate to close them and block the world out. What had just happened?

Eliza peeked through a gap in the curtains and watched Mr. Eustace Fallow lope down the street. A smile played on his lips as he gazed ahead.

I can see you, that smile said. *I know you're there.*

Eliza snapped the curtains closed, cloaking the room in darkness. Behind her, the books seemed to move on their shelves, watching her, a silent audience. She fled to the living room where the fire still blazed, but it offered little comfort as Eliza gazed through the window into the garden, wondering what to do.

Should she tell her mother? Was it worth opening that Pandora's box?

No. No need.

She'd wait until her father was alone and tell him about Mr. Fallow. And even though he'd make a joke of it, he'd keep a watchful eye on the house and keep her story to himself. He knew how to tread on eggshells just as well as Eliza.

The grandfather clock in the hall struck the hour, and now Eliza felt an overwhelming urge to find her father. She grabbed the back door, wrenched it open, and crossed the garden, heading for the dark bulk of the shed. She stood at its door, watching her dad root through a pile of tools. He gingerly picked each one up as if expecting a spider to run up his arm. Behind, her mum stood with a notebook and poised pen. She glanced at Eliza. "What's wrong?"

"Nothing. I just thought I'd see how you're doing." Eliza smiled. "The house seemed a bit empty."

"We'll be back home in a couple of days," her dad said. "Provided we make it out of this shed without being eaten alive."

"You don't look well, Eliza." Her mum dropped the notebook on the workbench as her large brown eyes flitted over Eliza's face. "What's the matter?"

"Nothing. Honestly." Eliza laced her fingers behind her back, torn between standing before her mum's inspection and going back in the house. "I'm just tired. And bored."

"We'll eat soon. Your father's cooking tonight. So it will be bacon. Again."

"With a garnish of tomato-based sauce," her dad added, affecting a posh voice. "And an accompaniment of organic butter on a bed of wholegrain bread."

"Can't wait." Eliza forced another smile. She gazed at her father, ignoring her mum's searching eyes. "I'll go and put the oven on if you like."

"Maybe you could put some bacon on while you're there, and I'll put the finishing touch to the bread when I get in."

Eliza rolled her eyes, but as she turned, she froze. There, peering over the fence at the foot of the garden, was the book collector. "He's back!" Eliza heard herself say.

Mr. Fallow stood, staring across the garden, his face an off-white blur in the growing dusk.

"Who's back?" her mum asked.

"There's a man at the end of the garden." Eliza moved out of her mother's way to give her a clear view.

"There's no one there," her mother replied.

Eliza turned to look back. He was gone.

Her dad filed out of the shed. "Probably just a curious neighbor."

Eliza watched her parents walk through the long grass towards the foot of the garden. "Don't go down there!"

Eliza caught the look of irritation on her mother's face. And the question. There would be more questions to follow. Best to tell her now. Eliza clumped through the grass, soaking her feet and ankles as she pulled herself up, glancing over the fence.

The lane behind the houses was empty.

Mr. Eustace Fallow had vanished. No doubt vaulting away like a locust. Eliza checked the trees just in case he was perched in one like some gruesome bird.

"Is this the return of Casper Mustard?" her dad asked with a wry grin.

"Cornelius Mustard," Eliza corrected him. Cornelius Mustard had been her imaginary friend when she was younger. Before her mum drove him away and banned Eliza from the distractions of her imagination.

"Don't bring that nonsense up again," her mum said with a dark look. "So, who do you think you saw?"

Eliza took a deep breath and crossed her fingers, an old habit. "There was this man. He knocked at the door earlier."

"A man?" Her mum asked. "Why didn't you say? Who was he?"

"He said he was a book collector. He was a bit...odd. So I told him that there weren't any books and shut the door. I didn't think it was important."

"Carrion." Her dad shook his head. "Vultures circling 'round a dead man's house. They read the obituaries in the news, and it brings them out like worms."

"We don't know Tom's dead," Eliza said.

"He's not coming back," her mum replied quickly with a tone that was almost pleading. Eliza wondered, once again, just what her grandfather could have done to make his own daughter hate him so badly.

"Come." Her dad placed a hand on Eliza's shoulder as he smiled at her mum. "Let's finish up. I'm beat."

"Eliza, go back to the house," her mum said. "And if anyone else knocks on the door, don't open it. Come and find us first. We won't be much longer."

Eliza bit her tongue. She was nearly thirteen, not six. "Yes, Mum."

But as they trudged back towards the house, Eliza took one last look behind her.

There was no sign of Mr. Fallow.

Just a dark stretch of lane punctuated by deepening shadows.

CHAPTER THREE

Dark House

*E*liza gazed up at the dark house. Strands of ivy curled across empty windows and choked the old brick walls. She shivered. Why did she find the place so unsettling? It was just a house, after all, and it was not as if she believed in ghosts or anything. Her mum had made sure of that. But her mum's lessons on ignoring *nonsense* didn't stop the feelings she got from time to time that the world wasn't always as it *should* be. That sometimes there were things lurking at the edges of her vision that had no business being there.

Eliza opened the back door and stepped into the welcome blast of heat that swaddled the kitchen like a warm, invisible blanket.

She filled the kettle, placed it on the stove, and wondered if her grandparents had been aware of such things as electric kettles. Probably not. Their lives must have been so different from hers—Eliza growing up in a clean, sterile bubble, her grandparents stuck out here in a bygone era.

She examined the framed photograph over the oven, its glass speckled with globs of fat from the stove. It showed Tom and Susan dressed smartly, standing attentively before the camera, the sea and sky a washed-out blue behind them, its colors faded with time. Her grandparents looked so young, far younger than Eliza remembered them. As she considered it, she realized it had never crossed her mind that they had once been her age.

She took a cloth from the sink, soaked it, added a splash of dishwashing liquid, and cleaned the glass over the photograph, her mind wandering and returning to an old, unwelcome memory. It was a recollection she knew better than to encourage, and yet it had called to her since she'd set foot in the house.

Now, as she gazed at her grandparents, she let it unfold.

Six years ago, she'd sat in this very kitchen, with the same low table covered by the same red-and-white-checkered tablecloth. It had been a balmy June day, the bright blue skies darkening at the edges as the threat of a storm smudged the horizon.

It was the first time Eliza had stayed alone with her grandparents; indeed, she had only ever met them once before. Her mother had been recovering from appendicitis in hospital, her father abroad at some sort of dentists' convention. She still remembered her mother's concern as she'd complained that there was no one else for Eliza to stay with.

Her grandmother had been out that day, visiting her mum in hospital, leaving Tom and Eliza in the house.

Tom had decided they'd have pizza for breakfast, fish and chips for lunch, and a Chinese takeaway for dinner, and he'd been more excited than Eliza at the idea. They'd sat in the kitchen, a slight breeze blowing through the back door as they picked through their lunch. Eliza could still smell the vinegar covering Tom's chips, could still see the strange, clunky rings he wore on his fingers. She'd asked him what they were.

He'd told her they were magical.

Eliza had laughed, but when she'd looked up at him, expecting to see him smile, he'd looked quite serious. But before she could press him further, they'd both jumped, as a huge crash had come from above.

Tom's eyes had strayed to the ceiling as he'd muttered a strange word that Eliza had never heard before. Or since. He leaped up. "Stay here," he had commanded her as he'd run through the kitchen.

Eliza had stayed in her chair, listening to the din of his feet on the stairs, her heart thumping. And then she'd peered at the half-torn label on the vinegar bottle. She had stared and stared at that label, fighting the urge to get up and follow her grandfather.

Eventually, her curiosity had gotten the better of her and she'd found herself tiptoeing up the staircase. She'd made it halfway up when Tom had run from his bedroom, flying across the landing, a bulky rifle clenched in his hand. Thankfully, he'd been too intent on the hallway to notice her.

Eliza had frozen, her instincts crying out to return to the kitchen, but her curiosity had taken her up the stairs because she'd *needed* to see what had caused the commotion.

She had needed to understand, because somehow, even though she'd been only six, Eliza had known that some distant part of her future lay at the top of those stairs. That this might be her one and only chance to peek through the curtain her mother had drawn across her world.

Eliza's steps had been slow and precise as she'd walked along the hall, avoiding the places that would set off creaks. Ahead, she'd heard voices speaking, hushed, urgent, and angry.

They'd been coming from Tom's *library*, a large room that, like most of the rooms in the house, was lined with bookcases. But his library was larger than most and usually its door was locked. Eliza had peeked round the corner.

It had been empty.

Yet she had been able to still hear voices—her grandfather's, low and threatening, and another, which had been deeper than any voice should be. From time to time it had hissed, putting her in mind of a nest of snakes.

Slowly, Eliza had stepped into the room, checking the window and finding it closed. So where had the voices been coming from?

And then her eyes had been drawn to a slight gap between two bookcases, an edge of a door she'd never seen before.

A *secret* door.

Eliza remembered clutching her sleeves as she'd stepped towards the gap, as the voices had grown louder. More urgent, more threatening.

As she'd reached the door, something had flitted past, a tall, dark shape. It may have looked a little like a man, but she'd known it wasn't. No, whatever it had been, it hadn't been a man. Or a woman.

It hadn't even been human.

She'd wanted to scream and run back down the stairs and out of the door and away across the street. To keep running until the world made sense once more.

But she hadn't. She'd taken another step, her eyes wide and unblinking as they drank in every detail.

"Get back to the city!" Tom's voice. Different now. Deep with authority.

"No," the other had replied, its voice low. "I'm going to live *here*. It's so much *nicer*. Brighter."

"You shouldn't have come. You know the rules. Go back to where you belong, or so help me, I'll shoot you dead where you stand."

The other had paused and sniffed. "Ah, I smell a drearspawn child. So succulent."

"Get out!" Tom had cried, and Eliza had heard a click. "One more step towards my house, and I'll paint the walls with you. Get back. Now!"

The other voice had growled as something sliced through the air, followed by the sound of books tumbling to the ground.

Once again, she had thought of running. But she couldn't have left Tom, and she had known, instinctively, that somehow, this moment was important. That one day she'd be forced to face such things as whatever lurked beyond the door. *Better to face it now and understand what lay in store.*

So Eliza had pushed the door open and stepped into the room.

The figure had been larger than she'd first thought, so tall it had to stoop to avoid its scorched head touching the ceiling. Its scarlet face had stood in stark contrast to its sleek black suit. Its eyes had been wide and bright yellow, two tiny black balls at their centers. It had grinned at Eliza, revealing a mouth lined with tiny, curved teeth.

"Eliza! I told you to stay downstairs," Tom had said, his eyes unwavering from the line of his rifle, which was aimed at the creature's heart.

"*Eliza,*" the other had said. Her name had sounded revolting coming from its lips. "Good evening, Eliza."

"It's afternoon," she had replied and swallowed, hoping it hadn't noticed her shaking hands.

"Is it? I shall have to find out what an afternoon is, shan't I? Perhaps you can give me a tour of your world?"

"Eliza, look away," Tom had said as he bought the rifle up, aiming it at the creature's head.

Eliza hadn't looked away. The creature had stared back with a look of rapt concentration.

And then it had bowed to Eliza with a theatrical flourish, turned and leaped upon a desk, bending low and climbing through a huge stained glass window.

Eliza had stared at the window, drinking in the strange fragrances that had seemed to pour through it until Tom had crossed the room and slammed it shut. He'd shaken his head as he'd pushed her from the room. "It's all my fault. I'm sorry. I forgot the binds and seals. I'm not cut out for this anymore."

"Cut out for what?" Eliza had demanded.

Tom had leaned over, his large brown eyes staring into hers. "Eliza. Whatever you think you saw, you didn't." He'd placed a hand on her forehead. "You're getting a fever. You're hallucinating. And if we ever have a hope of seeing each other again, you must never mention this to your mother. Now, please, go downstairs."

Tom had followed her from the room, pulling the wall closed behind him until Eliza had found herself standing once more in a study lined with books.

And if it hadn't been for the rifle in his arms, she may have believed that she really was coming down with fever dreams.

Eliza looked away from the photograph of her grandparents and into the garden. The shed door was still ajar, torchlight playing over the ground as the sky darkened. Night was setting in. Soon her parents would be finished. She glanced at the ceiling, thinking of the hidden room and the creature that may or may not have passed through a stained glass window.

Had that really happened?

It couldn't have. Her mum spent most of her life telling Eliza there were no such things as monsters. The very idea was nonsense.

But if that was the case, why did she feel the need to repeat this to Eliza at every available opportunity? And why wasn't she allowed to watch or read anything imaginative? What was the problem, if these things were just made up?

Eliza looked back to the shed. Once her parents were finished out there, the inventory would nearly be complete and soon they'd pile into the car and she'd most likely never see the house again. Then she would be back in the suburbs, in their concrete and magnolia bubble, spending her days being micromanaged by her mother while her father fixed people's teeth.

She took the stairs two at a time, flicking on light switches as she went, dousing the house in a soft yellow light to drive out the shadows.

As she passed along the hall towards the library, Eliza's heart thumped. She told herself it was just exertion from the stairs, doing her best to ignore the whispers that seemed to issue from the empty rooms.

CHAPTER FOUR

The Hidden Room

*A*s she passed the tall, arched window opposite the study, Eliza stopped.

The winter sun set heavy and red, the road below empty but for a few dead leaves skittering across the pavement. Despite there being no sign of the so-called book collector, Eliza yanked the curtains closed.

She stood before the study door; her hand faltered on the doorknob. She took a deep breath, turned it, and pushed the door open, reaching for the light switch.

The room was exactly how she remembered, a soft off-white carpet and deep-red walls lined with bookcases. The books filled the air with a musty scent, their thick spines colored in somber tones. Eliza examined the corner where the secret door had been, scouring the wall for the tell-tale sign of a crack, but there was none.

She pulled the bookshelf. It didn't move.

She scoured the bookcase for a switch and, after a while, began to question her memory. Perhaps Tom had been right. Perhaps she really had been coming down with a fever. Perhaps the whole nightmarish memory had been a figment of her heated imagination.

Eliza stopped searching. If the door had ever existed, she couldn't find it. But as she was about to leave the room, something caught her gaze.

A black-covered book stood out among a set of tan-colored volumes. It wasn't the book's color that caught her eye, however, but the gold embossed symbol on its side.

A rectangle within two circles.

"A closed door inside two circles," Eliza said, repeating the book collector's description.

She pulled the book, producing a soft click and distant clatter of gears. As the hidden door appeared, Eliza froze, her excitement turning to dread. What would she find on the other side? Tom? Was this where his dead body was? Was that why he'd gone missing? Perhaps he'd fallen and bashed his head and died alone in his secret room, hidden from help.

For a moment she considered running downstairs and fetching her parents. Let them deal with it. But if she did, the room would be emptied, sealed, and she'd never see it again.

Eliza ignored her trembling hands, threw open the door, and stepped into the hidden room.

CHAPTER FIVE

The Book of Kindly Deaths

*T*he room was empty—no corpse upon the floor and no sign of her grandfather. She took another step.

It was just as she'd remembered, a small room with a large wooden desk and behind, a huge stained glass window. The image embedded in the colored glass showed a tower and moon and below, a sea of sloped roofs.

Just like the painting above the fireplace downstairs.

Eliza was about to examine the desk when her eyes were drawn back to the stained glass. It couldn't be. It was impossible!

Distant light somehow illuminated a shard of pale blue glass representing moonlight.

She leaned closer, blinking, trying to clear the illusion. But it was no illusion. Somehow a light flickered through the window.

But there couldn't be light through the window, for beyond it should be a solid wall.

Eliza reached for the window latch and tried to unlock it, feeling a surge of relief as she realized it was jammed shut. Because, somehow, she knew she didn't want to see what lay beyond. That this was the place monsters came from. Monsters like the one she'd seen all those years ago.

She turned to the desk below the window. It was empty but for an old book and pen. She picked up the pen and dropped it as a jolt, like a shock of static, ran through her fingers. "Ouch!" Eliza examined the pen in its thick brass casing where it now lay upon the desk. She placed a cautious finger upon it, waiting for another shock, but there was none. So she picked it up.

The pen was quite plain except for a tiny engraving of the door within two circles. As Eliza unscrewed the tip, peering at the nib, a drop of blue ink fell upon the desk.

She put the pen down and picked up the book.

It looked like a handmade journal with a thick black cover and the now-familiar symbol. Soft gold lettering spelled *The Book of Kindly Deaths* across its cover, and below the title, the name Edward Drabe.

"Drabe," Eliza whispered. Drabe was her mother's maiden name. And her grandfather's name.

Just as she was about to open the book, her mother's voice cut through the air. "Eliza?"

She jumped, her head spinning as she stuffed the book under her sweater and ran from the room, pulling the hidden door shut. Bolting through the adjoining study, she slipped the door closed and managed to make it halfway down the hall before her mother appeared on the landing. "Didn't you hear me?"

"No."

"I was calling you. You said you were going to put the oven on." A suspicious look crossed her mother's face. "What have you been doing up here?"

"Reading in my room. Sorry, I forgot about the oven."

Her mum gazed at her for a moment. "Come downstairs, I don't like you being up here on your own."

"I'm nearly thirteen. What do you think's going to happen to me? Aside from being bored to death."

"Just come downstairs."

"I will. After I've used the bathroom."

Her mum muttered as she left the hallway, leaving Eliza free to slip into her room and stash the book between the pillows.

She ducked into the bathroom and flushed the chain, spending a moment to wash her hands. Eliza glanced at her reflection as she brushed her long black hair, stark against her pale white face, her dark eyes tired.

It was no wonder. Twelve years of dealing with her mother's neurosis would be enough to make anyone exhausted. "It's eaten her up," Eliza whispered. "And now it's eating me up."

Dinner, if a bacon sandwich could be described as such, was a mercifully short affair.

Eliza listened as her father made his familiar "dad jokes," wondering if there was a club for fathers where they sat around brainstorming awful jokes. If there was, her dad was surely president of the society.

"We're going to see if we can get the television working," her mother announced.

"I'm really tired," Eliza said. "I was thinking of having an early night."

"I know it's difficult for you here," her mother said, standing and giving Eliza a tight hug. "But we'll be home in a day or so, and then you can get back to your cello practice. I know you've really missed playing with your group. We'll be home in no time. I promise."

"I'm alright," Eliza answered. "I'm just really tired."

Her mum held a hand over Eliza's forehead and checked her throat. "Get an early night and wake me if you need anything. Okay?"

"Okay."

"Wake *her* up," her dad said, pointing to her mum. "But don't wake me. Not even if the house is falling down. Okay?"

"Okay, Dad. Goodnight, then." Eliza left the living room and filled a glass with water. As the tap clanked and sputtered, she opened the cabinet below and found exactly what she was looking for—a small, thin flashlight.

Eliza closed her bedroom door, crossed to the window, and peered out at the wintry night. A row of skeletal branches reached up, dark against the sky; above, a sliver of moon disappeared behind a bank of wispy clouds.

Eliza looked below, searching for a glimpse of the so-called book collector, but the garden and lane seemed reassuringly empty. She shivered at the thought of him and snapped the heavy purple curtains shut.

As she brushed her teeth, Eliza wondered about the book hidden between the pillows. What was it? Who was Edwin Drabe? Why was the book kept in a hidden room?

She climbed into bed, glad for the thick goosedown duvet and the plump pillows. Eliza pulled the cover over her head and switched the flashlight on, grinning as she retrieved the book and held it up in the soft light. She hadn't read like this in years.

The book was heavy, its pages thick and reeking of age and dust. She tried to open it, to rifle through its pages, but they were stuck fast. She pulled at them, but no matter how hard she tried, they wouldn't budge.

Was this some sort of joke? Had someone glued the book shut? Had Tom done this? But why?

And then the cover fell open and Eliza began to read the neatly curved handwriting on the first page.

November 11, 1809
Edwin Drabe, 1741-

For those in future years who read this account of my dealings with the Grimwytch, may the heavens protect you.

Herein, you shall find a collection of accounts, which describe my travels in our world and the places that border and overlap it.

These tales have been written to salve the tortured souls of the Ghasts and Ghoules who have crossed from their land to ours. And for their victims and those who are locked away in the Midnight Prison or lay slain by my hand.

May they find peace within this book of kindly deaths.
Edwin Drabe

Eliza shivered as she read and reread the passage. "What's the point in that if this is just a book of stories?"

Perhaps it was a part of the joke, a mock warning for a book sealed in order to taunt its reader.

But as she finished the first page, the next fell open.

CHAPTER SIX

Halfers Hollow

*T*he rough woolen gloves covering Robert Chandler's fingers were so full of holes that they brought little respite from the harsh November chill.

He stared down at the barrow as he wheeled it across the narrow path. It was almost full to the brim with potatoes, but it should have been empty. The potatoes would have sold at the market if it hadn't been for the unexpected competition from the smartly dressed farmer whom Robert had never seen before. He tried not to think of the bitter disappointment he'd find on his parents' faces when he got back to the farm.

Robert glanced back at the small market town, with its twinkling lights that made it look so cozy, wishing he'd had time to buy a bowl of soup before setting out for home.

Not that he could have afforded one.

Behind the town, twilight stretched over the horizon, as if reaching out for him. Robert gazed at the empty fields on either side of the path. They were blackening, like pools of night. Bessie, his grizzled old terrier, walked in front of him, her head down as if sharing her master's low mood.

Ahead, Gallows Wood engulfed the trail, a malevolent, ominous patch of black.

Despite his fears at the sight of the place, he wished he could take the path that cut straight through it instead of having to walk all the way around. But he was forbidden.

And if his parents found out he'd been in the woods...well, it wasn't worth thinking about.

As he drew nearer, the cart struck something upon the path, sending it tipping over. Potatoes spilled across the dark, stony ground. Robert swore as he squatted down to scoop them up. It was difficult telling potato from stone as the night set in. He gathered what he could find and hunched over the cart, peering down at his feet to see if he'd missed anything.

When he looked up, Bessie wasn't there.

And then he caught the white smudge of her fur in the distance. She was running towards the woods.

"Bessie!" he cried.

Ahead of the terrier was something else. A deer?

Robert hefted up the cart handles and ran, his eyes fixed on his dog as she disappeared into the gloom of Gallows Wood. As he reached the edge of the trees, Robert stopped. He couldn't help but think of his best friend Sam and the tale he'd told the other week.

Sam had said he'd cut right through the middle of Gallows Wood, and Robert had had little trouble believing him. Sam would do such a thing. Sam was older, braver, and smarter, and Robert would have given anything to own even an ounce of his friend's courage. But even Sam had balked at the sight of the ghost he'd seen passing through the trees.

It was a lady, he'd said, and no ordinary lady. This one had glowed as if fashioned by moonlight, her eyes as big as saucers and brightest yellow. The ghost—for what else could she have been?—held a lantern in one hand and a gleaming silver sword in the other.

She'd chased Sam from the woods, and only the wards and seals the villagers hung from the trees kept her from catching up with him. Sam had vowed revenge, promising to find a way to best her. And Robert had no doubt his friend would drive her from Gallows Wood.

But Sam was Sam, and Robert was...Robert. And now Gallows Wood stood before him, its dark, spindly trees like fingers reaching out of the night.

In the distance, Bessie barked.

"I ain't scared of you," Robert called to the trees. "I'm going to get my dog back." Clenching his teeth, he thrust the cart forward along the path that wound into the woods like a snake. He looked up at the bare trees with their tangled branches, empty, twisted things. "Just trees." He scoured the dark woods for a sign of Bessie, straining to hear the sound of her bark, but there was only the soft whisper of leaves.

When he glanced back, the path behind seemed to have vanished into the night. Distracted by the growing darkness, Robert lost control as the cart veered down a small incline, taking him with it. It splashed into a stream.

Robert fought to keep the barrow. As he righted it, a light flashed from the trees. He set the cart down, ignoring the ice-cold water sloshing over his hobnailed boots. "What was that?"

He stared into the trees, searching for the light, but there was nothing.

"Seeing things," he reassured himself, but as he considered calling Bessie again, he thought better of it. He didn't want to draw attention to himself.

Just in case.

Robert pushed the cart up through the frozen mud on the other side of the stream, throwing his weight behind it, glad for the exertion for it took his mind off the light. And its owner. Sam's ghost? The lady with the sword and the lantern?

He wondered how long it would take for the path to wind its way out of Gallows Wood. It couldn't be far, surely? The woods were more a dense copse of trees than a forest.

He stopped as the light flickered once more, this time brighter and *closer*. It seemed to be hovering in the air.

Robert was about to run as fast as he could, when he heard a bark.

Bessie.

He set the cart down, his own fear evaporating as he thought of his dog, frightened and alone in the trees. Was she injured?

"Bessie!" he called, not caring who heard. "Come here, girl!"

The light flickered again, yards away now.

Robert crashed through a thicket of brambles, his coat catching on the spiny branches. He pulled it free and fought on through the darkness. He found himself in a clearing. Feet away, the smear of white fur that could only be Bessie.

And behind her, a house.

She sat and stared intently at the building. Watching.

The light flickered once more. It was coming from a window in the upper floor. And then it went out again. What was it? A signal? Robert had heard there were smugglers living nearby. Perhaps they'd sought refuge in Gallows Wood? Whatever the light was, Robert didn't care, he just wanted his dog back and for both of them to be home and safe and warm, away from this nightmarish place.

As he stepped towards his dog, a branch snapped beneath his boot. Bessie turned, whining softly. She crawled towards him, low and flat on her belly. Just like she did when she was in trouble.

Or when she was scared.

"What is it, girl?" He reached for her and placed a hand on her head. She licked him, her tongue dry, as her tail beat nervously against his leg. He looked back at the house as a patch of moonlight fell across the building.

He'd never seen such a narrow place. Two windows looked out from the dark mass of brickwork. One window revealed the flickering light, while the one below remained empty and black. The front door was as narrow as the house itself, and even if Robert had wanted to enter the place, he would have had to turn sideways.

Why would anyone want to build such a strange place?

But as he continued to consider the building, he realized it wasn't a house. It was *half* a house. As if someone had taken a great knife and cleaved it in two, leaving one half standing and the other...gone. Robert glanced on either side of the building for a sign of its other half, but there was no rubble, only a thick carpet of wintry leaves.

The light flickered once more, drawing Robert's eyes, and this time he realized why it kept coming on and going out.

Someone was pacing before it.

He saw it—a tall, stick-thin silhouette. It raised a hand, beckoning to him. Bessie yelped as if she'd been struck and leaped up, running away with her tail thrust between her legs. "Bessie!" Robert called, but it was no use, she was gone, vanishing into the dark stand of trees.

He was about to follow after her when he heard the tapping.

The hairs rose on the back of his neck as he gazed up at the figure rapping its bony knuckles against the glass. It moved then and as it did, he could see the light behind it—a candle balanced on the arm of a chair. Something about the figure transfixed him.

What was it? What was *wrong* with it? Something was amiss.

It rapped its hand again, this time louder.

Robert stepped back, fighting the tide of revulsion that threatened to engulf his senses. Something tore into his knuckles. He looked down to find a tendril of bramble stuck into his hand.

Carefully, he unpicked the thorn from his skin while behind him the tapping grew, making his heart thump madly. He pictured the bony hand breaking the glass. Smashing through the only barrier between him and that misshapen thing.

He ran, plunging through the forest, wading through bushes, tripping over logs, and pulling himself up as he stumbled through the trees. He had no idea if the sound of skittering footsteps at his back was real or imagined.

But still, he could hear that tapping. That dread-white knuckle rapping upon the window.

Finally, he found the path and, in the middle of it, his cart. He grabbed its handles and fled, his lungs tight as he fought for breath. He didn't stop running, not until the trees thinned and he spotted the strips of dark red cloth hanging from their gaunt limbs. Scarlet wards and binds, left by the villagers to keep the evil of Gallows Wood at bay.

Only when Robert was past the wards did he stop, catching his breath and clutching his side. He glanced back, but there was no sign of the man at the window. At least, not that he could see, for Gallows Wood was a silent mass of spindly limbs and trunks, any of which might have been the figure. Robert grasped the cart with his frozen fingers and ran on.

The village was silent. A few lights flickered in windows as people settled in for another cold night.

When Robert reached his house, he spotted Bessie, her ears flat against her head as she lay sheepishly before the stout oaken door, her eyes unable to meet his. Robert set the cart down and stroked her head with his numb fingers. "It's alright, girl. I saw him, too. I saw him, too."

He raised his hand and thumped upon the door just as the lights of the world seemed to wink out and he tumbled into a black abyss.

Robert woke as a hand slapped him gently upon his cheek. He looked into a pair of eyes gazing down at him. It took him a moment to recognize his mother's concerned face. His father stood behind her, arms folded, face unreadable.

"What happened?" Robert's mother asked, her hand on his forehead. "You're frozen."

"I..." Robert looked back at his father. "I didn't sell anything at the market. Not a thing."

"Don't worry about that for now, son," his father replied. "What happened to you out there? Answer your mother."

"Bessie ran off. She ran into...Gallows Wood."

His mother's hand flinched away from him. "Tell me you never went in there. Tell me!"

"I went in."

Robert flinched as his father punched the low beam above his head, his eyes narrowed. "What did we tell you about Gallows Wood? What the hell did we tell you?"

"Not to go in."

"And so you did. I can't believe it, not after all the times we've told you," his father responded. "You're a fool, boy, a bloody fool."

Robert gazed at his feet as his father moved towards him. "Bessie went into the trees. After a deer. I couldn't just leave her, could I?"

"Never mind excuses," his father replied as he leaned down and examined Robert. "What did you see in Gallows Wood?"

"I saw a house with a man in a window. He looked starved. He looked like a skeleton. Who is he?"

Robert's parents glanced at each other. "Never you mind," his mother warned. "There's a bowl of stew on the hob. Eat it and go to bed. You need sleep. That's all there is to it."

"And forget what you saw," his father said, his voice low. "Because you saw nothing. Do you understand me?"

"I understand, Father."

Despite his father's order to forget what he'd seen, Robert couldn't forget, and that night, his sleep was fractured by terrible nightmares.

He found himself back in Gallows Wood, standing before a tall, grimy mirror. A row of candles surrounded him, and the darkness beyond their circle was impossibly black. Robert glanced into the mirror, holding a hand towards the filthy glass, reaching for his reflection. But there was nothing there. He reached further.

And then it appeared.

But the reflection wasn't his. It was the man from the window, reaching for him. And as he leaned closer, Robert finally saw what he'd failed to see before.

And now he knew exactly what was so wrong with the man.

Robert awoke, gasping for air, his heart beating frantically. With a dull, growing dread, he realized that the vision offered in the mirror was no nightmare. It was what he had failed to really *see* in Gallows Wood.

That the reason the man who had beckoned to him from the window had been so horribly disfigured was because he had no mouth.

As the soft light of dawn spilled through the window, Robert's parents rose from their bed, dressing quickly.

"Where are you going?" Robert asked.

"You should be asleep," his mother replied. "We're going to Hackwich Market to try to sell what's left of the potatoes. You'll have to look after yourself today."

"And don't even think about leaving the house," Robert's father warned. "Now, get back to sleep."

"I can't sleep. I had nightmares. About the woods and about that…man. Who is he?"

Robert's father shook his head. "Listen to me. You forget about it. I told you last night, it wasn't real, just your imagination. Do you hear me, boy?"

"Yes, Father."

"Keep the fire stoked and prepare dinner. We'll be back before sunset."

"Yes, Father."

Robert's father looked grim as he ushered his wife into the ice-cold morning, slamming the door shut behind him.

Robert stayed in the house, just as he was told, until mid-morning, when he took Bessie out.

It was a cold, dreary day with rags of mist obscuring the village. Robert allowed Bessie to run in the fields behind the house, but kept her close lest she run off again. As they passed through a gap in the hedge that led to the brook, Bessie began to bark, her fur standing on end.

Someone was walking towards them. A tall, thin figure passing through the mist.

"No," Robert cried. "Get away!" He began to run towards the house, glancing back to see the figure bearing down on him. "Leave me alone!"

But still it neared. Robert pounded across the furrows of frozen mud and all at once tripped over Bessie, falling onto the rock-hard ground. As he fought to pull himself up, the air filled with laughter.

"What are you running from, you idiot?"

"Sam?" Robert asked. He turned to see his friend standing over him, his face full of merriment.

"Who else did you think it was?" Sam asked. He stooped down, brushing a curtain of coppery hair from his eyes, and held his hand out for Robert, pulling him up.

"I shouldn't be out here, Sam. Something happened last night. Something bad."

Sam gave him a curious look. "What do you mean, something happened? Nothing ever happens around here."

"I went into Gallows Wood. I never meant to."

"You're lying," Sam said. "You'd never dare go into Gallows Wood! Never."

"No, I did, Sam, and I saw something, and it wasn't your ghost."

"So if it wasn't a ghost, what was it?"

Robert told Sam his story. As he described the house and the figure in the window, the fear began to rise in him once more.

"You're lying," Sam said. "You're just trying to outdo me 'cause I saw a ghost and you didn't. So you made your own phantom up."

"I swear it, Sam. I swear on my mother's life."

Sam studied him for a moment. "If there really is half a house in Gallows Wood, you can take me there."

"But my parents…"

"Are gone for the day. Leave Bessie at home, she's useless, and take me to this half a house. Only when I see it with my own eyes will I believe you."

Robert sighed. He would do anything for Sam usually, but he couldn't go back. Not there. "I can't, Sam."

"Of course you can't, 'cause there's no such place. You see, Robert, this is why I'm going to London. I need to find a new partner for my ghost-hunting business because you're scared of everything and just make stuff up." Sam walked away, throwing a limp wave over his shoulder. "So long, Robert."

"But I want to come to London with you, Sam. And hunt ghosts." He ran after his friend. "And I ain't making anything up, I swear it."

Sam gave Robert a hard look. "Like I said, if you ain't making it up, you'll be able to show me the house, won't you?"

"Alright. I'll show you." The thought of Sam leaving him behind was more than he could bear. They'd been friends for longer than he could remember. And at least it was daylight. Plus, there would be two of them this time. "But we'll have to be quick. I need to get back before my parents."

"We won't be gone long, I'm sure," Sam said. "Just long enough for you to pretend you can't find your half a house and the starving man."

"He wasn't a man. Not like you or me."

"We'll soon see, Robert, won't we?"

They locked Bessie in Robert's house and then took the long way round to Gallows Wood, for it wasn't just Robert's parents who forbade him to enter the woods. No one was allowed in.

As Robert passed the red tatters of cloth hanging from the trees, a jolt of panic shot through him. Thankfully, Sam was too busy talking to notice, but as Robert looked up at his friend he realized that some of the confidence had left his usually jovial voice.

"Did you really come here? Into Gallows Wood?" Robert asked.

Sam spat upon the path. "'Course I did. Why would you ask me that?"

"I just wanted to check. Because we don't have to carry on, you know. We could turn back." Robert peered ahead into the desolate, wintry wood.

"Let's just keep going. Show me your half a house, and *then* we can leave. But not before. And I promise you this— if it doesn't exist, I'm going to have to find myself another partner for the ghost-hunting business."

Despite the daylight, the place was just as unnatural as it had been at night. A carpet of dead leaves obscured the path, and several times they lost it. Robert gazed into the mist and crossed his fingers.

"What are you doing?" Sam asked, grinning as he looked down at Robert's fingers.

"Praying we don't see your ghost."

"Don't worry about that. If we see her, I'll punch her in the nose and send her on her way. So, where's this house, then?"

"I don't know. It was near a stream. We should be there any minute."

They soon found the stream and as they did, Robert noticed his friend tense.

"This man you saw, he's probably one of those smugglers," Sam said. "He must have some sort of disease which makes him thin, and the others use him to frighten people out of the woods. He got rid of you, after all, didn't he? If your house exists, it's probably where they hide their treasure. So, was it near here?"

Robert heard the slight tone of fear in his friend's voice. "Yes." He pointed ahead. "Through those bushes and up that hill, I think. It'll be up there somewhere. Look, we don't have to..."

"Let's just get up there and see this house, shall we?" Sam said and glanced at the sky. "It'll be dark soon, and I need to get back before it is. I've got a lot to do."

The house looked even stranger by daylight. Sam, who had been busily discussing how he planned to spend the money they got from the smugglers' treasure, stopped. "Oh."

"See, I told you, didn't I?" Robert said, taking courage from his friend's fear.

Thankfully, the windows were empty.

"So, where's the other half?" Sam asked as he stepped cautiously towards the house. Robert joined him, searching the forest floor for signs of it just as he had last night, but there was definitely nothing there.

"It's even got half a door!" Sam said. "And...it's open."

Robert shivered. The door had been closed last night, he was sure of it. So why was it open now? He looked around the trees. Was the man out here with them? "Let's get home."

"We can't." Sam said. "We need to see if we can find their treasure first, because I ain't coming back. I haven't got time. This could pay for us to get to London."

"This isn't anything to do with smugglers, Sam. I'm telling you, he wasn't an ordinary man!"

"Whoever he is, he probably ran away before you raised the alarm. But he might have left something behind. Let's just have a very quick look. Then we can go."

"How do you know there's no one here?"

"Look at it! It's empty, isn't it? There's not a sound."

"I don't know."

"There's no one here, you coward! Come on, just a quick look."

Robert knew from experience that it was better not to argue, but as they approached the house, his hands began to shake. Sam laughed at him and slapped him across the top of his head. "Get in there!"

"You first." Robert said.

Sam looked as if he were about to say something and thought twice about it. "Alright, then." He pushed the door open, turned sideways and stepped into the house.

Robert took a deep breath and followed him.

The hall was dark, its walls covered in lichen. Thick webs clung in the corners. Something crunched below Robert's feet. He looked down and cried out in horror. The ground writhed under a carpet of beetles, earwigs, and huge insects, the likes of which he'd never seen. He tried to turn away, but Sam grabbed him, pulling him on. "Hurry up!" he whispered. "Keep moving, or they'll crawl up your trousers!"

Robert walked on, his chest tight. It felt as if the hall had somehow grown a little narrower. A doorway stood to their right. Sam glanced in and then stepped inside, pulling Robert with him and sending him sprawling into what looked like an old kitchen. A row of pans hung from the ceiling on hooks. They were covered in rust and patches of moss, and the scorched brick hearth was empty but for dust and a sea of insects.

Robert gazed out of the window at the woods. Thankfully, the trees seemed still and empty. Something skittered against his hand, causing him to flinch. The window ledge was covered in a row of dead flies. There was such an air of desolation about the place, a terrible emptiness, and it felt as if it was beginning to seep inside him. "I want to leave, Sam. There's nothing here. Let's go."

"If you believe there's nothing here, why are you whispering?" Sam shook his head. "No, we're going to find the treasure first. Come on, let's look upstairs."

Sam walked ahead of Robert, blocking the hallway to the front door, and nodded towards the staircase. "Up you go."

Robert swallowed. He knew that if he refused Sam would never let him live it down. And if he didn't do what he was told, he was certain Sam would leave him to spend the rest of his life working the fields while Sam went to London to become a famous ghost hunter without him.

"Go on!" Sam whispered.

Robert nodded briskly and began to climb. The first step creaked loudly, sending his heart fluttering. He stopped until a finger prodded him in the back. Robert continued, placing each foot carefully upon the next step and praying it would remain quiet.

As he nearly reached the top, he turned to look back at Sam. His easy smile was gone now, his expression grim. He pointed ahead and whispered, "Hurry up."

Robert continued, ignoring the urge to turn and push past his friend. It would all be over soon. In no time, they'd be back out in the daylight and on their way home, with Sam having a newfound respect for him.

He reached the landing, the floorboards below bare and, thankfully, free of insects. He looked around the dilapidated hallway. Two doors stood at either side. One was open, the other closed. Robert stepped towards the open door and found a bare room with a rickety old chair and a candle perched upon its arm.

The same candle he'd seen last night from the window. In this very room.

Sam glanced about the room. "I didn't exactly expect a treasure chest to be sitting here waiting for us. No, they've probably hidden their gold. Come on, let's check the floorboards. One's probably loose." He got down on his hands and knees and began to run his fingers along the boards, testing each knot and hole as he went. He pushed down on a board near the window, and the other end rose into the air. He turned to Robert. "Get down here and help me out!"

As Robert crossed the room, he heard the faintest of sounds. A soft click. He was about to turn back to the hall when Sam swore softly. "It's just rubbish," he said, removing a tiny figurine from the hole in the floorboards, a toy knight in armor. He delved back into the hole and removed a withered rose inside a sealed bottle. "Why bother hiding this stuff?" He picked up the bottle and smashed it against the floorboard, and was about to reach back into the hole when he froze.

Robert stood, dumbly watching the color drain from Sam's face as he stared sickly past Robert.

Staring at whoever, or whatever, was behind him.

Slowly, Robert turned as the man stepped into the room. His emaciated face held a furious glare, his eyes boring into Robert's, exactly as they had in his dream. And where a mouth should have been, there was simply nothing. The flesh below his nose was completely smooth as it continued down his chin and neck.

Robert barely noticed as Sam pushed him aside, screaming and vanishing through the door.

In the daylight, the man's emaciated form was even more horrifying than it had been at night. His clothes hung off his skeletal body like those of a scarecrow. His face seemed to be a nest of bright blue worms, twitching below his paper-thin flesh. *They're veins*, Robert told himself, watching numbly as they ticked and pulsed below eyes swollen with hatred.

Robert was frozen in the tiny room, unable to move, and as he thought of running, the man turned and closed the door, sealing them inside.

"Let me go," Robert begged. "Please."

The man glared down at him, and a new look crept into those bright green eyes.

Victory.

He grasped Robert by the jaw, his bony fingers strong and firm, as his other hand reached towards Robert's face.

"Please. I have to get home. My parents…" Robert stopped as the man seized a corner of his lips and began to pull. He expected agony, but there was none.

One moment, his mouth felt numb, and the next, it wasn't there.

He tried to scream, but couldn't. He reached for his mouth, but it was gone, the flesh below his nose smooth and empty.

Robert stared dumbfounded as the man held his lips between his fingers and placed them carefully below his own nose. And then the mouth, Robert's mouth, opened upon the man's face, and he took a huge breath, like a drowning man fished from the sea.

He leaned over, resting a hand against the wall to steady himself, his other hand on his chest. And then he cried out, his voice full of a terrible energy. "Yes!" He slammed his fist into the wall. "Yes!"

Robert tried to look away but was transfixed. He breathed slowly through his nose, taking short breaths, fighting the terror that threatened to engulf him.

The man began to cough. He hunched over, hands on knees, his wracking cough filling the room. And then something passed from his mouth.

A tiny, bright amber being, fluttering like a butterfly.

It hovered in the air before the man, and he reached for it, letting it rest delicately in his palm. He held it to Robert. "Take it in, boy. Breathe it through your nose if you want to live. It shall sustain you. If that's what you choose." Deep below the man's ragged voice was the merest hint of compassion.

He held the glowing filament closer. "Take it now, boy, before your heart stops."

It fizzled and glowed and, as Robert breathed deeply through his nose, it flew up his right nostril. Such was its intensity that he clenched his fists, fighting to stay on his feet, for it was as if the sun had risen inside his head.

The pangs of hunger he hadn't even realized were there were instantly sated, his dry throat quenched.

"You won't want for food and water again, boy."

Robert watched his own mouth speaking to him from the man's face.

"It's no good fretting, either. You won't get your mouth back. It's mine now. I've taken yours just as my own was stolen. That's my right. And now I must go. I have a hunger like you'd never believe."

Robert grabbed at the man, clutching his wrist.

Gently, the man shook him free. "Don't bother fighting me, boy. Decades I've lived in this house. And now you've broken my curse and inherited it for yourself." His eyes softened, a little. "Still, it won't harm me to tell you what's what. What to expect. And *why*. Why is always the most important thing.

"Take a seat, boy. Breathe through your nose. Nice and slow. And listen to what I have to tell you. For there may be a chance for you yet. It is, after all, from your blood that this whole thing started."

The man guided Robert to the chair and made him sit. He stepped to the window and gazed out into the darkening afternoon. "The story starts here. In this house.

"A boy lived here. His name was James Maybury. He was born long ago, longer than you've been living. This was a proper house back then, and while it wasn't much, it was his home. James lived here with his mother, father, and a little sister called Anna. He loved them all very much.

"And then a winter came. A bitter cold wind blew across the land, bringing snow and ice, and everything was white, no matter where you looked. Beautiful. And deadly, for the winter was accompanied by a hideous thing that came calling at their door. It found James's mother and father and his little sister. But somehow, it missed him.

"It was a terrible malady. Fever, thirst, exhaustion, and hallucinations. Visions of imps and demons crawling up the walls and hammering upon the windows, visions such as would drive a person mad. And James could only watch as his family grew sicker and madder by the day. Soon their cupboards were empty. He scoured the house from top to bottom for sustenance, but there was none.

"As he watched his family waste away before his very eyes, he knew he must find food and supplies, for eating would surely lend them energy to fight the fever.

"So he wrapped himself warm and set out into the woods, ploughing his way through a snow drift almost as tall as he was. He wandered for hours, getting lost as everything looked exactly the same, a sea of white broken only by the trees and stumps.

"Eventually he broke from the woods and found himself before a large farm. He knew of the place and the person, if she could be called that, who lived there. With a heavy heart, he trudged through the snow towards the house in the distance. Smoke rose blackly from its chimneys and as he neared it, he passed a barn. From within came the sounds of chickens and pigs. As he heard them, he felt a little hope, for not everything was frozen, and there was still flesh, blood, and sustenance.

"So he knocked upon the door, and it was opened by a grotesque woman. If 'woman' could be a word befitting the creature. She was a huge thing, her stomach hanging low below her thick woolen dress, pale and distended. Her hair—long, gray, and listless—hung over her reddened face. Her eyes were large and pale, her mouth full and wet, her nose purple at its tip. It was the face of a glutton, a face red through overeating. The opposite of his own and those of the loved ones he'd left behind.

"'Please,' he said, 'I've come from the house in Gallows Wood. My parents and sister are weak with fever. We haven't eaten for days, and the snow has killed the few crops we had. Please, will you help me?'

"The lady gazed at him for a moment, before licking her lips and giving him a pitiless sneer. 'Help you, you say? And why would I want to do such a thing? To save a few peasants? Keep a few more beggars living?'

"'But they're dying, miss. My family is dying.'

"'So you said,' she replied and smiled. 'And it's no concern of mine. Now, if you don't get off my land, you shall pay a hefty price. One far worse than your current malady.'

"And then, with one last tantalizing blast of warmth and the succulent scent of roasting pig, she slammed the door in his face. James stood for a moment, the thought of turning and facing the white, merciless waste more than he could bear. But then he heard the sound of her laughter, and it squeezed his heart like the coldest, cruelest vise.

"And so he made his way back, trudging on through the falling snow, but as he passed the barn, where he could hear the soft cluck of hens and the snuffle of pigs, he stopped.

"He'd never stolen a thing in his life, but at that moment, he knew if he didn't take something back with him, he'd be burying his family in a snowy grave. One he'd soon be following them into.

"So, he unlatched the door, for only a latch sealed it, and he made his way into the barn. Here, the hay was free of snow. Pigs occupied the main part, their stench heavy in the air. And behind the pigs, a henhouse, crammed and packed with chickens. A row of birds sat roosting upon a bar, and it didn't take him long to find the plumpest and to wring their necks just like his father had shown him. He stuffed them, still twitching, into his coat, and as he turned to leave, he screamed. For there, standing before him, was the old woman.

"'I warned you, boy. Do you know, the only reason I spared you was to know you'd die of wretchedness and a broken heart? I like to see hearts break, for I have none of my own. Do you know what I am?'

"'A monster,' James Maybury replied.

"'Indeed. And the people in these parts usually know better than to cross me. But you didn't know better, did you? Even though you were warned.'

"'My family is dying. I had no other choice.'

"'Stop talking, boy. It will hurt less.' She stepped towards him, her smile violent and cruel.

"'Get away from me, you old hag. Leave me be!' James cried.

"'I told you not to speak,' she said as she reached up and snatched James's mouth from his face.

"I do not need to tell you how it felt, for you already know. He watched in horror as she dropped his mouth inside her pocket and then rubbed her corpulent fingers together. A spark of light appeared, amber and fluttering. She pinched it between her fingers and thrust it up his nose. He fought, his chokes catching in his throat as the light blazed around inside his head.

"She laughed as she watched him struggle. But she was not finished.

"She closed her eyes and bunched her fingers into tight fists and as she did, the chickens around them began to squawk and cry and one by one they dropped to the ground, dead as doornails. It was as if she'd somehow drawn up their lives into her fists. When she opened her eyes, they were pure white; below them, her mouth was a gaping hole.

"'So it's done,' she said. 'You are less than you were when you arrived. And so is your home in the hollow. Half a house you now have, and an eternity of starvation. But your hunger will not kill you, for the spark I have given you will keep you alive. And only I, or my kin, can free you...and that will never be so.'

"She pointed to the door. 'So go on your way, child. Go home.'

"James's feet began to take him away, and there was nothing he could do to stop them. As he glanced back with one last, pleading look, it was to see the creature leaning low and thrusting dead chickens into her mouth. Bones, feathers, and all.

"When he reached the hollow, his house, just as she had promised, was cleaved in half. The other half had vanished into thin air. He opened the door, waiting for the sound of his dying family, knowing he wouldn't hear them. For they were gone with half of the house, gone to whatever hell the witch had sent them to."

The man turned from the window and regarded Robert. "You know who the old hag was, don't you, boy?"

Robert nodded. It was one of his first memories. A giant old woman with huge eyes and terrible, black moods.

"She was your blood, boy."

No, she was not. She couldn't be.

"Ah, but she was. Your real mother. I knew from the moment I saw you in the woods. You have the same aura. The same bad blood. You've just never found it in you, not yet, at least. I'm sorry for you, boy, really I am. But this is what your kin did to me, for I am James Maybury, and now her curse is broken and met upon you."

Robert leaped from the chair and grasped the man's tattered shirt. *Please*, he thought, his voice screaming in his mind. *Please!*

"There is nothing I can do for you. I've served my time in this house, silent and alone, robbed of a means to feed myself, to speak and tell people of the curse. To find my family. Starvation would have been kinder than the punishment given to me, which is why *she* ensured I couldn't starve. But now the bond is broken, and I shall leave this tomb where it stands." James Maybury gazed at Robert for a moment and shook his head. He was about to say something else when the sound of barking dogs echoed through the trees.

Robert ran to the window, James Maybury close behind him.

Outside, in the dusk, he could see his father running, Bessie at his heels and two other dogs close behind. Sam and his father, who was clutching a rifle, followed, and behind them, more of the villagers. A pang of hope filled Robert as he watched them.

"Here they come," James Maybury said. "Fresh from the farm and baying for the blood of a monster. Ironic that the monster is one of their own. If there's help to be had for you, boy, I'll send it."

The front door crashed against the wall downstairs as the men raced into the house.

James Maybury ran from the room to the door across the hall as the sounds of feet pounded up the stairs. Robert chased after James as he kicked the door open and passed through a bare, desolate room, crossed his arms over his face, and threw himself through the window. He crashed through in a storm of glass and vanished from view.

Robert stood before the broken window, watching as the man who had stolen his mouth flitted through the trees, his stick-like figure vanishing among the tangle and weave of the twisted branches.

He turned back to find Bessie and the other dogs racing into the room. They stopped as they saw him and began to whine and howl, before scuttling away. Tears sprang into his eyes as he held a hand over the place his mouth had once been.

Robert's father appeared first, Sam and his father close behind. "Are you alright, son? What happened?"

Then Robert's mother reached the top of the stairs. As she saw Robert, she ran towards him, throwing her arms around him and clasping him so tight he thought he might snap. The men from the village checked the other room before joining them.

Robert looked over his mother's shoulder at Sam, who was staring at him in bewilderment. Robert let his hand drop from his face, closing his eyes, unable to bear seeing the terror on his friend's face.

The room filled with cries as the men, once standing brave with scythes and rifles, screamed like frightened babies. Robert's mother's hands slipped away, and she began to cry. "He's not a monster. Not Robert!"

Robert stepped through the crowd. They parted before him as he walked back to the empty room, lit the candle upon the chair, sat and gazed into the growing dusk.

Eliza closed the book, leaving her finger inside to mark her place. "That was horrible," she whispered.

She ran her fingers over her lips, wondering what it would be like to lose her mouth. She pictured trying to draw a breath only to find her mouth gone, panicking as she forced air through her nose.

Eliza shook her head, forcing herself to return to the present. Maybe her mother was right. Maybe imaginary stories were a waste of time and a useless distraction. She glanced back at the book. Where the story ended, another passage of writing started, in the same style of writing as the introduction. Her great-great-grandfather's hand? Edwin Drabe.

Eliza fought the urge to close the book and sneak it back to the study in the morning. To forget about it. But as she stared at the writing below her finger, she picked it back up and began reading.

Addendum

James Maybury found me in London.

He'd spent many weeks searching for someone who might undo the terrible thing that had been done to him and, in turn, to poor Robert. James placed a map before my young assistant and me and pointed. "Go here. And if you can, undo what has been done. I've heard you can write things away, things that are not as they should be. Write this story, make a kindly death."

"I shall judge whether or not it's to be a kindly death," I told him.

"Well, do whatever you can for him."

"You could do that. You could give him back what's rightfully his," I replied.

He tensed, his eyes traveling to the gun upon my desk. "Will you challenge me? I only took what was taken from me."

"You did. And only you can decide whether that was right or wrong. It's not my place, not in this matter. But you have come to me, and that shall stand for you, Mr. Maybury. Pack our bags, Sarah," I told my young assistant. "We shall leave at first light."

The Book of Kindly Deaths

I watched James Maybury as he left, shoulders hunched, the scars of his cursed life still weighing him down.

We arrived in the village of Buryton the following day. The villagers swore they'd never heard of Robert or his family. Their home, standing alone in the village, blackened and empty, told a different tale.

We left Buryton and soon found the house in Gallows Wood. It was exactly as described, half a building and no more. A light shone in an upper window.

I knocked upon the door. Moments later, it was answered by a drawn-looking man, brandishing a rifle. He glanced from me to Sarah.

"I'm here to see your son. I've heard of his...affliction and I wish to help," I told him. "I have experience of such matters."

He lowered the rifle, nodding for us to follow, and as we entered the place, we were forced to turn sideways through the narrow opening.

A waft of cooking smells issued from a dank kitchen, where a pot hissed and bubbled upon a hearth. Standing before it was a woman. She grasped her sleeves as we approached and nodded to the ceiling. "He's up there," she said.

"Before I go to Robert, tell me," I replied, "how did he come to live with you?"

"We adopted him when he was little more than a baby," his mother said, "after his real mother fled, if you could call her such a thing. She'd been caught eating another family's livestock. Such a terrible hunger. We all knew she was a... monster. And we were scared of her. The others from the village chased her from her home; when they did, Robert's father and I went and rescued him."

"And what happened to his real mother, the malefactrix?" I asked, as tenderly as I could.

"No one knows," Robert's father replied. "They cornered her in a tunnel near Portdown. They covered it from both ends, but there was nothing to be found, nothing in the middle. She was gone, vanished into thin air."

"I will need to see this tunnel, and then I may need to destroy it," I told him. I glanced around the disheveled kitchen. "So, why are you out here, hiding in the woods?"

"Because the other villagers think we might be tainted, like him," the father said as his eyes traveled to the ceiling.

"Well, they are wrong," I told him. "I hunt for the beings that we call monsters. I send them back to where they belong. Or I write their tales into my book and they find peace. A kindly death, if you will. I can write Robert's tale, if you and he agree to it."

"Please," his mother begged. "Whatever you need to do. We can leave once we know he is at peace."

"I will ask him. If Robert agrees, it will be done and you can go and start over. Somewhere else. But never, ever utter a word of this matter to anyone."

We found Robert upstairs, sitting in his chair, staring out the window. He turned and looked at me, his face gaunt, his stare hard.

I left Sarah to her business. She had a gift for communicating without speaking. Slowly, she noted down Robert's story in her journal as they gazed at one another, talking in silence but for the scratch of her pen on paper.

When she was finished, I asked Robert if he wanted to be written away, or to venture to a place where monsters dwelled. A place he wouldn't be judged. He asked to cross over.

I took the book from my bag and began to write his story, just as you have read it, Sarah relaying each word of his sorrowful tale. And when it was done, I took my pen and handed it to Robert and he signed on the place just where he should.

And then he was gone. Gone from this world and into the other.

CHAPTER SEVEN

The Watcher

*E*liza switched the bedside lamp on and set the book down. She was glad for the light as she glanced at the book with its cracked black cover. She pushed it aside. There was something very wrong with it. It wasn't normal, and that hadn't been a normal story, either. And even though she hadn't read anything even slightly imaginative since early childhood, Eliza knew stories didn't work like that.

Stories remained on paper. But that one felt as if it had followed her into the room. And it wasn't written like a normal story, but more like someone recording an event that had actually happened.

Outside, the birch tree's branches scraped at her window, taking Eliza back to Gallows Wood. She could still see Robert's face, his skin blank beneath his nose, his eyes bulging with terror as the stick-thin man darted through the trees, taking Robert's mouth with him.

The scene was broken when a light blinked through the gap in Eliza's curtains.

Eliza gazed ahead, and it blinked once more.

Slowly, she crept across the room, drawing the curtains and peering through the window. Beyond the dark expanse of her grandfather's garden, a light shone in a neighboring house. The light came from a bare bulb that shone harsh and sickly yellow in an empty room.

Or was it empty?

No, someone was inside. They passed across the light, a perfectly black silhouette, pacing back and forth, as if agitated. And then they flitted to the window, cupping their hands against the glass as they peered out. At her.

Eliza's breath caught in her throat, mesmerized as they watched each other across the night-filled garden. Time crawled to a stop as neither moved, until Eliza finally managed to summon the will to close her eyes and break the connection. She grabbed at the curtains blindly and snapped them closed. When she opened her eyes, the watcher was gone, sealed away behind the curtains. She allowed her breathing to calm before climbing back into bed.

"Just a neighbor," she whispered. "Forget it."

The black book rested on the soft white sheet. She thought of returning it to the hidden study, but knew she wouldn't. Because even though her heart was still thumping, Eliza knew she'd never be able to settle until she knew what the book was.

And what it meant.

And why her grandfather had left it out upon the desk. Did it hold a clue to his disappearance and where he'd gone?

As she placed a hand on the book's old cover, Eliza knew she would read it until the end. That this was what she was somehow meant to do. Her curiosity, so often curtailed by her mother, was beginning to grow, and with it, an almost insatiable lust for knowledge was building inside of her. Even if the knowledge was terrifying.

"Be brave," she told herself. "You're part Drabe, after all!"

Eliza turned the flashlight on, switched the lamp off, and picked up the book.

The pages she'd just read were sealed once more, but as she tilted the book, it fell open to the next story.

CHAPTER EIGHT

A Pocketful of Souls

*V*ictoria Stapleton chose not to cover her mouth as she yawned. Usually, she'd at least attempt to hide her boredom, if only to avoid a stern lecture in the way polite young ladies should behave. But today, on the anniversary of her thirteenth year on this dismal planet, she didn't care a jot for manners as her anger boiled like lava in her veins.

The main focus of Victoria's malice stood before her.

The *magician.*

She tutted as he flipped his gloved hands into the air, producing yet another puff of green smoke from the hat balanced on the stool.

The village children, a sea of filthy brown clothes and greasy heads, sat cross-legged before the magician, crying and cooing with delight as he baffled them with his tricks. When he pulled a scrawny white rabbit from his hat, they screamed with wonder, clapping as fast as their hands would allow.

In a strange way, Victoria almost envied the audience their simple amusement. The only time she ever felt even a vague sense of happiness was at night when it was time to go to sleep.

"Amazing!" cried a scraggly boy, as the magician pulled a bright red handkerchief from his sleeve.

"Is it?" Victoria asked, her irritation drowned by another chorus of applause. She glanced away from the children and the grime of their clothes and the bitter stench of their poverty. How she detested their eagerness and wretched energy. Didn't they realize what life had in store for them? Were they really so easily distracted from their impoverished lives?

All of it was her father's fault. He was the one who had invited the little beggars into their home, insisting they share in her birthday celebration. But the invitations weren't sent out of goodwill or his paper-thin sense of charity. No, they were simply given to raise his standing in the community, the benevolent patrician bestowing an act of kindness upon the local paupers.

Had her parents given Victoria the birthday present she'd truly desired, they would have gone away for an extended period of time and left her alone.

"Please, finish soon," Victoria begged as the magician reached for another prop. She glanced towards the windows, but the thick velvet curtains were drawn, sealing her inside the room.

But boredom wasn't the only reason Victoria wanted the magician to leave.

No, there was something else that set her teeth on edge about the man. He was like a carrion crow swirling around the room, his long black cape like wings hanging from his tall, wiry frame. Above the cape, his bald head gleamed like a pale pink ball, with only his thin, pointed beard lending his face definition.

His red-rimmed eyes kept roving across the audience, as if searching for something to feast on. They rarely settled on any one child, constantly darting from here to there.

Occasionally his eyes would fix on Victoria, and she'd be forced to look away. For while his voice was full of cheer and bluster, there was another tone below its surface—

haunted, needling, and desperate. How could her parents have allowed him into the house?

But the young girl who accompanied him was, perhaps, worse than the magician.

Victoria had never seen such a morose-looking child. Her ash-grey hair, which was surely more fitting for a woman two score years her senior, hung limply across her slumped shoulders. Her pale, emotionless face appeared carved like a statue's. Heavy black circles lay beneath her watery blue eyes, and she looked as if she hadn't slept for weeks.

She should be in bed, thought Victoria. *And he should fetch a doctor for her, because clearly she's not long for the world.* And then it occurred to Victoria that the girl looked even more miserable than she was, and she almost felt pity for her.

The girl handed the magician two large silver hoops, which he held up. "These rings are made of solid metal, and I shall use them to show you a sight which is so miraculous that it may still the beating of your heart!" An excited gasp came from his audience. "Now, I shall need a clever little lad or lady to come here and test the strength of the rings. Who shall step forward?"

A forest of grimy hands reached into the air with such force that they seemed intent on pulling the ceiling down.

Victoria rolled her eyes. Her uncle, who fancied himself something of a showman, had performed the very same feat at Christmas.

"So many eager young ladies and gentlemen!" the magician said to the sickly girl, who gazed back with dead eyes. "It's almost impossible to choose. But wait, I know!" He fixed Victoria with a smile. "We should let the birthday girl come and take part. She's remained in the shadows for the whole show, so let's bring her into the light and shine a beam upon her pretty little face."

"No, thank you." Victoria forced a tight smile, trying to break the pull of his insistent eyes.

"Oh, come now," the magician protested. "You're only thirteen once in a lifetime! Why squander the chance of fun and excitement on such an auspicious day?"

"Thank you for the offer," Victoria replied, "but no. Ask one of *them*." She pointed at the village children as each tried to raise their hand higher than the one beside them. "They look like *they're* enjoying themselves."

The smile faded from the magician's face, and he flashed Victoria a furious look. And then the anger was gone, and he offered a brief, insincere smile, pointing to a boy who got up in such a hurry that he tripped.

The room was instantly filled with raucous giggles, but Victoria ignored the spectacle. Instead, she watched the magician's assistant. The girl stared back at her and, with the slightest movement, shook her head.

What was that? A warning? Victoria continued to gaze at the girl, hoping to provoke a further response, but instead, the girl stared lifelessly into the distance.

Finally, after what seemed like forever, the show ended and Victoria guided the children from the room, herding them into the large hall outside. They stood around on the black-and-white tiles, scuffing them with their hobnailed boots until she ordered them to fetch their coats. The children ran to the cloakroom, grabbing at their rags and tatters of cloth, yanking them on with an eagerness to leave now that the show had ended.

Victoria didn't blame them. They had no interest in her or her birthday, and why should they? It was not as if she'd ever attempted to hide her contempt for them.

Outside, snowflakes fell. She wondered how long it had been snowing. As one of the children spotted the weather, another excited chorus rose, and soon the front door was thrown wide as they pushed and shoved their way outside. Victoria stood beneath the doorway. The countryside was covered in a thick layer of white, its glare harsh and bright below a spotty gray cover of clouds. The children scooped up the snow, forming it into balls, shrieking as they hurled them, their excitement turning to occasional yelps of pain.

"It's called snow," Victoria shouted. "And it comes every winter. You may have seen it before!" She slammed the door, shivering as she went in search of her shawl. As soon as she found it, she would have the magician paid and escorted from the house, and finally she might find some peace.

Victoria returned to the room where the show had taken place, grabbing her shawl from the back of her chair. As she turned, she noticed the magician standing on his makeshift stage, his assistant beside him.

He gave Victoria a cold smile. "Well, well, it's the birthday girl."

"I came back for my shawl," Victoria replied. "Don't let me keep you and your assistant from packing. I'm sure you're both keen to be on your way with the snowfall. The path to the village is already covered."

"We shall be on our way soon," the magician said. "And this is not my assistant, at least not in an official capacity. She is my dear daughter, Sophia." He placed a hand on the sickly girl's shoulder. She didn't respond. "So, *Victoria*, were my obligations fulfilled today? Did I entertain the birthday girl?"

Victoria flinched. He spoke her name warmly, as if they were old friends. "No. I was thoroughly bored. But the village children seemed to find your show passable."

"Ah, the children. Of course, you wouldn't count yourself a child, would you, Victoria? Not at the grand old age of thirteen. I rather doubt you've ever considered yourself a child though, have you? For someone so young, you seem so *tired*." He raised his hand to the chandelier hanging above him. "Such an affluent, opulent life, and yet you appear to carry the weight of the world."

"I am tired," Victoria responded. "Not that it's any of your concern."

The magician stepped towards her. Victoria fought the urge to step away. "Oh, but Victoria, it *is* my concern. I came to entertain, to baffle and bewitch you with my magic. And yet, I found the most important member of my audience the least entertained. I've failed to give the service I was paid so handsomely to provide."

"Don't let it concern you. You freed my parents and me from the burden of each other's company for a few hours. I'd call that a success. And now you may go on your way."

"But I wonder," the magician replied, gazing into her eyes. "What *would* excite you? Let us say, for the sake of argument, that I were able to perform any feat of magic. What would you choose?"

From the corner of her eyes Victoria saw the girl, Sophia, glance towards her.

"Well?" he asked.

"Magic doesn't interest me. It's just tricks and sham," Victoria said, trying to ignore Sophia's steady gaze.

"You're right," the magician agreed. "Most magic *is* trickery and diversion. But what if I were to tell you I could summon *real* magic? Ancient magic? And what if I had the power to grant you any wish? Tell me, what would you choose?"

Victoria sneered, determined to call his bluff and make him look just as stupid as he was. "I'd choose to be invisible so village fools would leave me alone."

"Really?" he gazed even further into her eyes. "But I don't think you're telling the truth, Victoria. I can see something else…a long-held dream that has nothing to do with invisibility. You're keeping it from me because you believe talking about it will make you seem foolish. But there's nothing foolish about dreams and desires."

Victoria was about to command him to leave the house and take his sickly daughter with him when her words failed her and her mind turned instead to her dream. The dream that haunted her both in sleep and during her waking hours. The dream of flight, and of flying far, far away. "I…I've always wanted to fly. Like a bird. But without wings. To go into the clouds or wherever my will takes me."

The magician smiled. "Interesting. Helping you fulfill that dream is not beyond the scope of my ability. But I warn you—you will only have a short time. Stolen moments in the grand scheme of things. But how many other people have the opportunity to say they've soared through the clouds?"

"I don't believe you," Victoria said. "You're just a showman. And not a very good one."

If her insult had an effect, the magician hid it well. "But let's say," he continued, "just for the sake of argument, that I *could* lend you the ability to fly. What would you give me in return for such a gift?"

With a growing sense of hope and unease, Victoria realized he was perfectly serious. Delusional, perhaps, but serious. "I have no money, if that's what you want. My parents only give me a meager allowance."

"Money is something I used to covet," he responded, an air of melancholy creeping into his voice. "But nowadays I find coins weigh so heavily in my pockets. And the more I accumulate, the greater the burden. But there's something else you have that would serve as payment. Something it appears you have little use for."

"What?" Victoria found herself genuinely curious. Was he really going to give her the gift of flight? Of course it was quite impossible, and yet strangely, she found herself immersed in the conversation.

"Well, I could take your name. Or perhaps a precious memory, if you have any. Or maybe that beauty spot on your cheek. And yet I don't think any of those things are worth the gift of flight."

"So, what is?"

"Well…" The magician shrugged. "How about your soul?"

"My soul?" Victoria shivered as the candlelight flickered.

"Well, *soul* sounds so grandiose, really, but that, in essence, is what I'm asking for. I may be wrong, but I suspect you have very little use for yours. Tell me, has your soul ever brought you a modicum of comfort or joy?"

Victoria shook her head. "Not as far as I'm aware. I'm not even convinced I believe in souls, much less own one."

"We do," the magician assured her, glancing at his daughter. "But some of us, and in this case I mean you, have very little connection with our souls. Your life, if you don't mind me saying, appears to be one of bile, spite, and boredom. I hardly think you'll miss the loss of your soul."

"But what about...about when I die?"

"You don't need a soul for dying, Victoria; death will come calling on its own. What *would* change is that, without your soul to take you any further along the road, there would be nothing more. You'll simply wink out of existence as if you were never here. Does the idea of nothingness bother you?"

Victoria thought for a moment. Would oblivion be such a bad thing? And how would she know, anyway? One minute she would *be*, the next she wouldn't. "I don't care about oblivion. But what about damnation? And Hell?"

"Do you believe in damnation and Hell?" the magician asked.

"Not really. I don't really believe in anything."

"There you have it, then. But you do believe I can give you the gift of flight, now, don't you?"

"Maybe. We shall see, shan't we?"

"We shall."

"You say I have no need for my soul. So why do you need it?"

"Sophia made a similar deal to the one I'm proposing. She made hers with a lady she met in the city. I was in more *troubled* circumstances at the time and languishing in debt and prison. The lady gave Sophia enough money to free me from my captivity, in return for her soul."

Victoria glanced at the magician's daughter. "Is that what's wrong with her?"

"In a sense. But she had a passion for life, Victoria, whereas you have none. I've been looking for someone like you for what seems like an age. So, what do you think? You give up your soul, and I bestow the prize of your wildest dream. The gift of flight."

"Are you the Devil?"

The magician laughed. "If I were, I think I'd have grander plans than trading magic with a bored little girl, don't you? No, I'm merely offering a deal on behalf of my daughter. But the day grows old, and the snow is falling, and we must be on our way. So quickly, before we leave, I shall ask you once again. Will you trade, Victoria? Something you shall barely miss in return to be able to take to the skies, to glide and soar wherever your will takes you?"

As the magician turned away, Victoria wiped her tears with her sleeve. She'd always told herself she'd give anything to be able to fly, and here was her opportunity. Of course, it hadn't happened the way she'd dreamt. She wouldn't just be able to take wing and fly from the house. To glide away from her parents and her cold, detached life.

Or would she? Perhaps...perhaps she would.

But what was she offering in return?

Nothing, as far as she could see. She had long come to understand her future was bleak. Her hatred and boredom were so ingrained that she knew little else, and if she'd ever had a passion for life, she'd long forgotten it. She knew her spite had turned her into a loathsome creature and that no one wanted to be around her.

And she couldn't blame them. Which was why she was resigned to spending the rest of her days in the house. She'd wait for her parents to die, inherit the place, and sack the servants so she could be alone. That was how she would end her days, haunting the rooms and halls, a ghost waiting for its end.

A clatter broke her thoughts as the magician packed the last of his props. "What are you doing?" she asked.

"We must be on our way. I have no more time to wait on your answer. There will be someone else to accept my offer."

"I'll do it," Victoria blurted. Her heart thumped as she realized what she'd agreed to. "As long as it won't hurt."

"You won't feel physical pain." The magician reached into his battered trunk and produced an old ledger and a black pouch. "But before I grant you your gift, you shall need to sign this book. Then, once your wish is fulfilled, I will collect your soul and place it within this pouch. From thereon you shall take the pouch and ledger and our dealings will be done."

"What will I do with it?" Victoria asked, gazing at the pouch. Something seemed to move within its soft black lining.

"Keep it safe, in case the Collector calls."

"What's inside it?"

"Souls. And the book carries the signatures of those who have forsaken them."

"Who is the Collector?" Victoria asked. "Is *he* the Devil?"

"I doubt it." The magician gave her an insincere smile. "We've never met the Collector, so I couldn't tell you for sure. All you need to know is that, while you carry the book and the bag, the Collector may call to claim his debt. You can be released from this burden at any time, however, by finding another."

"Another what?"

"Another person to trade with. Just as we are. And if you do, then you shall be rewarded."

"What with?"

"Oblivion."

"Is that what she seeks?" Victoria glanced at Sophia's dead eyes.

"More than anything. Her body and mind hanker for her soul, but then, Sophia loved life. You, on the other hand…"

"Hate mine," Victoria finished. And it was true. She despised it all—the house, her parents, and the bleak stretch of countryside beyond the windows. It was an emptiness she could no longer bear. "Where do I sign?"

The magician opened the book, smoothing it and pointing to a space below a long line of names. He took a pen from his pocket, dipped it into a small bottle of ink, and passed it to Victoria.

Above the list of names were lines of thick black writing in a language she'd never seen before, the letters a series of looping accents and hacks and slashes. She wondered if it was a variation of Latin. "What does this writing say?"

"I cannot read it. But the gist of its meaning was explained by the lady my daughter traded her soul with. She told Sophia everything I have told you—in essence, that you shall forsake your soul in exchange for a gift of your choosing, and that you will keep the book safe until either you've passed it to another, or its owner collects it. Sophia was told the agreement is binding in the most ancient of courts."

"What court?"

"I don't know, and I do not care to find out." The magician glanced at Victoria's hand as it hesitated over the page. "Sign now, or we shall be on our way and you will never hear from us again."

Victoria glanced at the other names in the ledger and wondered where the people who had signed were now. Dead, most likely. Gone from the world and into oblivion. She glanced at the magician's daughter. Victoria was stronger than she. She wouldn't miss her soul. How could she miss something she'd never known? It was impossible.

Victoria looked up at the large oil painting that dominated the wall. She sat with her parents, fake smiles artfully painted on their faces—one big, happy family.

She turned back to the book, her hand trembling as she signed her name. And then she held out the quill to the magician.

But he wouldn't take it. "The pen, the pouch, and the book are yours now. Thank you for freeing my daughter, and may your journey be easier than hers has been. Now, I need to give you your gift and show you, should you choose to pass the debt on, how you may give it to another." He opened the pouch, and as he did, a light filled the room.

Victoria leaned forward. Inside were a number of brightly colored eggs, far smaller than a bird's. Each egg carried a light, its color glowing through a glass-like shell.

A warmth rose from the bag, and Victoria was about to reach in when something scuttled through the eggs. She caught a glimpse of a hard, black creature with many legs and two huge pincers.

She stepped back. "What was that?"

"I didn't see anything," the magician replied.

"Yes, you did."

"Do you want your gift or not? Either way, you've signed the book, so whether or not you claim your wish, I must collect your soul."

"I'll take my gift," Victoria replied.

A thought crossed her mind, a way of escaping the *burden*, as he had put it. She buried the thought as deep as she could, just in case he could read her mind.

The magician reached nimbly into the bag and removed three shining eggs. They rested in his palm, one vivid blue, the other gentle lavender, while the third was a rich gold.

"Take two and carefully place them in your pocket. Once you've fully focused on your wish, place the third on your tongue. See yourself flying in your mind's eye, and you shall. After a while, there will come a time when the magic wears off. When it does, place the next egg upon your tongue, and it will keep you airborne. When the second egg fades, use the third to return to solid ground. Do not fly too high. We don't want you to come to harm." He placed a hand on her arm, lightly pinching her skin. "To be clear, Victoria, when the power from the last egg diminishes, you will return to me and keep your side of the bargain."

Victoria snatched her arm away. "I know."

She flinched as the magician tipped the three eggs into her palm. They were as hot as sand on a summer day and strangely light, like knots of wool. She transferred the eggs to her other palm and, gradually, they began to cool. Their shells were hard and smooth, like marbles. She gently lifted two of the eggs and placed them in her pocket before holding the third between her fingers.

Victoria closed her eyes and concentrated on the idea of flight.

"Picture your wish," the magician said, his voice seeming to come from some far-away place. "Make it real in your mind's eye, and when you can see it as clear as crystal, place the egg upon your tongue."

Victoria did as she was told. She imagined her polished shoes taking off from the carpet and saw herself gliding effortlessly across the room. There were no wings attached to her back, for she had no need for them. All she had to do to fly was focus on where she wanted to go, and her mind would take her there.

"Can you see yourself flying?" the magician asked.

"Yes."

"Can you feel it?"

"Yes."

"Then place the first egg in your mouth."

Victoria did as she was told. The egg rested upon her tongue for a moment before cracking, and all at once her mouth was filled with a multitude of flavors: peppermint, salt, sage, chocolate, and citrus.

Victoria gasped as a wave of power broke across her mind. It felt as if a star had burst inside her head. And then the energy began to build. It started in the crown of her head, running along her spine and bursting through her body.

I must be shining like a beacon, she thought, *the light bursting through my pores.*

"There," she heard the magician say.

Victoria opened her eyes to find herself looking down at him. She was floating in the middle of the room!

For the first time in her life, Victoria felt a surge of excitement and she couldn't help but grin. Her head was inches from the chandelier, and she reached up and spun it just for the sheer fun of it. It turned, sending the dust from its crystals raining down upon the magician.

Below, in a corner of the room, stood a pile of colorfully wrapped boxes. Birthday gifts. She hadn't bothered opening them and wouldn't now. Because not one could compare with what she had in this moment. The only thing she'd ever dreamt of.

"You've done it, girl," the magician said as his daughter slumped in a chair beside him, her breathing shallow. "You have your wish. Use it wisely while you can."

Victoria barely heard him. All she could focus on was levitating in the air.

Flying!

"Don't forget to return as soon as you use the third egg. You must keep your side of the deal."

"I said I would, didn't I?" Victoria coughed, praying he wouldn't see the blush she could feel blossoming across her cheeks. He was staring right into her eyes now, as if trying to read her intentions, so she looked instead to the thick drapes covering the windows and flew to them, wrenching them apart. Outside, the ornamental garden was dusted with snow, the hills in the distance soft and white. They looked as if they were covered in a layer of icing sugar. A giant birthday cake just for her.

She opened the window and recoiled as a blast of cold air rushed into the room. Victoria dipped back down and swept her shawl from the back of the chair and pulled it on, grinning as the magician continued to study her.

"You must come straight back here, girl," he reminded. "Don't forget."

"Of course I won't," Victoria said, sailing from the room and soaring through the window.

As Victoria left the shadow of the house, snowflakes fell around her, swirling to the ground, which was now several feet below. She rose into the air and spun like a ballet dancer, catching snowflakes in her outstretched hands and crying out for the sheer magic of it all.

Victoria glanced back to the house, wondering if anyone could see her. She pictured the look on her father's face, his eyebrow raised ever so slightly, her mother's expression a mask of outrage. Victoria laughed and waved to the house as she swept round and sailed up into the air, higher now that her initial caution had faded.

The garden below looked like a miniature scene. The rosebushes were like tiny models, the row of hawthorn trees leading to the pond stunted and white, their branches bare, twisted limbs.

Victoria soared down, shooting inches above the tree tops as her breath billowed from her lips like smoke. She imagined she was a dragon and roared, picturing everything burning in her path, the staid symmetry of the ornamental garden ablaze. Her father's favorite haunt, the place he cherished more than his own flesh and blood, now cinders against the snow.

Victoria's mocking laughter filled the air as she flew over the great pond at the end of the garden, its waters a solid disc of ice. It looked as if a giant silver-blue coin had been dropped from the heavens, and at its center that tired old statue, a distant ancestor frozen in time.

Victoria waved and flew on.

But as she climbed back into the air, an almighty flash ripped through the center of her head, blinding her with a bright white light. Victoria froze as the sky above and the land below vanished.

She found herself running through a poppy field. Only it wasn't her. It was a young man, and he was chasing a girl, and both of them were laughing. All the boy could think about was how he'd give anything for this girl, and as he looked at her, his heart felt as if it would explode.

And then the boy was somewhere else, stooped in a room of shadows. Before him rested a book with a row of signatures and heavy black writing in a strange, foreign language. The boy was terrified, but his longing for the girl forced his hand as he signed his name upon the page. And as he placed a dot next to his name, Victoria was transported away, shooting across the countryside and into a tunnel and through a rotten door into an entirely different place.

An entirely darker place.

The vision continued to soar at a terrible pace, shooting across the center of a street of blackened stone. Up it went, flying towards a tall dark house at the end of a row of disheveled buildings. From one of the cracked windows, someone whistled a strange, haunting melody.

Victoria tried to fight the vision, crying and screaming, pleading not to be taken into that room, not to see its terrible occupant...

Another flash scorched her eyes, and Victoria found herself hanging above the countryside once more, treading the air as if it were water. She took a deep breath, rubbing her eyes and wishing she could scrub the images of that cracked window from her memory.

"It was nothing," she told herself as she focused on smothering the dark and insidious vision, which still tried to take root in her mind.

The energy that had initially coursed through her was ebbing. Victoria reached into her pocket and withdrew one of the remaining two eggs, placing it upon her tongue. Moments later, it burst, filling her mouth with an abundance of flavors and fragrances. She could taste toffee, thyme, and lemon, and her head was filled with the scent of old books, freshly mown lawns, and the earthy damp of an autumnal forest floor. As the light coursed through Victoria, she gasped, kicking her feet and forcing herself to remain aloft.

And then she stretched out, wheeling in the air.

Victoria glanced down at her house; from up here it looked like a dollhouse with tiny lamps burning within. Nothing like the home she'd grown up in, that dark, looming place that had smothered her in terrible, maudlin despair. But she was free of that now, free of her mother and father and the grim faces of the long-suffering servants.

Free from all of it.

She filled the sky with laughter. "I'm never going back!"

Above, dirty white clouds lay heavily across the sky, their underbellies gray and swollen with snow. Victoria climbed towards them, determined, just for a moment, to stand upon one. It was her childhood dream, and today was her birthday, and what better day could there be to see her dream made real?

Victoria clamped her arms tightly to her sides, flying faster and faster. As she rose, her clothes billowed about while freezing air battered against her. The temperature was dropping further, but the remaining egg in her pocket, coupled with the energy surging through her, enveloped her in a powerful heat.

Victoria looked down. The ground was so far away that the garden was little more than a small white patch with distant black specks for trees. And then she found herself passing through a cloud.

It felt as if she were wrapped in a soft, damp fog.

"Hello!" she called, snatching at the cloud, trying to grab a part of it. But all she was left with was wet, chilled hands.

The novelty of being inside the cloud soon wore off. It was no different from being in mist. Victoria focused on climbing up and, moments later, she shot through the cloud, emerging into sunlight.

It was so bright that she threw her hands over her eyes, slowly releasing them as she drank in the sight of the deep blue sky. "It's beautiful." How strange it was, she thought, to be surrounded by sunlight while the land below was covered in snow.

As she soared towards the sun, a second flash ripped through her head, forcing her to stop.

Victoria found herself back in the dark street, her vision hovering once more before the cracked window, the sight of it filling her with a nauseating terror. No matter how she screamed and yelled, nothing seemed able to break the vision.

And then she saw herself. Or at least, she saw the owner of her vision, its black wings beating furiously as it hovered near the window, a dark reflection in cracked glass. It was the thing she'd glimpsed in the pouch of colored eggs, a thing of many limbs and a shiny black shell. Hundreds of tiny legs raced below its body, each covered in spurs and spikes, viscous green liquid dripping from their tips. Its head was long and narrow, two feelers reaching out above a row of tiny black eyes. It clutched a vivid, cherry-red egg within its pincers.

This egg was so much brighter than the ones Victoria had glimpsed in the pouch. It brimmed and hummed with intensity and vitality.

At least for now. Knowledge began to seep into her mind, no doubt from the creature whose vision she shared. In moments it would take the egg, which was a soul, into the room where it would be harvested. Soon after, its color and sparkle would dim.

The creature landed on the wall beside the window and slithered across the dark brickwork. It hesitated for a moment before slipping through the shattered pane, taking Victoria with it. They scuttled together down a damp, mold-ridden wall and onto a filthy, bare floorboard before stopping.

The room was covered from floor to ceiling with all manner of bric-a-brac. Heaps of empty sacks sat next to piles of house bricks. A series of chipped cups rested upon a mound of ragged clothes; above them hung an ancient wheelbarrow. The creature flew over a chamber pot full of broken china dolls, joining a throng of bulbous, buzzing flies.

Somewhere within the grime and squalor, someone, or *something*, whistled a melancholy tune. All at once Victoria knew, beyond a doubt, that she mustn't look at the whistler—for it was the *Collector*, and one look at it could shatter her sanity.

The creature flew now, taking Victoria through the mountains of rotten, discarded things as it sought its master, his haunting whistle growing as he called his servant. As they drew closer, a great itch grew inside Victoria's skull and she summoned every part of her will to come away from this hellish place.

To be taken back to where she belonged.

It worked, and the scene faded before her eyes. The last thing she saw of the room was an immense, warty hand with long strips of yellowed nails reaching for the creature and the fresh soul it carried.

Victoria clamped a hand over her mouth. Her stomach convulsed as she retched, but nothing passed her lips. She tried to block out the nausea, instead focusing on her surroundings. She was still hovering in the air above the clouds. "I have to get back to the ground."

She'd flown as far away from the magician as she could. And she would do anything now but surrender her soul to the *thing* that burrowed within the pouch. The creature that hid beneath the souls of the other poor unfortunates who had forsaken themselves.

Victoria had lived today. *Really* lived. And she wasn't ready to die or face oblivion.

The energy pulsing within her began to ebb, her grip in the air faltering. At any moment she could plunge back to earth.

Even if she let that happen, it would make no difference. Death would elude her, of that she was sure. The *Collector* would never let her off so easily.

No, she had to get away, to run. Not for her life, but for her very soul.

Victoria reached into her pocket, withdrew the last egg, and placed it upon her tongue. This time, when the flavors came, she ignored them, their taste bittersweet with the knowledge of what they were.

Someone else's life. Someone else's soul.

The power surged through her with such force that it felt as if her blood were on fire.

Victoria didn't waste a moment, turning in the air until she was upside down. And then she let herself fall, piercing the cloud below like an arrow. She urged herself on, shooting through the other side of the cloud and emerging back into the bleak winter afternoon.

Down and down she swept, the land growing and rising before her. She waited until she was thirty or so feet from the ground before slowing her descent and hanging still over the thick layer of snow.

In the distance, her house loomed like a black box upon the landscape, its lights so inviting in the wintry gloom. Victoria looked away towards the nearby hill. A ring of beech trees crowned its peak. If she could reach them, she could use the trees as cover before making her way to the village nestled below.

The magician and his dying daughter would come after her, of course, eager to claim Sophia's prize of oblivion. But she would find somewhere to hide. Perhaps she could reach sanctuary in the home of some god-fearing soul and wait until the magician and his Devilish wrath passed them by.

All she had to do was survive the night, and tomorrow at dawn she would make her way to the city. Then she could start a new life, become someone else altogether, someone *they* would never find.

But what of her signature in the book of souls?

Could the Collector somehow use it to find her? Victoria crossed her fingers until they ached, praying to never have to see that beast again, to never go back to that squalid room.

She flew towards the circle of trees and was close to the hill when something urged her to turn. A thrill of horror coursed through her as distant light spilled from the doorway of the house.

The magician.

"He knows," Victoria whispered. "Knows I'm running away!"

Her terror seemed to affect her power of flight. She turned back from the house, dipping low and soaring over hedgerows, praying the last of the energy would take her to the circle of trees. Victoria landed as the last of the power ebbed away. Her feet struck the icy ground, sending her stumbling on as she fought to stay upright.

She threw a glance back across the white fields to the house. A black speck was moving away from the building, crossing the snowy waste and heading towards her.

The magician's carriage.

He'd seen her, of course. He'd probably been watching her all the way up into the clouds. And like a fool, she'd come back down to the same place. And now he knew exactly where she was. His carriage sped on. Victoria dug her nails into her palms, picturing the horses churning through the snow, their master poised furiously above as he cracked his whip.

Victoria made for the trees. She only needed to hide until nightfall, which was surely minutes away, and then she could make her way to the village. She looked down, her eyes smarting with tears as she saw her trail of footprints dark against the snow. She wasn't going to escape. There was nowhere to hide from him, for all he had to do was follow her tracks.

But still she ran, her lungs aching, her breath snagging in her throat.

When Victoria could run no more, she stopped, standing below the meager shelter of a tree, its bark solid at her back. She fought to control her breath, wiping her eyes as the carriage bore over the crest of the hill. The clatter of its wheels seemed so loud in the silent snowfall, the frozen air filled with the steam of the horses' ragged breaths.

The carriage came to a halt before her, and the magician jumped from the cab, his cape flapping blackly against the snow. Behind him, Victoria glimpsed Sophia's pale face through the grimy window.

"You stupid, stupid girl." The magician's eyes narrowed as he bore down on Victoria. "Did you really believe you could just run away from me? Did you think I'd let you go? You signed the book. You agreed to the terms. Do you think I'll let my daughter suffer that half-life for a moment longer than she needs to?"

"Please. I shouldn't have... I want to live. I felt alive this afternoon. *Really* alive. For the first time in...so long."

"Too little, too late. You signed the book and forsook your soul." He clutched the pouch in his gloved hand and held it before her. "And now you need to give the Devil his due."

"You said he wasn't the Devil!"

"I don't know what the Collector is, and I don't want to. All I know is that it's not of this earth. But that's not my concern anymore. It's yours now."

"This is all wrong," Victoria protested. "Those things you gave me...I swallowed someone's *soul.*"

"I didn't hear you complain when you got your wish. Yet now that it's time to settle up, you cry foul and protest. But it's to no avail, girl. You *will* relinquish your soul and take the accursed bag and book with you to damnation."

As he opened the pouch, Victoria's eyes were once more drawn to the glow from within. It was so bright that it lit up the trunks of the trees around them. "So beautiful," she sighed.

The spell of the colors was broken as the magician closed his eyes and reached a hand towards the crown of her head. When he yanked his hand away, something deep within her cracked. Victoria fell to her knees, clutching her sides. It felt as if something inside had been torn in half.

The magician clasped an intense blue light between his gloved fingers. *Her* light, *her* soul. As she gazed at it, she knew she'd never get it back. That it could never be returned.

But the craving she felt was so powerful she grabbed for it, her hands clawing at thin air. Tears froze on her face as she stared at the light. It was the brightest, most gorgeous blue she'd ever seen.

Perfectly oval. Just perfect. Like the eggs she'd swallowed, only brighter.

The farther it moved from her, the deeper her emptiness grew. And now it felt as if the world had turned gray, the last of its color contained within the glowing jewel in his hand.

The magician held it over the pouch, its color vivid above the other souls inside. Brighter because it hadn't been harvested. Yet. But it would be soon enough, when the creature within the bag took it to the room in the charcoal-black house.

"Please, give my light back," she begged.

The magician gave her a brief look of pity and shook his head. He dropped the light into the pouch and, all at once, the creature emerged and snapped her soul between its pincers. Victoria flinched as the creature flew out, two ragged black wings beating furiously as it hovered before her.

"No!" she screamed, snatching desperately as the creature evaded her, moving just out of reach, as if mocking her.

It watched her for a moment before wheeling around and landing on a tree trunk, where it skittered across the bark. The tree was diseased, clumps of sickly brown fungus growing from its trunk and at its center, a great black hole. The creature crawled inside, taking her light with it.

And in that moment, Victoria knew she would never see her soul again.

At least not until it had been devoured by the monster in the room with the cracked window, its vitality sucked away. Only then would her soul be returned to the pouch. She wondered if she'd know which one had been hers once it was among the other lights in the bag. Victoria sank to her knees, the chill of the snow absent as numbness spread across her.

The magician placed the pouch and the book of pledged souls in her hands. "Keep them safe, girl. Guard the bag with your life, lest you bring the Collector's wrath. Find another person, Victoria, seek another to take the burden so you may find peace."

She couldn't have replied even if she'd wanted to. She could only watch as the magician walked back to the carriage. And then a dull thud came from within as Sophia's lifeless body slumped against the window.

The magician stood for a moment, his head dipped in the twilight, and then slowly he climbed upon the carriage, took the reins in his gloved hands and snapped them. Victoria watched emptily as the carriage rolled away, a dark blur in the growing night. She stood on the hill, oblivious to the bite of the cold, and glanced back to her house.

The lights still shone in the windows, but she knew she would find no warmth within. Already the pouch felt heavy in her pocket, the harvested souls weighing her down. She wondered how long it would be until the creature returned with the remains of her soul. How long it would take her to find someone else to take on the burden.

Victoria trudged down the hill, her darkening eyes fixed on the distant lights of the village below, the snow around her ankles as white as a cloud.

Eliza closed the book for a moment, leaving her finger inside to mark her place. "What a hideous story."

Despite her instant dislike of the nastiness and malice of Victoria Stapleton at the beginning of the tale, by the end she felt strangely moved by the girl's horrible fate. It didn't seem fair. After all, Victoria had woken up to herself. She had realized her mistakes. She'd wanted to live and perhaps to make amends, and now her life and soul had been viciously snatched away.

Of course, it was a moral story. For despite Eliza's mother's ban on all forms of fiction, she recalled the *Grimm's Fairy Tales* she'd managed to read when she was younger, and she knew a lot of the old stories served as cautionary tales. Surely this was just another such story.

But it felt like more than that. Like the one before, it felt like an account of something that had actually happened.

Following the end of the story was another block of writing, another addendum. She wondered if it was a theme of the book, to follow each story with an imagined document from the writer.

Eliza began to read, silencing the tiny voice inside her head urging her to stop.

Eldritch Black

Addendum

Immediately after taking the role of custodian of *The Book of Kindly Deaths,* via the Grimwytch guild, I knew there must be a more effective way of tracing breaches up and down the country. At least, other than using their rather archaic compass.

So I paid a handsome sum to employ an agent in each city who, in turn, employed informants in the towns and villages across our land. And within days of anything unholy or monstrous occurring, I was told.

Which is how I came to learn of poor Victoria Stapleton. There had been several sightings of her just outside a small village. Always at dusk and always offering a person's heart's desires in trade for the price of a soul.

Thankfully, the people of the village were superstitious, and not one took her offer. The moment I was told of this Devilish event, I set out for Upper Caddlebury with my assistant, Sarah.

Upper Caddlebury was a small village with a welcoming inn, thatched roofs, and a sense of general cheer—quite the opposite of the dark occurrences within its midst.

My informant took me to the place on the road where Victoria had been sighted, and the three of us waited. As twilight fell across the woods, she appeared, winding her way through the trees. Her clothes were in tatters, her hair lank, and her face pale and drawn.

"Please sir, please madam, what do you wish for? What does your heart desire? I'll grant you anything if you'll just give up a little something you have no need for." Her filthy hands grasped my sleeve.

I took Victoria to the inn and requested Sarah help bathe and dress her before dinner. The poor girl barely ate the food, her lifeless eyes staring into the distance, and it took some time to draw her story from her. But eventually, as I wrote it into *The Book of Kindly Deaths*, the whole sorry tale was told.

"We shall end your burden," I told her. "But it will mean summoning the Collector."

"What is the Collector?" she asked, flinching as she said its name. "Is it a demon?"

"I'm not certain," I told her. "But yes, it's probably a demon, although not in a biblical sense. I believe it's most likely a lesser demon known as a hoardspike. They like to collect things. Especially things precious to humans. Like souls."

"My soul's in the pouch." Victoria pointed to the bag. "But it doesn't sing to me anymore."

"The hoardspike removes the soul's vitality before it passes the remains back. While these husks are of no use to the hoardspike, they're potent magic for us. They can be used as bait, to offer potential victims anything they want. And the demon thrives on the fear carried by the bearer of the pouch. Terror is just one more thing it collects. We need to end this cycle tonight."

"There's something else in the pouch," Victoria said. "A creature."

"It's called a fetcher. It hatches within the hoardspike, burrowing from its chest in the place a heart should be. The fetcher has the strongest affinity for its master, both parasite and host thriving on the actions of the other. The hoardspike nourishes the fetcher, and the fetcher does its bidding, collecting whatever it desires. We shall use this fetcher to bring the hoardspike to us. In its own dimension, it would be formidable, but ours shall weaken it."

"You're bringing the Collector here?" Victoria asked, scratching her arm until her nails drew blood.

I placed a hand over hers. "Do not worry, I can deal with the hoardspike. And before dawn rises, you will be free of your burden."

"Will I get my soul back?" The tiniest spark of hope gleamed in Victoria's eyes.

"You will get back what the hoardspike rejects. But I'm afraid it will be of no use to you."

"Will I die?"

"There are things I can do that will make your life more bearable," I explained. "But first we must bring the demon to us, and for that we shall need to find a more suitable place. Do you know of any buildings that lie abandoned? Tumbledown and deserted? These are the places the occupants of the Grimwytch favor."

"The occupants of the Grimwytch?" Victoria asked.

"The things we call monsters and demons," Sarah explained as she wrote an account of our meeting in her journal.

"But I don't want to meet monsters or demons," Victoria protested. "And I don't want to see the Collector."

"You may not have a choice," I replied. "The Collector can come to our dimension at any time to collect its book and pouch. Would you rather meet it with us by your side, or on your own?"

"There's a place where I sleep," Victoria said. "It's as you said, abandoned and tumbledown. It's an old building in the woods, and I've never seen anyone else there. But I've seen tracks and animal bones."

"It's probably used by poachers and hunters in the summer months. I will gather my equipment, and we shall be on our way," I told her, rising from the table.

"You want to summon this thing at night?" Victoria asked. And I could see it wasn't just emptiness that consumed her, but also fear.

"I do. You're safe with us, Victoria. I've dispatched more monsters than I care to remember. Now wait here until I return. Finish your supper; you will need all the energy you can muster."

The house Victoria brought us to was perfect for my purposes. It was a low, squat building with walls choked by ivy and a pervasive stench of rot and mold.

We lit a fire in the middle of the room and swept the floor as best we could, clearing away detritus and muck. I took my bag and removed several magical seals, which would hopefully bind the hoardspike within the four derelict walls. Sarah took a piece of chalk and inscribed symbols on the wall, glyphs and spells to weaken the creature once it passed into our realm. And then I took the old bones we'd collected from outside and placed them in a crude circle.

Finally, by the light of the fire, I asked Victoria for the pouch and book. She held on to them for a moment, a doubtful look on her face as I gently took them from her.

I placed the book in my bag and removed a pair of iron tongs. "When I nod, Sarah, I want you to open the pouch. Make sure you hold it away from you."

Sarah nodded grimly and did as I requested.

I could see the glow of souls within the bag long before she opened it, and when she did, the colors and the light were almost overwhelming. I was hypnotized by those lights for a moment as they shone like tiny, jewel-like eggs.

But the spell was broken when I caught sight of a barbed black tail sinking inside the bag.

Quickly I thrust my tongs inside, and from within came a dreadful din, like a living beast placed in a pot of boiling water. The bag writhed and spun in Sarah's hands as the fetcher desperately fought to free itself, and all at once I pulled it forth, holding it high above the pouch. It continued to shriek, a terrible sound bursting from its maw as the tongs clung tighter to its tail, its tiny feet twitching as its wings flapped. I threw it to the cold, hard ground with all my might.

A loud cracking sound came from deep within the fetcher, provoking another hideous cry.

I unsheathed my knife in a trice and leaped down, cleaving off its head and flicking it into the fire with my blade. It continued to scream inside the flames for a moment, until I threw its writhing body beside it.

And then the temperature in the room dropped.

The hoardspike was crossing over.

The shadows lengthened in the corners of the room and broke away, flowing across the floor like rivulets of dark water and gathering within the circle of bones.

The hoardspike grew before us, a male, far larger than any other I'd encountered. He towered at least three feet over me, wearing a heavily stained shirt and a pair of tattered, brown woolen trousers. These were his only concessions to humanity.

His feet were bare, horrible things covered in warts, their yellowed toenails curled many times over. His thin face carried a look of fury, his putrid green flesh covered in boils and liver spots. He raised a long finger, pointing to me as he hissed, "The air is...too clean."

"It must be a change from your squalor, hoardspike. Do you know why you've been summoned?" I asked, one hand on my knife, the other on the holster of my pistol.

"Summoned?" He laughed with a sound like a hacking cough. "You didn't summon me. I heard the cry of my fetcher." He gazed at the fire and a fleeting glimpse of pity crossed his gnarled face. "You killed it, human. You killed my fetcher!" He thrust a finger into the bloody red hole in his chest where the creature had once lived.

"I did. It had no business in this realm, as you well know. And neither do you. I've seen your journal, hoardspike, and I know how many souls you've taken." I pointed to Victoria, who was cowering in the corner. "You will face your punishment, but first you will free the girl."

"I shall do no such thing." He licked his lips and gave her a smile. "Even though her soul was quite delicious."

"You will free her from the burden you've imposed, and I shall destroy your book of pledged souls. What remains of them shall be buried in a sacred place. And then I shall end your miserable existence, for I cannot permit you to live."

"I thought it would be the Midnight Prison for me," he said, with no little amusement. "That's how our law works, unless I'm mistaken?"

"Only if the Midnight Prison was my judgment. But you've destroyed many, many lives, and I feel not an inkling of mercy for you."

"Then I am in a corner, little writer. Holed up like a rat. What incentive do I have to agree with your wishes if I face execution at the end of them?"

"I can make your passing painless."

"And the girl?" He grinned at Victoria. "What will happen to her?"

"That's no concern of yours." I held the gun openly now.

"Listen to me...Victoria," he said. "You had your wish, and I gave you power, and so you are bound to me. This writer will destroy you. He wears a velvet glove, but believe me, it hides an iron hand. Take the journal and pouch and go and fetch me a soul; then, and only then, will I release you from your endless wandering."

I aimed the gun at the vile creature's head, but before I could release the trigger, he moved with an inhuman speed, and my weapon was thrown across the room, discharging into the wall. I ran forward, unsheathing my knife, and slashed at the hoardspike, opening a great wound in his side. Vile, sticky, indigo blood poured from the gash as he howled. Before I could bring my blade down across his loathsome throat, he hit me across the face with the back of his hand and sent me crashing to the ground.

To my horror and against all instruction, Sarah ran forward to grab my gun, and the hoardspike bore down on her, lifting her into the air and shaking her before throwing her aside.

And then he moved towards Victoria.

She stood before the fire, the vile creature's book of pledged souls in her hand.

The hoardspike stopped, a look of horror crossing his cracked old face. "That's my property, girl."

"But you gave it to me to look after, remember?" Victoria replied, a tone of insolent fury creeping into her voice. "Or have you forgotten my burden?"

The hoardspike laughed. "Do you think burning my book will save any of the souls inside, least of all your own? It's too late. I have them all, deep, deep inside." He rubbed a grotesque finger over his belly.

"I know what you've done," Victoria continued. "And I know what you are. And I know the book is worth nothing, but you still want it. Still need it. You hoard. Like a common rat."

The hoardspike swallowed, his beady eyes resting on the book. "Just give it back."

I crawled as slowly as I could, reaching for the place where my gun had fallen.

I was halfway there when the hoardspike snapped his head in my direction. "I thought you were out cold. A shame, I was looking forward to feasting on your eyes before I killed you. Oh well."

He splayed his fingers, his long, curled nails as sharp as knives, and loped towards me. And then Victoria laughed and he stopped, screaming as he saw his book tumbling into the flames.

He lashed out at Victoria with a savage blow and her scream was cut short. There was nothing I could do for her.

I dove for the gun, cocked the trigger, and shot the demon.

He fell where he stood, straight into the fire, an acrid stench filling the air as he joined his fetcher.

I ran to Victoria. She clutched her throat, and I could see by her eyes that the wound was a mortal one. She slumped to her knees, falling into my arms.

I held her, weeping and weeping until, finally, Sarah placed a gentle hand on mine. "It's over," she said.

And it was.

At dawn, I returned to the abandoned house and set about my grim task. I dismembered the hoardspike, placed him within a series of sacks, and threw them into the back of my hired carriage. Sarah and I removed the binds and chalk markings on the walls of the building and destroyed all evidence of our presence.

I took out the compass the guild had given me and used it with my map to find the nearest crossing place to the Grimwytch.

It was an old bridge over a dried-up river; below it was a door in the wall. I opened the door into the other world and put my Solaarock necklace on to counteract the harsh rays of their moon before entering.

I found myself deep in a part of Blackwood, a haunted, wretched place. Surrounding me stood Watcher Trees. Or at least that is how they appeared with their tangled limbs adorned with softly glowing eyes. But this place was known to be haunted by shapecasters, and so I took a piece of iron from my pocket and touched each of the trees with it. Their eyes blinked rapidly and their limbs recoiled, but had they of been shapecasters, the iron would have scorched and sizzled their revolting flesh.

I dumped the remains of the hoardspike below two entwined Watcher Trees.

And then, crossing back to our world under cover of night, I returned the body of Victoria Stapleton to her parents.

I wrote to them, certain my words would offer scant comfort. Had my occupation permitted, I would have told them what had happened to their brave daughter. But my job is to move by shadows and stealth, to sweep away all evidence of the other world.

We travelled west and buried the pouch of harvested souls deep beside a spring, paying our final respects to the poor unfortunate victims within.

CHAPTER NINE

No Such Thing

"So, what was the point?" Eliza whispered. Why follow a story with a journal entry? Why not just make it a part of the story?

Unless the author, Edwin Drabe, was trying to make the story seem more real. Perhaps it was all a part of the atmosphere, such as fixing the book to only turn one page at a time.

But as her unease grew, as she tried and failed to tell herself it was just a book of fairy stories, something slithered across Eliza's foot. She clamped a hand over her mouth, stifling her scream. Her foot itched madly. It felt as if it had been tickled by a series of tiny feet.

Eliza leaped from the bed, pulling back the duvet, to see something black and shiny scuttle over the edge of the bed.

It couldn't be…could it?

The fetcher?

Had it somehow escaped from the book and found its way into her room? Perhaps it had been secreted inside a hidden compartment.

"Don't be ridiculous. There are no such things as fetchers!" she told herself. But whatever had crawled from the bed, Eliza knew she needed to find it if she hoped to get to sleep. Eliza flipped the main light on and the room

Eldritch Black

brightened for a moment, before the light bulb dimmed and extinguished with a soft *pop*.

Movement in the center of the room caught her eye as something wriggled towards the curtains. Eliza took a tentative step forward, wondering what she'd do if she managed to catch whatever the hell it was—because aside from mosquitoes, Eliza didn't like to kill anything. Not even the enormous spiders that appeared each autumn.

But if this thing *was* the fetcher, she'd kill it in an instant.

"It can't be the fetcher," she whispered. "It's just a story and..."

Something clambered up the wall below the curtains, just as the book described—a series of skittering legs, a black shell, two folded wings, and a pair of horribly large pincers.

And then it vanished below the curtain line.

Eliza grabbed the curtains, sweeping them apart just in time to see a long black tail disappear down a hole in the windowsill.

A beam of moonlight illuminated the sill, and now she could see it wasn't a hole but a large knot in the wood. She ran her hand over it. It was quite solid. There was no hole, no place for the creature to wriggle into.

So where had it gone?

She was seeing things. No doubt through tiredness and her imagination freshly awoken by *The Book of Kindly Deaths*.

But as Eliza began to pull the curtains, her eyes were drawn to the window across the garden, where she'd earlier seen the figure watching her. It was still there. Standing in the window as the bare bulb blinked, and as it did, the light in Eliza's room came back on.

For the briefest moment. Before winking out once more.

As the figure clamped a hand to the window, its light bulb flickered and faded. And as its light went out altogether, the light in Eliza's room came back on.

Eliza stared at the window across the way, but she could only see a square of darkness. She shivered, wondering if the figure was still there with its hand upon the glass, before she snapped the curtains closed and adjusted them until there wasn't the slightest gap.

Eliza snatched the duvet from her bed, examining it to make sure nothing was caught within its folds. Then she flipped her pillows over and checked beneath them before switching off the main light and climbing into bed.

CHAPTER TEN

Into Grimwytch

*E*liza held the book up before the bedside lamp. As she gazed at its cover, she began to understand why her mum had forbidden her to read fiction. It played havoc with the mind. *Particularly this book, she thought, with its nasty little stories.*

They seemed so real. Or at least, they seemed as if they might be real *somewhere*. And the darkness they brought had brushed against her world, making a neighbor decorating an empty room a menacing silhouette, a faulty light bulb a threat, and a shadow a mythical creature.

And now her imagination, long ago quashed by her mother, was growing wild like weeds in summer.

Eliza jumped as a floorboard outside her door creaked. *Someone* was outside.

The first thought to spring into her mind was of the book collector, Mr. Eustace Fallow, standing in the hall. She stashed the book below her pillow, her heart thumping as the handle turned and the door swung open.

A shadow fell against the wall.

And then her father poked his head into the room. "I saw a light under your door. And if *I* saw it, so will your mother, and she's on her way up. So, to prevent an argument of brutal and epic proportions, I thought I'd give you a heads-up. It's pretty late and…are you okay, Eliza? You look awful!"

"Thanks, Dad," Eliza said, offering a smile. "I'm fine. Something woke me up. It felt like a spider crawling across my leg. So I turned the light on, but there was nothing there."

"That old chestnut, eh?" Her father grinned.

"What do you mean?"

"I mean, I have that same nightmare myself. Most nights. Only it's not just the one spider in my dreams. It's several hundred thousand." He shivered. "I must have passed my nightmares to you somehow. Sorry!"

"I won't hold it against you, Dad. It's probably this house. It's a bit weird, isn't it?"

"Oh yes!" Her dad nodded. "Just a tad! I'll probably have nightmares myself tonight. Well, there's something to look forward to. But look, if you get really, really, really freaked out, wake me up."

"How freaked out?" she asked, allowing a slight smile as she wondered what kind of ludicrous creations her father would come up with this time.

"Really, really, really, really freaked out. I mean, if you wake thinking there's a squadron of killer midgets loose, don't wake me. But if you wake thinking there's a squadron of killer midgets loose with tarantulas on their shoulders and meat cleavers for hands, then you can wake me. Okay?"

"What about tarantulas with meat-cleaver hands and midgets on their shoulders?" Eliza asked.

"The same thing will probably apply. Anything else, let me sleep. Alright, goodnight, darling."

"'Night, Dad."

As the door closed, Eliza switched the bedside light off. The book felt hard below her pillow, so she grabbed it, placing it beneath the pile of clothes on the floor. She'd finish it in the morning. When it was daylight and the stories wouldn't be half so scary. That way, she could discover what happened in the end and maybe a clue to why Tom had left it on the desk.

Providing there was an end.

Eliza was still wondering what the stories meant when she fell asleep...and found herself standing at the top of a ladder in the middle of thick, swirling fog. Except as the fog parted, she saw it wasn't fog, but a cloud. And close, so close it almost hurt her mind, was a great red moon. Eliza reached for it as if it were a balloon and almost had it in her grasp when the ladder began to shake. She clutched it, climbing down its rungs as fast as her feet could go, glancing beneath and wishing she hadn't.

Below, stretching for as far as she could see, was a great black city, its ancient buildings bathed in darkness, snakes of gray smoke rising from its chimneys. In the city center stood seven colossal black towers. Eliza gazed at the closest, marveling at its immensity. But beyond the towers' awe-inspiring size and gothic grandeur, there was also something deeply disturbing.

She thought about climbing the ladder, going back into the sky, but the shaking started once more. Eliza renewed her efforts, climbing down faster and looking away from the tower.

As she neared the bottom, which somehow seemed to happen much faster than it should have, she saw people in the street below. Eliza caught a glimpse of pale skin, lank hair, hard angular faces, and flashing red eyes. She looked away, focusing instead on the cobblestone street.

Time jumped, and she found herself at the foot of the tower, pushing its great arched doors open, their color blacker than black. And then she was inside the tower, standing in the middle of a huge chamber. At its center was a tall chair. Eliza felt a curious and immense sense of relief to find it empty.

But of course it's empty, she thought. *The man who sits there is in my world now. And I'm in his.*

Quite how she knew this, she had no idea. Except that she did, and the knowledge was as real as the ladder she had descended.

Someone hissed. She turned to find a series of cells running along the room's circumference—and behind thick black bars, people. At least, they looked like people, until she spotted the tall, disheveled lady with great long, curling nails and warts across her face. Eliza stepped back.

It's a Collector.

And then the other prisoners began to call—some laughing, some howling, while others wept. "Stop!" Eliza cried, and somehow she was more disturbed by hearing her voice in this world than she was by the cries of the prisoners.

Eliza looked for the doors, her eyes falling on the staircase that rose round and round in ever-tighter circles, vanishing towards the tower's summit. The staircase beckoned to her. "No. That's not the right way," she shouted, her voice rising over the prisoners' din.

Eliza turned until she found the door, fleeing through it and passing into the street, which for some curious reason was painted with blue letters. She searched for the ladder to her world, but it was gone, and as something screamed, Eliza ran, flying down the street and into another and on and on she went. The streets passed in a blur as here and there she caught snapshots of bizarre and terrible sights and all manner of misshapen figures.

She ignored them and ran on.

Eliza stopped as she passed a street illuminated by a great white light. The glow was pouring from a tall house in the center of the street, its very bricks ablaze with light. Outside, a crowd gathered, keeping to the shadows, unwilling, it seemed, to step into the light.

Someone watched from a window in the light house, and all at once Eliza felt a strange, powerful surge of affection for him.

She knew the watcher.

Or had known him.

Many, many years ago.

As Eliza stepped towards the house of lights, the crowd turned to her, and a figure whose face seemed to be formed of one huge, snarling mouth prowled towards her. Its intent was clear as she glanced at the curved dagger clutched in its hand.

Eliza ran, down a murky tangle of roads filled with old, crumbling buildings, emerging onto a long street lit with gas lamps. At the end, a grand building stood. She ran towards it, doing her best to ignore the howling, which seemed to draw closer by the second. She ran up a small flight of marble steps and came to a door, stopping short as her gaze fell upon its knocker. .

It was a gargoyle.

And dimly, she realized she'd recently seen its twin. At her grandfather's house.

Eliza looked away from the revolting brass, impish face as she placed her palm upon the door and pushed. It swung open and Eliza stepped inside.

The interior was grandly decorated, with polished marble floors and a thick, plush carpet running up a wide staircase. The building was lit with gas lamps and moonlight, which filtered through a series of stained glass windows. Each window boasted a different image—here a deformed figure with what looked like tentacles for hair, there a cowled man gazing into a sundial. But in every picture, Eliza found images of pens, books, and towers.

Eliza turned as voices echoed along the corridor below the stairs. She followed them, avoiding looking directly at the two armored guards standing before a large room. She knew, somehow, that she mustn't look at the guards. At least, not directly.

The guards stepped into the shadows as she approached, just as she'd known they would. Eliza emerged into a large room lined with bookcases.

The books whispered as she entered, but she knew better than to answer them. In the center of the room, she found a large glass case. Something moved within. Eliza stepped closer as its occupant slithered into a patch of moonlight.

The creature was the size of a rabbit, its flesh the deepest, darkest blue she'd ever seen. It reminded her of a squid, a squid crossed with a slug. Two feelers extended from its bulbous head and as they found her, its soft, yellow, cat-like eyes swiveled to regard her. Eliza felt a compulsion to cradle the creature. For somehow, despite its hideous appearance, she knew it was a magical thing. But as she opened the case and reached for the creature, it sprayed a fine blue mist from its mouth, coating her face. Eliza grimaced as she frantically wiped her eyes and found her hands covered in ink.

And then the voices returned, drawing closer.

"You know he's not *right*. Don't pretend otherwise. Some of his recent judgments have been…evil," said a man's voice.

"Right or wrong, we elected him. What would you have us do, conspire to remove him from office? Do you want to commit treason?" a lady's voice asked, low and full of authority.

"It's only treason if it's against the king," the other pointed out.

"He was endorsed by the king, Mr. Bumbleton."

And then they stepped into the room. The first was a lady, tall and reed-like, with long, deep black hair and a pair of bright lilac eyes glowing from her harsh, lined face.

The man beside her looked like a barrel, with a thick auburn beard and a pair of bespectacled black eyes set into a pudgy, pale face.

Both wore official-looking black robes.

They gazed in silence at Eliza as she frantically scrubbed her face, until finally the lady spoke. "It seems the Drabes know no end of meddling. We have another, it appears, Mr. Bumbleton. An*d* he told us there were no more. He lied."

"Indeed he did, Mrs. Sallow, indeed he did." Mr. Bumbleton peered at Eliza through his pince-nez glasses. "But this one isn't wholly here."

"I don't understand?" Eliza said. And she didn't.

Nothing in this dream, for she realized that was what it was, made sense. Although, in another way, it all made perfect sense.

"She doesn't understand," Mr. Bumbleton said, sighing loudly.

"No, she doesn't. Because if she did, she wouldn't be here snooping," Mrs. Sallow said with a low, cat-like hiss. "Don't think ignorance makes you exempt from punishment, Miss Drabe."

"I'm Miss Winter," Eliza replied.

"You're a Drabe, through and through," said Mrs. Sallow. "Just like your grandfather. Did you see him on your journey? Hiding in his house of light?"

"Hiding might not be the best word to use, Mrs. Sallow." Mr. Bumbleton chuckled. "Everyone in the Grimwytch knows he's there. I mean, he's not exactly difficult to miss!"

"Your grandfather will have to come out eventually. And when he does, there will be consequences." Mrs. Sallow's eyes narrowed. "For you, Miss *Winter*, as well as him."

"But not now," Mr. Bumbleton said. "Because she's not really here."

"No," Mrs. Sallow agreed. "She's not."

"But…" Eliza stopped.

She found herself at the top of the ladder once more as it began to totter, threatening to fall to the city below.

Eliza reached out, finding an edge in the swirling fog, and pulled herself up. She stepped carefully across a short stone walkway towards the faint door that had just materialized. Beyond the door, a dim white light.

Eliza grasped the edge of the door, which had now become the hard cover of a book. She peeled back a heavy paper curtain, taking great care not to displace the trembling blue words jiggling upon it as she stepped inside.

Another page brushed against her, and she gently tugged its corner, stepping into the next page.

Only it wasn't a page, but a sheet.

And then she found herself lying in her bed.

For the briefest moment, Eliza could still hear the distant cries emanating from the city far below, could still feel the Grimwytch's curiously scented breeze upon her cheek.

She gazed at her hands. They were free of ink. "But it's real," she said. "That place is real. Somewhere."

Eliza reached for the bedside lamp, switched it on, and picked up *The Book of Kindly Deaths*.

It fell open to the next story.

CHAPTER ELEVEN

The Wrong People

*A*s Katherine Meadows opened the door, she found the village of Tattleton covered in thick, slate-gray fog. "Damn you, David," she muttered as she made her way down the hill.

Within moments she was engulfed in swirls of fog. Katherine shivered, wondering if she should return to the house for her coat; instead, she bunched her hands into the sleeves of her thick woolen jumper and walked on.

The sooner she found her brother, the sooner she could return to the thick vegetable soup her mother was preparing on the stove.

Katherine gritted her teeth as she wondered where David had gotten to. At thirteen, she was only four years his senior, and yet it often seemed as though a lifetime separated them.

As she passed through the village, its houses little more than dim, dark blocks, she strained to hear anything that could give her brother's location away. She stopped in front of the church as, somewhere in the distance, someone shrieked.

Katherine waited, and moments later another shout came. It was instantly swallowed by the fog, but it was enough for her to change course.

The cry had come from the old bridge.

"He wouldn't," Katherine told herself, praying she was wrong. The huge stone bridge that ran the length of the gorge was strictly out-of-bounds—not only to David and his friends, but the whole village.

It was a place to avoid. A place best forgotten.

But now, as Katherine took the old trail leading to the bridge, she could hear voices, and they were getting louder. "Surely they wouldn't be that stupid," Katherine muttered. But she'd seen the recent changes in her brother as he'd made his new friends, and she knew it was only a matter of time before something bad happened to him.

As the dark bulk of the bridge loomed through the mist, the voices were clearer as they rang out below it—one the arrogant, commanding boom of Richard Tattleton, the other the rather less assured voice of her brother David.

"Get on with it!" Richard demanded.

"Go on, David, you lost. You have to do it." A girl, perhaps Alice Westam or her sister, Claire.

"Please." David now. "I'll do anything. Just not that."

Katherine ran faster as she spotted the three smudges in the fog and, looming above them, the bulk of brickwork that formed the old bridge wall. Just past the three figures, she could see a dark rectangle.

The ancient black door.

Katherine glanced at the scene of devastation in front of it. They'd pulled aside the heavy sacks and debris that had covered the door, leaving them strewn across the ground. David stood directly before the door, the others a slight distance away. His hand hovered in the air, knuckles ready to knock.

"Get away from there!" Katherine shouted.

David flinched, surprise and guilt spreading across his face. "I didn't…"

"Just get away from the door," Katherine said, shoving him away, but moments later Richard Tattleton pushed David back.

"This has nothing to do with you." Richard glared at Katherine. "We made a bet and David lost. Now he has to pay his forfeit."

"You're not allowed to be here," Katherine said, looking from David to Alice and finally Richard. "None of you. Do you know how much trouble you're going to be in?"

Richard crossed his arms. "None, if you keep your big fat mouth shut."

"How dare you speak to me like that!"

Richard stepped towards her. Despite being a year her junior, he was big and strong and he knew it. "Like I said, this is nothing to do with you. David made a bet, we all did. And he lost. And now he has to knock on the door. And if he doesn't, the whole village will know about it."

"And then everyone will know you've been here," Katherine replied. "And apart from the fact that this place is forbidden, look at the mess you've made." Katherine pointed to the debris strewn across the ground.

"I don't care," Richard said. "I can take punishment. But David's going to be known as a coward for the rest of his life. No one will trust him. *No one.* And he knows it, which is why he's going to knock on the door."

Katherine looked to her brother. He gave a slight nod, his face a mask of misery and fear.

"I don't know what's so scary about that stupid door, anyway," Alice chimed in. "Unless you believe the stories, and I don't. They just tell them to make us do what they want."

"So why don't *you* knock on the door, then?" Katherine asked Alice, who simply shrugged.

"Because she didn't lose the bet," Richard said. "Ignore your sister, David, and get on with it, because I'm getting bored now."

David nodded, walking towards the tall black door like a man condemned to execution. As Katherine watched him, she felt a terrible conflict. On the one hand, she wanted to grab David and lead him from the door, but on the other she knew that if he didn't follow through with his forfeit, his reputation in Tattleton would be forever blackened.

Richard Tattleton's parents were well-respected within the village. Indeed, the Tattletons were the village's founding family. Their opinions were listened to even though, to Katherine, most seemed to be deeply malicious. The Tattletons had driven many people from the village over the years, for anyone who disagreed with them soon found that their status fell lower than that of a mongrel dog. Only last month, a farmer whose cow had given birth to a two-headed calf had been accused by the Tattletons of communing with the Devil. He'd fled in the night as someone had set fire to his farmhouse, engulfing it in flames.

As David raised his hand before the door, Katherine shouted, "Don't! I'll do it."

She swallowed. All eyes were on her.

"Really?" David asked.

Katherine felt sick as she nodded. "It's just an old door. But the bridge is unstable. You shouldn't be near it. I'll knock on the stupid, bloody door, and then the three of you can put all this stuff back across it. And we'll never speak of this again." Katherine looked at Richard. "Agreed?"

"I suppose it doesn't matter. If you want to take his place, then so be it."

Katherine bit her tongue. She didn't want to take David's place or be anywhere near the door. Just the sight of it, uncovered now, was making her flesh creep. She peered at the large keyhole set into the dry, cracked black paint and held her breath.

Had she heard someone on the other side giggling?

Katherine looked over to Richard. "This is ridiculous…"

"Your sister's a chicken, David," Richard said. "So you'd better go and knock on the door right now. Or your family will be ruined."

Katherine held up her hands. "Leave him alone. I'll do it. It's only a door." But as she approached the door, the legends about the people on the other side of it began to tumble through her mind.

The Wrong People.

"Get on with it!" Richard shoved Katherine towards the door, stepping away.

She swallowed, raised her hand, and before her mind could talk her out of it, brought her knuckle down. Katherine flinched as a huge cracking sound filled the air, as if the heavens were being rent in two. She clamped her hands over her ears as brick dust rained down upon her head.

Behind her, the children were stepping away, their faces full of horror while David's turned ashen. Katherine turned back to the door, her heart thumping wildly as she looked at the woman who stood within the doorway.

She was clad in a black dress and wore a battered old hat with a dead flower drooping from its band. Greasy black hair framed her face, and her skin was like old, yellowed parchment. The woman grinned at Katherine, revealing rancid black teeth as she used her hand to shield her ditchwater-gray eyes. Something squirmed below her lip.

A maggot?

An obese man waddled out from behind her; he, too, was clad in black, his bald head the same waxy yellow. He raised an odd-looking brass device to his lips and began to blow. Music filled the air, its sound low and melodic in a distinctly broken way. There was something deeply hypnotic about the sound, and as Katherine listened, all ideas of running away left her mind.

She found herself walking towards the door. Behind the obese man and the lady, other shadowy figures lurked, one of them tall in the gloom.

Katherine stopped and turned as she thought she heard someone calling to her. There were three children behind her, one of whom looked quite familiar. They seemed to be shouting, but she could hear nothing, only music.

The smiling lady in black guided her through the door, and Katherine knew, distantly, that she was walking into a place that was very different from the world behind her.

A very wrong place.

The tall man appeared in the gloomy passage beyond; he was so tall he had to stoop. His long, greasy black hair was plastered to his yellowed, papery face. His gray eyes found hers, and he offered a crooked smile and bowed.

Behind him stood an elderly man with a long black beard and a thatch of wiry hair. His eyes, already huge behind his broken spectacles, grew even larger as they settled on Katherine, and he gestured for her to hurry in.

Katherine could see little in the passage, but she could smell it and her stomach turned. Despite her thumping heart, all Katherine could focus on was the swell of music. She watched numbly as the tall man took an immensely long key from his pocket, threw the door shut behind her and locked it.

The last thing she saw was a boy whom she now recognized as her brother, screaming and yelling as he stood in a bright white mist.

"You're a Keepsy now!" the elderly man said as he snapped forward and prodded his finger into her forehead, as if drumming his words into her mind.

And then the music stopped, its spell broken as the obese man put his instrument into his pocket and gave Katherine a theatrical bow.

"Where am I?" Katherine asked.

The woman in the hat brushed her hand against the side of Katherine's face. "Home now," the lady said, stroking her cheek once more.

Katherine glanced at the passageway with its crumbling brickwork coated in moss and pungent black fungus. The overwhelming rot and other odors that Katherine preferred not to focus on made her retch. She leaned against the wall, flinching as her fingers sank into a soft, cold, slimy patch of fungus. It broke, covering her hand in a vile, sticky substance.

"No eat," the obese man told her. "Food at new home."

"You think I want to eat that stuff? Do you eat it?" Katherine's stomach convulsed again.

"We do not eat that," the elderly man explained. "Not good. You learn things now you're Keepsy."

"Not Lendsy!" the tall man said, patting Katherine's head with his immense hand. "We got a normal. Real normal!"

"You belong to Eiderstaark, now," the elderly man told her.

"I don't belong here. And I don't know anything about the Eiderstaark. I just need to get home, through that door."

"We are Eiderstaark!" the lady announced. "Old family. Very old. Live in Greshtaat district. Take you there. Take you home. For cakes and rain."

"Cakes and rain," the elderly man repeated. "Then work."

"I just want to go home," Katherine begged. "Please!"

"Will go home," the obese man told her, mopping his sweating forehead with a filthy rag. "New home."

"Come!" The elderly man gave Katherine a shove in the small of her back. She sprawled into the darkness. A pair of bright white eyes flashed in the murk as a haggard old lady lurched towards her. She was hunched, her face a mass of lines, her intense white eyes gazing into Katherine's. The old lady opened her mouth, revealing a set of fangs, and lunged forward with surprising nimbleness, her clawed hands outstretched. "New blood for old bones!" she cried.

The tall man batted her hands away from Katherine. "Get back, vympaar. Get back! Girl Eiderstaark, not blood drink."

The old lady hissed, vanishing into the shadows, her eyes flashing once more. As Katherine passed her, she stayed where she was, the Eiderstaark clearly outnumbering her.

Katherine felt numb as she walked, the old man clamping his hand around her shoulder and whispering, "Keepsy stay with us. Safe that way. But if Keepsy run, worse things than vympaar in Grimwytch."

They left the murk of the passage, emerging on the crest of a hill.

The sky above was filled with stars. Katherine gazed at them, shaking her head. "That's impossible. It's only afternoon."

But impossible or not, the night sky was above her. Amidst its weave of blinking white stars, a huge red moon leered down. Katherine had never seen the moon so large. Below the moon was a city with thousands of buildings of all shapes and sizes, a mass of slate-gray roofs pouring smoke into the air. Through the smoke, seven great towers rose like shards of black flint.

Something about the sight of the towers made Katherine shiver.

"What is this place?" she asked, "And how can it be under the bridge?"

"Midnight City. Heart of Grimwytch," the elderly man replied. "Greatest city there is. We live in Greshtaat district."

"Told Keepsy that already," the obese man huffed.

"Yes. Told Keepsy that already," the elderly man agreed, prodding Katherine in the back once more. "Question less, walk more."

They made their way down the hill, the grass wiry and sharp. As Katherine tried to focus on the hill and the city, she found she couldn't quite take it all in. It was as if her mind couldn't comprehend its immensity. And impossibility. For a moment, she thought of running back to the door, until she recalled the thing in the passageway, the thing thirsting for her blood. And besides, the door to Tattleton was locked.

They entered a warren of narrow streets, the cobbles as black as tar. All around, buildings reared up, each one different from the next, like a set of mismatched teeth. She found window frames placed over brick walls, while dimly lit figures stared from empty holes. Front doors opened up into the street while people left their houses via pulleys and ropes, or simply dropped from the holes where windows should have been.

Alleys bisected the streets, curls of thick fog licking from the darkness. *Perhaps*, she thought, *this is where the fogs that plague Tattleton come from.* Her thoughts were interrupted as she spotted a huddle of figures watching from the shadows, their eyes flashing red in the gloom.

I need to be able to find my way out of this place, she thought, searching for road signs, but there were none. Panic began to grip her as she realized she was already hopelessly lost within the tangle of streets.

As they walked on, they passed other pedestrians, and while most had the same waxy, yellow skin and grime-encrusted faces as the Wrong People, some were unlike anything she'd ever seen.

Or ever wanted to see again.

Like the stick-thin boy who appeared to be missing a mouth, who darted into an alley. Or the pair of colossal figures with human bodies and the heads of wolves who swished their walking canes at Katherine in disgust.

And then a squat creature with a head so red it looked as if it were ablaze weaved through the wolf-headed figures. It was dressed in fine scarlet clothes, and as it spotted Katherine, it cried, "Who would have thought it? The Eiderstaark have finally found their normal and brought it into the Grimwytch!"

The elderly man held up his finger, warding off the creature. "No show now." He swept his hand towards Katherine. "Show tomorrow."

They turned a corner, walking into a dead-end street. At the end of the street stood a group of derelict houses, their walls coated in soot, their ramshackle roofs looking as if they'd fall in at any moment. As soon as she saw these higgledy-piggledy buildings, she knew they must surely belong to the Wrong People.

"Home," the woman said, tittering as she released a blast of putrid air from her mouth.

"You will like," the obese man told Katherine, his cheese-like face full of pride. "Very own cellar."

"Lucky, Keepsy." The tall man winked at Katherine.

They led her to a series of uneven stone steps. The tall man loped up them, pulling two old wardrobes aside to reveal an entrance into the house. "Come."

Katherine stepped through the hole in the wall, her spirits sinking as she saw the state of the house. It must have lain derelict for years, its walls bare but for patches of peeling wallpaper, its hole-ridden floorboards coated in dust. A set of stairs led up into darkness, their boards spotted with the same black mold that dressed the ceiling.

The tall man ushered Katherine into a large room. A series of crates was set in a circle, illuminated by black candles flickering in their seats of wax. As Katherine smelled the bitter stench rising from the candles, she wondered what the wax was made from before realizing she'd sooner not know.

The Wrong People filed into the room, the woman guiding Katherine to sit upon a crate that was just as hard and splintered as it looked. The elderly man stood before Katherine and gave her a bow. "First night for Keepsy. So Keepsy eat with us. After tonight, no more luxury."

Luxury! Katherine nearly laughed until the full implication of what he'd said sank in. For if he considered this luxury, then what could she expect after tonight? She wiped her tears with the back of her hand, promising herself she would run away at the first opportunity. Katherine looked up at the glassless windows. It should be easy to climb from one down into the street. And then she'd run as far away from these repulsive people as she could. Once she found the key to the door under the bridge. And a weapon in case the *vympaar* still lurked in the passage.

That was, if she made it through the monster-lined streets.

"Keepsy like Grimwytch?" the lady asked with wide, hopeful eyes.

"I…" Katherine began. She swallowed. "Yes. It's very… nice. And I'm sure it will look nicer by daylight." *And easier to find my way home.*

"No light," the elderly man said. "Always moontime."

"It never gets light?" Katherine asked.

"Never," the elderly man replied, fishing into his beard and seizing something that writhed in his filthy fingers. He popped it into his mouth, chewing thoughtfully. "Juicy pustulekiss fly. Fired my hunger. Fetch feast," he said.

The obese man got up, vanishing into a murk-filled room lit by a solitary candle.

"When can I go home?" Katherine asked.

"Never," the elderly man replied, spitting a husk onto the back of his hand and examining the gooey remains.

"You *are* home," the tall man said. "Keepsy's new home."

The obese man returned moments later, a curtain of drool glimmering on his lips as he regarded the large tray in his hands. He set it before Katherine, who glanced at the *feast*, cupping a hand over her mouth, praying they wouldn't expect her to eat it.

Upon the tray were six plates and a platter with what looked like a great pie formed of mud. Each of the Wrong People cut a slice of the pie, releasing a stench of rotten vegetables and dirt, and held it expectantly as the obese man licked the drool from his lips and opened a box of squirming maggots. He poured the maggots liberally over his pie before seizing another handful, shoveling them into his mouth.

"Bad!" The tall man cuffed the obese man around the head. "Share!"

"And don't forget plate for Oldsy," the woman said, pointing to the staircase.

Katherine followed her finger, but there were only shadows. Was there a fifth member of this strange family in the house? And if so, why were they hidden away?

The lady passed a slice of pie to Katherine, who held it as far away from her nose as possible.

"Eat, girl. Need strength. Work tomorrow," the obese man said.

"I ate before...before I came here. Thank you, anyway," Katherine said, passing her plate back to the obese man, who snatched it away.

As the Wrong People devoured their revolting meal, Katherine did her best to ignore the sound of crunching maggots and the stench rising into the air.

She glanced at the cups upon the tray. "Is that water?"

"Rain." The elderly man said. "Four year old. Vintage. Special for Keepsy's first night."

Katherine picked up the glass, gazing at the scum floating on the water. The Wrong People stopped eating as they watched her with expectant looks. Katherine mimed drinking and rubbed her stomach. "Oh, that is delicious!"

"Delicious," the tall man agreed and pointed to the remains of the mud pie. "Eat, too."

"I can't eat," Katherine said. "Or I'll be ill."

"Soon you eat. And love our food. Soon you be like us. Moonlight will turn you," the elderly man told her, cramming the last of the pie into his mouth.

What does that mean? Katherine gazed at the moon through the hole in the wall before peering at the skin on the back of her hands, inspecting it for signs of change.

It was as pale as always.

Not a sign of waxy yellow.

Yet.

The tall man burped, causing the woman in the hat to giggle. The elderly man shook his head. "Quiet. Late now. Keepsy to bed. Tomorrow work. Tomorrow show. Many come to see Keepsy."

"What do you mean, *show*?" Katherine asked.

"You will see. Bed now. Quiet Keepsy." The elderly man mimed sleeping, nodding to the tall man, who picked up a candle and a plate of "food." He gestured for Katherine to follow him. As Katherine did as she was told, her eyes strayed to his pockets. Somewhere, he held the key to the door below the bridge.

"New room for Keepsy." The tall man gave her a rotten grin before opening a sturdy door beneath the stairs. A flight of steps descended into darkness. The tall man passed her the candle, shoving her towards the stairs. "Down." As Katherine took the first step, a small, squat figure bolted past her. She caught a glimpse of a boy with a mess of black, tangled hair and waxy skin as he flew past with a hiss.

"Bad!" the tall man yelled, grabbing the boy and flinging him back down the stairs. "No food for Oldsy now."

A cry of fury and despair rose from below.

"Bad!" the tall man said again, pulling a stick from his coat.

"No!" Katherine held out her hands. "Please, don't hurt him." For while she'd found the boy perfectly repulsive, the idea of him being beaten made her sick.

The tall man glared below, before turning his attention to Katherine. "No beat Oldsy tonight if Keepsy want. But will beat Oldsy tomorrow if Oldsy bad."

"I'm sure he won't be bad," Katherine said as the tall man pushed her through the door, slamming it behind her. Katherine took the first step, the candle lighting the gloom as she held a steadying hand on a damp wall. "Hello?" she called, wondering where the boy had gone. For as feral as he'd appeared, he'd also seemed quite harmless.

Somewhere below her came a sniffle.

She stepped onto a hard stone floor, finding herself in a tiny room. Moonlight streamed through a grate from the street above. Two filthy blankets lay in the middle of the room. In the far corner the huddled figure of the boy nervously watched her.

"Don't worry, you're safe," Katherine said. "I won't hurt you."

The boy stared in silence, before eventually nodding as he asked, "New Keepsy?"

"I'm not a '*Keepsy*,'" Katherine said, setting down the candle and gazing through the grate. "And I'm getting out of this abysmal place the first chance I get. Do you want to come with me?"

The boy slowly nodded. "Go with Keepsy."

Katherine reached up for the grate, seizing one of the bars. It was rusting, but was surprisingly solid given the building's general state of disrepair.

She turned to find the boy drawing a blanket over himself and resting his head on the floor. "Keepsy sleep. Not much time 'til work."

Katherine yawned. She was exhausted. She would try to sleep, despite the hideous circumstances, and awaken alert and ready to escape. "My name's Katherine," she whispered. "What's your name?"

The boy looked at her emptily before shrugging and pulling the blanket over his head.

As Katherine closed her eyes, noise began to filter through the grate—a peal of raucous laughter, a sobbing wail, a squeal that sounded like a pig being slaughtered. She shivered, trying to blot out the images filling her mind. "I'll be out of this terrible place soon enough."

Someone began to walk up and down the street, pacing, before stopping beyond the grate.

"Human!" a voice whispered.

Katherine glanced up, but all she could see were a pair of black leather boots. And then she heard a cry of anger. It sounded like the tall man, roaring something incomprehensible into the street from the window above.

The boots hurried away, and as Katherine listened to them recede, she fell into a deep sleep.

Katherine awoke to a sharp pain as something jabbed her shoulder. "Get off, David!" she begged, before she remembered where she was. Katherine flinched as the tall man jabbed his finger into her arm once more. "Wake, Keepsy. Work time. Garden time."

Katherine held out her hand. "Alright, I'm getting up. Just please stop poking me." She gazed to the blanket beside her, but it was empty, the boy gone. Katherine untangled herself from the bedding. Darkness still filtered through the grate. And then she remembered that it was always dark in this wretched place.

Her stomach rumbled.

"Breakfast above. You eat," the tall man said.

"No, thank you," Katherine said, recalling the revolting meal they'd shared the night before.

But she was starving and thirsty; her mouth felt as if it were coated in moss. She realized she'd have given almost anything for a cup of water and a means to clean her teeth.

I won't be here for long, she reminded herself, *and I won't spend another night in this place.*

"Come," the tall man said, leading Katherine from the cellar and through a series of squalid rooms. They stopped in a large room with a patch of wall covered by a tatty blanket and a pile of decrepit furniture. The tall man pulled the furniture aside, ushering Katherine through the hole on the other side.

Outside, she found a small patch of dirt filled with black flowers of the type the woman with the hat wore. Here and there, dotted amongst the flowers, were anemic weeds. A large wall enclosed the garden, far too tall for Katherine to climb.

"Clean." The tall man pointed to the garden.

Katherine nodded, reaching for a weed. But as she pulled it, its stem sank into her finger, making her shout with pain.

"No!" the tall man gasped. "No! Clean this." He pulled up a flower, tossing it over his shoulder.

"You want me to throw away the flowers and keep the weeds," Katherine said. "I should have known."

The tall man watched Katherine from the steps as she set to work, yanking the flowers and throwing them onto a pile. After a while, he vanished into the house.

Katherine continued, stopping when a loud squawk made her jump.

A crow the size of an owl watched from the wall, its black eyes studying her raptly. Something about the bird made her shiver. She picked up a stone, tossing it at the crow, narrowly missing its great body. It squawked once more, turned, and flew off, merging with the night sky.

Katherine continued pulling out the flowers until she spotted something beneath the dirt. She fished it out, holding it up. It looked like a vegetable—half-turnip, half-potato. She glanced back to the house, glad to see the holes in the walls devoid of watchers.

As her stomach rumbled once more, Katherine closed her eyes and bit into the vegetable. It was just as vile as it looked, and tasted like an overripe, half-rotten mushroom. She gagged as a pungent aroma filled her mouth, but despite its taste she chewed and swallowed. Before praying it wasn't poisonous.

Katherine waited for a moment before delving into the dirt and finding another. She wiped the earth away, biting into it and ignoring its acrid taste. She finished her meal before tossing the roots over the wall and continuing with her work. Only when the garden was clear of every last flower did she stand and stretch, flinching as she turned to the house.

The tall man stood against the wall, watching her.

How long had he been there?

"Finished?" he asked.

"Finished," Katherine replied.

The tall man stepped into the garden, lifting the piles of dead flowers and throwing them over the wall. "Good job, Keepsy," he said, escorting her back inside the house before handing Katherine a small pouch.

"What's this for?" Katherine asked.

The tall man pointed at the windowsills and floor and said, "Put dust in pouch."

"It would be quicker to sweep it up. Have you got a broom?"

"No!" he cried in alarm. "Dust best this time of year. Keep dust. Dust for cakes." He rubbed his stomach, smiling.

"Of course." Katherine sighed, setting to work.

"Good, good." The tall man grinned. "Keepsy gather dust in all downstairs rooms."

"What about upstairs?"

"Never go upstairs." He shook his head violently. "Never!"

"As you wish." Katherine gave him a disarming smile. "So, where are the others?"

"Other Eiderstaark?"

"Yes."

"At door under bridge. Go every day and wait for invitation. For Keepsies."

"But you have me here now," Katherine said. "Why would you need another *Keepsy*?"

"Keepsies don't last long. Now stop talking and gather dust," he ordered, striding from the room.

As she worked, she wondered what he meant by Keepsies not lasting long. What happened to them? And what might happen to her?

Katherine ran her fingers along the windowsills, sweeping thick clumps of dust into the pouch while plotting her escape. All she needed was the key to the door below the bridge. And then to find her way back to the passage. *But how?*

She wondered if the Wrong People slept. And if so, where did the tall man sleep? Did they have bedrooms?

She glanced to the ceiling.

Their rooms had to be upstairs. Perhaps that was why the tall man had been so firm in forbidding her from venturing up there.

She gathered dust until she heard the sound of the Wrong People climbing back into the house. They were alone. It seemed no *Keepsies* had offered themselves today.

No wonder, Katherine thought bitterly. The story of her abduction must have spread across Tattleton by now, and the ancient black door would have been covered over.

She looked up as the obese man gave a shrill cry and waddled over, the others following. He seized Katherine by the chin, examining her face. "Has girl been outside?"

"Your friend," she nodded to the tall man, "whatever he's called, sent me to work in the garden."

The elderly man barged his way through, peering at Katherine, before giving the tall man a furious look. "Fool! Girl worked in garden and moon worked on girl. Keepsy turning."

The Wrong People chattered angrily amongst themselves, and from what Katherine could understand from their garbled conversation, their chief concern was her *spoiling* and *turning*. It appeared to be a problem for "*the great show*," and that soon, Katherine would turn altogether.

Katherine wiped the tears from her eyes, holding her hand before one of the candles. Was it her imagination, or was her skin slightly yellow? And a little waxy? Katherine finger-combed her hair. It was lank. But she hadn't washed it for who knew how long, and this house was full of dirt and grime.

She ran a finger across her teeth, expecting it to come away as black as the Eiderstaark's teeth.

"Come, Keepsy," the lady with the hat said, motioning for Katherine to sit on the crate beside her.

This time when the obese man brought the "food," there was no ceremony. They tore into the revolting pie, chewing maggots as they slurped their rainwater.

When Katherine refused to eat, they barely gave her a second look.

As the Wrong People finished their meal, the tall man picked up a plate with a small slice of pie and a cup of rainwater, taking it to the cellar door. As he opened it, the boy appeared, trying to shove past and receiving a great blow to the side of his face.

The boy howled as the tall man removed his stick and, before Katherine could stop him, beat the boy across his arms. "Bad Oldsy. Bad!"

Katherine ran, throwing herself between them and begging the tall man to stop.

Finally, he did, turning to the Wrong People with a grin. "Keepsy likes Oldsy."

As they howled with laughter, Katherine had to stop herself from kicking the tall man in his bony shins. Instead, she passed the food to the cowering boy, helping him through the door. The tall man shut the boy in and gave Katherine a stern glare.

"Why do you keep him in the cellar?" she demanded.

The elderly man, who had joined them, gave her a quizzical look. "Oldsy punished."

"Why?" Katherine asked.

"Tried to escape," the obese man replied, adding, "Keepsy should learn lesson."

The elderly man clapped his hands, smiling at Katherine. "Be happy, Keepsy. Be happy." He pointed a finger. "Show tonight. Big show for peoples of Greshtaat. Much riches. Much dust."

"What is this show?" Katherine asked, even though she had a perfectly good idea of what it might entail.

The woman with the flower in her hat giggled as she pointed at Katherine. "You are the show. Normal in the normal show. Keepsy come with me." The lady guided Katherine into a huge room lined with candles. At the end of the room stood a grimy old curtain, which the lady swept back, revealing a crate. Katherine felt a swell of disgust as she realized its purpose.

The elderly man hobbled up to her, pointing to the crate. "Stand," he ordered.

Katherine did as she was told, as the other Wrong People watched her with rapt concentration.

"When show begins," the elderly man explained, "curtain opens. You turn all way round. So they see you. And poke tongue out. Your tongue funny. And show teeth. Your teeth funny."

"That's so good to know," Katherine said, only just containing her fury.

She was leaving tonight, if there was such a thing as night, after their "normal show." Come what may, she would find the tall man's key and leave this dreadful place.

The elderly man continued his instructions, ordering her to keep turning and poking out her tongue, as he whipped back the curtain and presented her to the others. Katherine turned and twirled to their hilarity and applause, round and round until an insistent knocking came from their makeshift door and they scuttled across the room.

The elderly man remained, closing the curtain and whispering, "Stand still. Stand quiet. Like dead statue."

Katherine wanted to ask him what a dead statue was, but instead took a deep breath as from outside came a clamor of voices, whistles, laughs, and growls.

The room beyond the curtain sounded full and, over the hubbub, she heard the obese man's voice. "Hello!" he called. "Hello! Tonight you see *normal*! Chalk-white face! Clear eyes! Normal teeth! Normal hands and toes! And," he paused, "normal tongue!"

A gasp rose from the crowd, followed by cries of delight.

"I can't..." Katherine's terror grew as the din of the audience increased.

"You will," the elderly man said, pinching her leg. "Keepsy will do as told."

"Tonight!" the obese man announced. "We present horror. And fun. Tonight I give you...*the normal girl!*"

Katherine peeked through a gap to the long line of figures, their misshapen faces even more monstrous by candlelight.

And then the first stepped behind the curtain, a pallid-faced lady with three eyes on her forehead and a slit for a mouth. She hissed at Katherine as the elderly man pinched her once more until she turned and twirled, presenting her hands and fingers and then her tongue. The ashen-faced lady gasped and began to applaud.

"Next!" the elderly man rasped, shoving the woman back through the curtain.

One by one, the city's monsters appeared, and as each stepped through the curtain, Katherine had to contain her horror at their nightmarish mutations. Soon she learned that the best thing was to look at her feet and, after twirling, stare directly ahead as she showed her tongue.

That way she could avoid their leering, inhuman eyes.

Some of the creatures were not content just to look at her. A few prodded her arms and grasped her hair as they sought a lock or two for a keepsake. The elderly man slapped their hands, cursing them before calling for the next spectator.

After what seemed like hours, the din of voices beyond the curtain began to quell and Katherine glanced through the gap.

There was only one spectator left, a tall lady dressed in black with a mane of long, dark hair and a huge crow balanced on her shoulder. Katherine gaped at the bird, wondering if it was the same one that had watched her from the garden wall. As the lady stepped behind the curtain, the elderly man gasped, looking at his feet.

"Away, Eiderstaark," the lady said. "Give me a moment with the normal." She had a low, measured voice. One that was clearly used to being obeyed. The lady handed the elderly man a black velvet bag, causing him to exclaim with pleasure as he tugged his forelock and skittered away.

"Look at me," the lady said.

Katherine did as she was told, swallowing as she gazed down. Something about the lady commanded instant authority. It was there in her straight posture and her intensely grey eyes. She held a black lacquered fan over the lower half of her face, swiping it gently and causing the crow to squawk. "Hush," she whispered. "I know, the stench is appalling, but we should expect no less of the Eiderstaark. I'm sorry they caught you, girl."

"I hate it here," Katherine said. "I just want to go home."

"And you will," the lady replied. "And I shall help you. My name is Yarrowiska. The Eiderstaark call me a queen."

"Are you a real queen?" Katherine asked.

"Of sorts. But that's quite unimportant. All that matters is that we get you away from this terrible place, back to where you belong. I'll meet you by the grate in the cellar tonight."

"Were you out there last night?" Katherine asked, glancing at the lady's boots.

"I was. An associate told me a human girl had been caught by the Eiderstaark. I waited until tonight to be sure."

A loud, exaggerated cough came from beyond the curtain. Yarrowiska leaned closer to Katherine, whispering, "I need to get out before they become suspicious. Look for me later." She stepped around the curtain, taking great care not to touch it. Katherine listened to the clack of her boots on the floorboards until they faded away.

She allowed herself a smile. Now she had a guide across the city.

Then the curtain was suddenly whipped open, and the Eiderstaark watched her from the middle of the room.

The elderly man prodded her in the side. "Good Keepsy. Good show. Much dust." He pointed to a rickety table with a collection of pouches.

"They paid you with dust to gawp at me?" Katherine asked.

"Yes. Good normal. Good dust!" the elderly man said. "More shows. More dust. Before Keepsy turns."

"Turns into one of you?" Katherine scowled, jumping from the crate.

She was relieved as the tall man opened the cellar door, ushering her inside. This time Oldsy stayed below, whimpering in the shadows.

"Sleep now, Keepsy," the tall man said.

"I will. Goodnight." Katherine stopped herself from adding, "*And goodbye.*"

She descended into the gloom. The boy sat in the corner, his eyes wide as he glanced past her. "Don't worry," Katherine said. "He's not coming down. And he's never going to hurt you again. At least, he won't if you come with me."

The boy stared blankly.

He's simple, Katherine thought, probably from being beaten around the head so many times. "Do you want to leave this house for good?"

The boy nodded.

"Then come with me tonight."

"Where Keepsy going?"

"Back to my village. You can come, as well. Or go back to wherever you're from. Do you want that?" Katherine gave his hand a consoling squeeze.

The boy nodded and was about to say something when a voice hissed through the grate. "Girl!"

Katherine flinched as the boy's nails dug into the palm of her hand. He skittered away with a yelp, hiding in the shadows. "It's alright, Oldsy," Katherine said. "Yarrowiska's a friend. She's going to help us escape."

Yarrowiska peered down. "I'm going to help *you* escape. Leave him here."

"No!" Katherine said, a little louder than she intended. "I can't leave him behind. I won't."

Yarrowiska glared at Katherine, before giving a sharp nod. "Very well." She held up a long, black key. "I haven't found a lock that this key cannot open. Well, aside from one, but we don't need to open *that* door just yet. I heard the Eiderstaark's banal conversation as they went up to their rooms. They should be asleep by now. Use this key to get out of the cellar and leave by the first hole you find."

Katherine caught the key as Yarrowiska dropped it through the grate. "Thank you. Will it open the door which leads...?"

"No. Believe me, I've tried. Don't worry, we will find a way to get you home. However, we must go to my house first, so I can treat your condition. Your flesh is turning from the moonlight. Tell me, was your hair always so black?"

"No." Katherine ran her fingers through her hair. "It was...*is* chestnut brown."

"No matter," Yarrowiska said. "I shall help you."

"Thank you, Yarrowiska. You're so kind," Katherine said. "Where shall I meet you?"

"Meet me in the street. I have a carriage waiting. We will be long gone before the Eiderstaark awaken. Be quick."

"I'll be as quick as I can. But first, I need to find the key to the door under the bridge. So I can get home."

"No," Yarrowiska protested. "There isn't time."

"But how else am I going to get back to my world?"

Yarrowiska looked as if she were about to say something but thought better of it. She muttered and shook her head. "Very well. Go now, be quick," she said, melting into the gloom.

Katherine ran to Oldsy, placing a hand on his shoulder. "Come on. We're leaving."

"No," he said, his eyes filled with fear. "Not with *her*."

"I told you, she's a friend. She's going to help us get away."

"Not with her," Oldsy repeated, shrinking further against the wall.

"Very well," Katherine told him. "If you want to stay here, then that's your business. But I'll leave the door open in case you change your mind and decide you don't want to spend the rest of your days being beaten in this rancid cellar. It's up to you."

As Katherine slipped the key into the cellar door lock, she heard a soft *click*. She opened the door and stole into the house, leaving the door ajar for Oldsy.

As she spotted a patch of moonlight issuing from a hole in the wall, Katherine was tempted to climb through and join Yarrowiska. But the key to getting back to Tattleton lay in the pockets of the tall man somewhere above.

Katherine climbed the stairs, gingerly testing each step for creaks. The upstairs was a mirror of the house below—bare floorboards, walls full of holes, and a set of doorways.

Muffled snores came from behind the first door. As Katherine pushed it open, she shivered. The elderly man lay in a bed in the corner of a room and before him, a row of buckets. As the stench of the room washed over Katherine, she retched, stepping into the hall, trying her best to put the vile contents of those buckets from her mind.

Katherine tiptoed to the next door. She turned its handle, but froze as a voice murmured within. She ducked down, gazing through a hole in the door.

A large bed filled the room, and lying in its center, in a filthy pair of long johns and matching nightcap, was the obese man, his nightclothes fluttering in a breeze. On the wall opposite him was a huge hole and beyond it, the city. A plate with a slice of pie rested on his rising and falling stomach as he mumbled, "Big cheese, little cheese, round cheese, smelly cheese." Katherine left him to his strange list and listened at the next door.

Silence.

Katherine searched for a hole or crack to peek through, but there was nothing, so she placed her hand on the doorknob, ignored her fluttering heart, and turned it.

She eased the door open to find a small desk with a hat placed upon it, a wilting flower in its band. Next to it, the lady slept on a jumble of blankets and clothes, her brow furrowed, her black teeth bared. She hissed and turned, letting out a low, feral growl. Katherine closed the door and stepped towards the final room.

This one had to belong to the tall man. The door was ajar, and beyond, a great pair of yellow feet showed through socks that were more hole than cloth. Beyond the feet, a pair of legs stretched, and far behind them, the tall man's face, his hands resting on his chest as he stared at the ceiling.

He was awake!

Katherine's heart thumped. Had he seen her?

But he remained perfectly still, and as she heard his soft snore, she realized he was sleeping with his eyes open.

No stranger, perhaps, than she should have expected from an Eiderstaark.

The tall man lay upon the floor on an old sheet. Every now and then, something dark and shiny scuttled from beneath it, vanishing between the cracks in the floorboards. She inched into the room. In the corner was a rickety chair with clothes heaped upon it and, resting right on top, the tall man's coat.

Katherine crept slowly forward, taking great care to step as far away from the tall man as possible. She was halfway to the chair when he lifted his hand and pointed at her. She clamped a hand over her mouth, swallowing her scream as his eyes continued to stare at the ceiling.

"Tell him," he whispered.

Katherine shook her head. Was he talking to her? Was he awake?

And then he continued. "Tell him to flog his weary soul in old market. Eiderstaark not want it here. Hoardspike pay."

What's a hoardspike? Katherine wondered.

Whatever it was, it sounded unpleasant.

She waited until his hand fell back to the sheet before she continued to the chair, slipping her hand into his coat pocket, the scent of stale sweat filling her nose.

The first thing she found was a crust and grains of what felt like hardened mud. And then something slithered against her fingers. Katherine stifled her shriek, fighting to rid herself of the image of squirming maggots.

She glanced towards the other pocket and thrust her hand inside. Something cold and soft obstructed her hand and below it, something metallic.

The key?

But as she removed the object, she yelped. It was a dead mouse, one of its eyes missing, its mouth contorted in a grimace.

Katherine watched in horror as the tall man's eyes moved from the ceiling and focused on her, confusion on his sleepy face. She thrust her hand back into the pocket, grabbed the key, and was halfway across the room when one of his hands grabbed her leg. "Keepsy? How…"

"Get off!" Katherine yelled, bringing her other foot down on his hand.

He let go with a howl.

"Bad Keepsy!" he yelled, struggling to his feet.

Katherine ran out the door, freezing at the sight of the elderly man rushing from his room, a candle in one hand, a knife in the other. "Keepsy!" he yelled. "Come here!"

Katherine ducked towards the stairs but he barred her, his blade slicing through the air. She turned, pushing through another door, and found herself in the obese man's room.

He was awake now, and as she flew into his room, he covered the plate of pie, yelling, "Secret pie! Not for Keepsy!"

She ignored him as she made for the huge hole in the side of his bedroom wall and climbed through, as the tall man cried, "Stop, Keepsy! Stop!" She turned back to look out across a panorama of thousands of grimy rooftops and above them, the great black tower. Below the hole in the wall, the cobbled street looked hard and cold as it glistened in the moonlight.

Katherine lowered herself, clinging to the edge of the wall. The tall man grabbed her wrist, causing her to scream. With a clatter of hooves, a horse and carriage swept from an alley, its driver wrapped in darkness. It stopped below Katherine as she clung to the ledge, and Yarrowiska emerged from within. "Jump to the carriage roof. It will hold you."

"Inside, Keepsy!" the tall man demanded as behind, the rest of the Wrong People stared at Katherine with sleepy-eyed disdain.

"Pie thief!" the obese man growled as he, too, seized Katherine's wrist, his sausage-like fingers clammy against her skin.

"Get off!" Katherine cried. She let go of the wall with her other hand, hanging and praying her weight would overwhelm them.

It didn't.

Something black and feathered swept past her. It took a moment for Katherine to realize it was the great crow. It cawed, pecking the obese man's fingers and causing him to wince. He let go of Katherine with a high-pitched squeal.

The tall man batted his free hand at the crow as it raked the back of his other hand with its claws. "No!" he cried as it slashed at him and finally, with a howl of rage, he let go of Katherine.

She fell and struck the carriage's thick canopy, bouncing and falling before Yarrowiska seized her, guiding her to the ground. "Get in, girl. Quickly!"

Katherine opened the carriage door, climbing into its plush interior. Yarrowiska joined her, petting the crow that had just returned to her shoulder. Above, the driver cracked his whip, and as the horses began to canter, something else struck the carriage roof.

Yarrowiska opened the door, half climbing out and arching her neck to look up before clambering back in. "They must have thrown something."

In the distance came the sound of the Eiderstaarks' screams and above them, a tinny, musical sound.

It was the obese man's trumpet, and as Katherine heard it, she had an overwhelming urge to leap from the carriage until Yarrowiska clamped her hands over her ears.

Katherine glanced from the window as the carriage rattled through the foggy streets, and here and there, she glimpsed the city's denizens. Not one approached the carriage, as if they were keeping a respectable distance.

Katherine shrank from the carriage window as cold moonlight beamed down upon her with the same intensity as a summer sun. She looked at the skin on her hands and noted with horror that it was becoming as dry and brittle as old paper, its color lit with a slight yellow hue.

"Don't worry," Yarrowiska told her. "I will cure you just as soon as we reach my house."

The coach sped on, and as it climbed a hill, Katherine recognized some of the buildings. "Are we near the passageway that leads to Tattleton?"

"It's not far. I shall take you there soon." Yarrowiska placed a cold hand upon Katherine's wrist. If the gesture was designed to bring comfort, it failed.

"Why are you helping me?" Katherine asked. "Not that I'm ungrateful."

"I despise the Eiderstaark and their petty-minded ways. They should never have been selected to liaise with your kind. It was our old king's decision. Little wonder for the gossip saying he was part Eiderstaark himself."

"Is that why the Eiderstaark have the key to the door?"

"Many, many years ago, the people of Tattleton traded with the Grimwytch, until a flame of righteousness swept across your realm and such dealings were outlawed. But the door between our world and yours remained, perhaps in secret. And ever since, the Eiderstaark have lurked in the passage each day, waiting for someone to knock and invite them to open it."

The carriage began to rumble as it left the street and rolled through a pair of iron gates and across a graveled path.

"We're here," Yarrowiska said. "Now, let's make you well."

The driver opened the door, holding out a gloved hand for Katherine. She took it, doing her best to avoid the blazing red eyes shining from the swaddles of the man's hooded coat.

The house before Katherine was immense. She recalled how the Eiderstaark elder had acted towards Yarrowiska, how he'd called her a queen. Looking at the building, it was no wonder.

The facade was hewn from black marble, with four great pillars supporting a portico that stretched above a set of red lacquered doors. The turreted roof was decorated with gargoyles, each leering down at Katherine. Were they ornaments? She wondered as one seemed to turn its head to regard her. She looked away. Yarrowiska led her up the steps towards the door. Something struck Katherine in the back.

She turned to see a figure splayed out beneath the carriage. Oldsy.

What was he doing? She was about to call to him, but he shook his head, pointing to Katherine and away from the house.

"Is something wrong?" Yarrowiska asked.

"No. I was just admiring the view."

"You should admire it from indoors, where it's warmer and the moon won't turn your skin. I can see it changing even as we speak. We must reverse the effects now, before it's too late."

The driver opened the doors and stepped aside, admitting Katherine into a grand hallway.

Eldritch Black

"Fetch the potion at once," Yarrowiska told the driver. "We need to counteract the moon's effects."

As Katherine watched the driver vanish into the shadows, she shivered, wondering what type of creature resided within that voluminous cloak.

Yarrowiska guided Katherine into a large room with a huge fire blazing in a hearth, illuminating the paintings above it. They were horrible pictures. Spiders devouring prey; hunched mourners in black beside graves; figures standing in empty, desolate places, their faces filled with melancholy.

Katherine approached one of the many tables filling the room, each holding a glass case. Inside, dead insects, animals, and tiny figures floated in amber liquid.

"You like my collection?" Yarrowiska asked, a thin smile playing at her lips.

"I…" Katherine was glad of the distraction as Yarrowiska's driver hurried into the room, a tall silver goblet in his hand.

"Let's get your beautiful skin back to its natural color," Yarrowiska said. "Drink."

As Katherine reached for the goblet, her heart began to pound. She'd sensed from the start that there was something both strange and a little frightening about her rescuer and now, looking back to her art collection, she realized why.

Every picture and exhibit suggested cruelty.

Katherine peered at the liquid in the goblet. It was a dark, oozing substance, bubbles breaking upon its murky blue surface. She didn't want to touch it, let alone drink it.

"Drink, girl. Or end up an Eiderstaark forevermore." Yarrowiska fixed Katherine with a steely glare.

The driver murmured something as he stepped towards her.

Katherine raised the goblet to her lips, for what other choice was there?

Suddenly there was a blur of motion from the corner of the room as a figure rushed forward, leaped into the air, and knocked the goblet from Katherine's hand, sending it tumbling to the ground.

It was Oldsy, with a victorious gleam on his battered face. He grabbed Katherine, yanking her across the room as Yarrowiska let forth a furious scream.

"Keepsy follow quickly!" Oldsy grabbed Katherine's hand. They ran to the end of the room, flying through a door.

Katherine glanced back to see Yarrowiska and the driver pursuing, her crow sweeping over their heads as it soared towards them. Oldsy slammed the door shut and grabbed a chair, jamming it below the door handle.

Katherine's breath felt as if it had been swept from her chest as she took in the room before her. A large, black-winged chair stood at the center of the room, angled to face a gallows, a menagerie of dead animals noosed and hanging from the ceiling. Katherine didn't recognize the creatures, but she recognized the looks of pain and anguish upon their features as they turned slowly in the air.

"Careful," Oldsy warned, pointing to the plants set out in pots across the lushly carpeted floor. Each of the deep green plants was covered in a profusion of spiny leaves. "Killostax flowers. Poison."

They made their way slowly and carefully across the room. Katherine kept her eyes on the floor as the dead animals rocked and swayed above, their shadows falling across the carpet and plants.

The sound of splintering wood filled the room. She glanced back at the door as the chair juddered. They'd be through any moment.

At the end of the room was another door, but Katherine's relief at the thought of escape was short-lived. The chamber beyond was bathed in gloom and filled with headstones, and below, a layer of dank, musty earth.

"What is this?" Katherine gazed at the headstones. It was as if someone had moved a graveyard from its rightful place and set it inside a house.

"Bad place," was all Oldsy said as he gripped her hand and led her through the graves, taking great care not to touch any of the stones. Katherine gazed up at the huge chandelier illuminating the room and swallowed as she saw what it was formed of—hundreds of bleached white bones reflecting a ball of blue fire at its center.

Katherine turned as the door behind opened and Yarrowiska called to her from across the room, "I tried to make things easy for you, girl. Had you drunk the potion, you would have become petrified where you stood. No pain, no suffering. But there will be plenty now."

Oldsy squeezed Katherine's hand, leading her on as Yarrowiska followed, threading her way nimbly through the graves.

Her driver wasn't so fortunate. As the hem of his great cloak brushed against a headstone, he gasped, clutching his chest, and toppled over with a hideous scream.

"Fool!" Yarrowiska pointed to Katherine. "Fly, Euryok, take her eyes lest they guide her further!"

The crow flew from her shoulder, sweeping below the bone chandelier, beady black eyes trained on Katherine, claws outstretched.

As Oldsy pulled her through the next door and slammed it, she heard the crow hit the other side with a satisfying *thud*.

The room before her was empty but for a raised platform at its center. Lurid red figures stood upon the stage, their limbs bent as if broken, heads cast down to face the ring of candles spread before them. At first Katherine assumed they were statues, until she looked at the strangely colored wallpaper decorating the room and gasped.

It wasn't paper.

It was skin, and as she gazed back at the twisted tableau at the center of the room, she realized why the figures were so red.

"Why?" she asked as Oldsy led her through the room, keeping as far away from the figures and the walls as he could. "Why has she done this? So much suffering."

"Cruesha'rl," Oldsy said as the door flew open behind them. "She feeds on suffering. A darkling. Very bad."

As they reached for the door, a dagger thudded into the wall beside Katherine's head. When it pierced the wallpaper, the room was filled with the most terrible shrieking.

Katherine looked back to see the red figures at the center of the room writhing and screaming, the sound of their agony unbearable. Before them, Yarrowiska stood, hands clamped over her ears, her face contorted with rage.

Oldsy opened the next door, pulling Katherine through, and slammed it against the terrible din. They were in another corridor. Oldsy dragged Katherine to a nearby window, opened it, and leaped through.

Katherine was about to follow when she glanced at the heavy moon hanging over the city. "The moonlight…"

"Keepsy come. Moonlight better than dying."

The door flew open behind Katherine, and Yarrowiska appeared, her crow on her shoulder, her eyes narrowed. "I'm going to make you a living exhibit, girl. It shall take *years* for you to die."

Katherine leaped through the window, landing heavily on the stony path outside.

Oldsy grabbed her hand, pulling her up as they ran down towards the pair of black wrought-iron gates. They squeezed through. Katherine glanced back to find Yarrowiska stalking after them, her crow soaring up, an extra pair of eyes in the night sky.

"How far is the door to Tattleton?"

"Tattleton?" Oldsy asked, leading Katherine across a wide road and into an alley.

"The other place. Where I come from."

"Not far," Oldsy said. "Keepsy quiet now. Keep energy for running."

They ran, threading their way through alleyways, each narrower than the last, while above them Yarrowiska's crow followed, cawing as it guided its mistress to them. Katherine threw another look behind to see Yarrowiska's silhouette stalking towards them. "She's catching up, Oldsy!" Katherine cried as they emerged into a street.

Another passage loomed across the street. They ran towards it but stopped as dozens of soft blue lights shone from the alley.

But they weren't lights. They were eyes that belonged to a number of figures that stepped from the shadows. Katherine's first thought was that they were children, with their stunted limbs and unsteady gait, until a gleam of moonlight caught the edges of the blades they wielded in their tiny hands.

"Slicers!" Oldsy whispered. "Nasty."

The slicers ran from the alley, stumbling towards them, hacking and slashing the air with their blades. A chorus rose from their mouths, a noise like a cross between a baby wailing and someone humming.

It was a horribly arresting sound.

"Leave them be, slicers. They're mine!" Yarrowiska stepped from the alley behind Katherine, her crow sweeping down and landing on her shoulder.

The slicers hissed as they regarded Yarrowiska, waving their knives towards her.

"Really? Well then, I'm going to enjoy taking your shiny heads for my collection." Yarrowiska reached into her cloak, withdrawing a small, glinting axe. She revealed its serrated edge and grinned. "Come and help me paint this street with your blood and innards. Euryok, you may take their eyes."

As the slicers ran to meet Yarrowiska, Oldsy squeezed Katherine's hand and they broke through the tiny waddling figures, shooting into the alley.

Behind, screams seemed to engulf the entire city.

Katherine looked back to see Yarrowiska bent low, surrounded by slicers, her axe slowly rising and falling.

Katherine gasped as she ran, her chest aching, but as she reached to wipe the sweat from her eyes, she stopped, gazing at her hand.

Oldsy pointed to the hill before them. "Keep running. Not far!"

"Look." Katherine held out her hand. "My skin is... It's like yours." She rolled up her sleeve. Her arm was the color of a tea-stained parchment.

"Keepsy keep going."

Katherine nodded numbly. What else could she do?

As she climbed the hill, she looked at her hand clenched by Oldsy's, their skin as one.

Katherine gazed at the passage that led to Tattleton, a dark patch between two derelict buildings. She wondered how much time had passed since the Wrong People had taken her.

Somehow, it seemed like a lifetime ago.

She trudged on, and as they stepped into the passage, someone within the gloom giggled.

"Quickly, Keepsy, quickly!" Oldsy pulled her into the passage, and if he'd heard the laughter, he showed no sign of it.

As they hurried between the dark walls, Katherine tensed, waiting for the vympaar she'd seen on her first visit to reach from the shadows and grab her. But they reached the door without opposition. Katherine took the long key from her pocket and thrust it into the lock. As she turned it, a dreadful din shook the passage, and dust and lichen fell from the ceiling.

Katherine pulled the door ajar, a sliver of light spilling through and searing her eyes. She cried with the pain, holding her hands over her face as she stepped through. "Come, Oldsy, follow me," she shouted above the noise. "Quickly!"

The grass beneath her feet was so soft, the air almost unbearably sweet. She opened her eyes and there, before her, the old, familiar blanket of fog. As she turned back to pull Oldsy through the door, she stopped.

Oldsy stared back, his eyes wide as a gnarled hand with long, curved nails sank into his neck. Behind him, the vympaar stood, her eyes flashing white, a sadistic smile on her gnarled old face.

"Let him go!" Katherine demanded.

"Come to me, child. Come, and I shall let this one go," the old lady promised. "And spare a little blood for these tired old bones."

"Keepsy close door," Oldsy said. "Keepsy close door!"

Katherine stepped towards it, clenching her hands into fists. "Let him go now!"

The old lady shook her head. "When you come to me, I shall let him go"

"I won't let her take you." Katherine offered Oldsy a weak smile. "You belong with me. Away from that ghastly place."

Oldsy shook his head, his eyes filled with tears. He looked beyond her. "Oldsy remembers now. Oldsy lived there once. Too long ago. Keepsy close the door. Vympaar doesn't want Oldsy's blood. Not fresh like yours. Old like dust."

Katherine flung the door open, flooding the passageway with light. The vympaar hissed, stepping back and releasing Oldsy.

"Come on!" Katherine cried. But Oldsy raised a yellowed hand to his tear-filled eyes, covering them. "Too bright. Please close door, Keepsy. Please close door."

Katherine took one last look at Oldsy before doing as he asked. She slammed the door, its sound like a thunderclap rolling across the village. She fumbled with the key as she locked the door before slipping it into her pocket. As she began to trudge home she was glad for the fog as it enveloped her, shielding her from the world.

Gradually, her eyes adapted to the light, the village appearing before her. It hadn't changed. Strangely, it was just the way she had left it. Katherine didn't know why she'd expected it to be any different. "It's just me that's changed."

The village was silent, and judging by the patch of light in the east, it was early morning. As Katherine reached her door, she stopped, looking down at her hand as it grasped the knocker. All traces of her old self had gone; her skin was as yellowed as a page from an old book. She wiped her tears, raised the knocker, and brought it down with three loud taps. Within moments, someone ran down the stairs. She knew the sound of his footsteps. David.

He opened the door, flinching as he caught sight of her. "Katherine?"

"Let me in, David."

He stepped away from her, his eyes wide with fear. "Katherine? Is that you? You're…"

"Of course it's me. Where's Mother?"

"Resting. She's been waiting at the door under the bridge all night. We all have. Some of the men tried to pick the lock, but it was impossible. What happened? Where did they take you? And…Katherine, you don't look well. You…" He paused and swallowed. "Have you come for me? Are you going to take me with you?" He turned from her and fled up the stairs.

Katherine stepped into the house, catching her reflection in the large mirror next to the door.

A stranger's face stared back. A stranger's face with dark, hollow eyes and waxy yellow skin. Her nose was covered in sores, her lips had thinned, and as she opened her mouth, she saw that it was filled with rotten stumps. She ran a hand through her hair, once chestnut-brown, now long, black, and lank and sticking to her crooked shoulders.

Katherine screamed, lashing out and smashing the mirror into hundreds of glittering shards.

Eldritch Black

Addendum

When my father, himself a writer and protector of our realm, retired from duty, he took me to the Guild in Grimwytch. I started my apprenticeship the same day, and over time they gave me a number of curious tools.

Along with the pile of blank journals that would become my Books of Kindly Deaths, I received a sword, pen, map, and a necklace of Solaarock.

The cartographer who created the map was born in the Grimwytch and had never visited our world, but had based her map on one of ours. The purpose behind her map was simple. Each time an illegal crossing was made from their world to ours, blots would appear on my map, giving their locations. Thus, I could see where the monsters had crossed and how to find them.

From time to time, the village of Tattleton had darkened upon my map, but the blot signified only a minor breach and occurred so infrequently I paid it little attention, for I had more pressing concerns.

In reflection of the tragic events that overtook Katherine Meadows, I wish I'd travelled to this dismal, foggy village sooner.

Word of the events in Tattleton reached me via my network of informants. They told how Katherine's mother, Elizabeth Meadows, had been searching for a doctor to cure her daughter's terrible, monstrous condition.

Immediately upon hearing the report, I packed my belongings, summoned my assistant, Sarah, and we set off.

I remembered the name Tattleton from my father. It was one of the few places where crossings from the Grimwytch to our realm had once been allowed, originally for the purposes of trading. But that was many years ago. Sadly, some of the villagers who traded with the peoples of Grimwytch had been so entranced by their strange and exotic lives that they had passed through to see the Midnight City. for themselves.

A tragic mistake.

Once the Grimwytch moon had wrought its terrible power upon them, the villagers became known as the Eiderstaark, which means "they who have turned."

As we reached the outskirts of the village of Tattleton, Katherine's mother Elizabeth and her son David intercepted my carriage. They were keen for their business to be kept private.

Once Elizabeth Meadows finished telling me of Katherine's circumstances, I could barely contain my rage. "Where is she now?" I demanded.

Elizabeth pointed to a large hill overlooking the village. "There's a cave..."

"Your daughter's living in a cave?" I asked.

"We all thought it best," David explained. "After the other villagers saw her, they turned on us. Threatened to burn our house down if we didn't send her away."

"I didn't want her to go," Elizabeth said. "It was Katherine's idea. We take food to her every day."

I glanced at the village of Tattleton, my anger raging. "What a soulless, vindictive place."

Elizabeth Meadows began to speak, but I held up my hand. "Just take me to Katherine. Now."

I found Katherine sitting by a smoldering fire, and I'd never seen such a pitiful, dejected figure. Having met the Eiderstaark in my travels, I knew what to expect, but poor Katherine hadn't completely turned. Indeed, I could still see the vestiges of the girl she once was.

I told her who I was and showed her my Book of Kindly Deaths.

"You want me to go back?" she asked, her eyes wide. "To that dark city?"

"You cannot spend your life in this cave, Katherine," I told her.

"I won't. I'll leave. I can disguise myself... I can..."

"You cannot stay in this realm," I said with heavy heart. "It's not permitted. But you will not have to return to the Eiderstaark. I can find you shelter at the guild. There are some beautiful quarters, and you will be well looked after. And I shall come to see you from time to time, I promise."

"But I'm not...I'm not a monster," Katherine said through her sobs. "I'm not like them."

"You're not a monster," I told her. "Not at all. But I cannot allow you to stay in this realm. Sooner or later you will meet with even worse people than those of Tattleton. And your appearance will be your undoing. People are cruel. Sometimes crueler than monsters."

It took a huge amount of persuasion for me to convince Katherine I had her best interests at heart. Eventually, through her despair, she agreed to cross over.

When I had finished writing her story, Katherine handed me the key to the door between our world and theirs and turned to her family. For a moment, I thought she'd rush to embrace them, but instead she looked away, her eyes filled with tears. She faded then, until she was little more than a ghost. And then she was gone, but for a solitary tear upon the page of my book.

I walked from the cave, leaving Sarah to console Katherine's mother. I had no wish to do so myself. I stormed down the hill, filled with fury, malicious thoughts writhing in my mind. I found the door beneath the bridge, covered over with all manner of junk. I threw it aside, pulling a hammer from my satchel, smashing great holes in the wood. Then I pried what was left of the door from the wall. Without the Eiderstaark key to open it, there was nothing behind but discolored brickwork and rotten black fungus.

I turned to face the villagers who had gathered, silently watching my act of destruction. "You will burn what's left of the door," I shouted. I must have looked like a wild man, for they shrank away. "And you will never speak of this matter again. Do you understand?"

They looked blankly from one to another, and so I repeated myself. "Do you understand me? Or do I need to return and raze this despicable place of gabble and judgment to the ground?"

They nodded and set to work, gathering what was left of the door.

As I walked from Tattleton, glancing at the now-empty cave upon the hill, I could not recall a time when my heart had felt heavier.

CHAPTER TWELVE

Visitings

*E*liza set the book down and gazed at the back of her hands, focusing on her skin with its map of freckles and blemishes. Anything to bring herself out of the story, to fix herself back in her room. In the real world.

She stared at the curtains as something scratched at the window. And held her breath when it came again.

A tiny chink in the curtain revealed darkness. It was still night, or early morning.

Another scratch. Eliza thought about calling for her parents, but knew she wouldn't. Not if she wanted to know what was really going on. No, whatever was happening between her and the book was her secret to keep, her mystery to solve.

"I'm not afraid," Eliza said, climbing from the bed and crossing the room, trying her best to ignore her rising dread as the scratch came once more. She snatched back the curtains and sighed with relief to find the branches of the birch tree scratching against the glass. In the east, a dim blue light grew. Dawn.

The window in the house across the way was still dark and empty. Thankfully, there was no sign of the emaciated figure she'd seen earlier that night. Eliza was about to return to bed when something shifted in the gloom.

She stared down, aghast, as four faces peered up at her.

Four perfectly still ovals.

"Garden statues," she whispered. "Not the Wrong People. The Wrong People don't exist." She glared down, angry at her cowardice. "You're not real. None of it's real!"

But as she drew the curtains, one of the ovals twitched. Eliza pulled the fabric tighter, ignoring the panic tugging at the edges of her mind. "It's just illusion," she said. "And imagination."

She wondered what other storybooks were like. Her dim memory of the Grimm's fairytales didn't help. Because they had been frightening, just as frightening as *The Book of Kindly Deaths*. And yet, as much as they had haunted her young dreams, they hadn't felt as if they were real. Had actually happened. Unlike these stories, which now seemed more like historical documentations, as ridiculous as that idea was.

She picked up *The Book of Kindly Deaths*, eager now to finish it, to close its covers. For she hoped that, once she did, her world would get back to normal.

CHAPTER THIRTEEN

Grim Shivers

*A*ugustus Pinch sneered as he perched upon a barrel and watched the people floundering about the market. His vivid blue eyes glowed like lamps in the dark of the winter's afternoon as he scoured this way and that for a prospect. He tapped a grimy hand against his coat pocket, taking comfort in the feel of the swell beneath, all those wallets and purses he'd managed to liberate already today.

Despite only having had a cursory glance through his takings, it seemed there should be enough money to keep him in gin and tobacco for the next few weeks. And yet the money he received was only a mere reward, for the real pleasure he took in thieving was the idea of his victims' anguish.

He glanced at a middle-aged couple as they passed by. They reminded him a little of his parents. As he thought of his parents, he spat upon the ground.

Augustus wondered where they were now. Hopefully in the poorhouse, for he hadn't left them a single penny when he ran away all those months ago. *It was their own fault, anyway*, he mused. He'd warned them he was leaving. Told them he'd had enough of the dry, dusty tutor they employed. And as for their expectations... Augustus sneered. They'd worked all their lives, setting aside enough money to be considered respectable.

And now they had nothing.

No money and no respect.

"Look at you," Augustus muttered, glancing at the shoppers in the market. "Spend those pennies while you can, for all the good it will do you." As the shoppers passed him, they glanced away. It didn't bother Augustus one jot, for he knew well enough his face was disquieting. Despite being only thirteen years of age, he had the drawn, lined face of a man many decades his senior.

Occasionally, he wondered if his appearance was punishment for the distress he'd caused others, their anguish reflected on the face of its creator. If it was, he was quite happy to live with it.

He turned to watch an old man stride towards him, his well-tailored clothes and coat hanging from his tall frame. The old man offered a smile, dug into his pocket, and flipped a coin.

Augustus let it fall to the ground.

"Merry Christmas," the old man said as he passed. Augustus ignored him, his eyes on the bundle of gaily wrapped boxes that seemed about to burst from the old man's satchel.

Presents, thought Augustus. *Maybe for grandchildren not much older than me.*

There would be sorrow aplenty when the recipients of those presents discovered their gifts were gone, their grandfather robbed.

"Merry Christmas," Augustus replied, spitting once more upon the icy street before leaping from the barrel and following the old man. He was careful to keep a fair distance as they passed through the marketplace and into a dark, narrow street.

A familiar surge of anger grew as Augustus followed the elderly man and studied his slow pace, the way he used his walking cane to check for ice. He often thought the elderly walked exaggeratedly slow on purpose. That they did it for attention and sympathy. Sometimes, he gave them a good shove to help them on their way.

"You can walk as slow as you like," Augustus whispered, "but it won't delay the Reaper. You were born into this desolate place, and you'll die in this desolate place, and that's all there is to it."

He looked back.

The street was empty. Augustus ran, and as he reached the old man, he grabbed his satchel strap and pulled it over the man's head before pushing him aside.

The old man slid on a patch of ice. Augustus heard a loud *crack*, which might have been the man's walking cane or his bones snapping upon the street.

He glanced back to see his victim sprawled upon the icy ground, fighting to get to his feet. "Bring my satchel back, boy," the old man shouted. "You don't realize what it carries!"

"Oh, yes I do! Presents, and plenty of 'em. Merry Christmas, you old rotter!" Augustus ran on, leaving the man's protests far behind. He ducked down a series of alleys, staying off the main thoroughfares, and was so elated with the weight of his haul that even the cloying stench of the sewerage couldn't dampen his mood.

Nine people robbed today. Nine lives touched by the hand of Augustus Pinch. He passed another alleyway, skirting through figures slumped on the ground.

He wondered if they were dead or drunk. Not that it mattered.

Ahead, a group of men huddled around a body, blocking the alleyway. Augustus seized a drainpipe and began to climb, pulling himself up the side of an old building. He emerged on the roof and lay still for a moment, his breath forming heavy white clouds. Above, the moon was full, glowing softly through the early evening fog. Augustus climbed to his feet and peered down at the alley.

It was empty now, the figures gone, the body left slumped in the mire. *The rats will eat well tonight*, Augustus thought as he jumped from rooftop to rooftop and made his way across the city. Eventually he found his way to the wharf, stopping at the dilapidated warehouse that served as his occasional home. The river stretched out below, black and pitiless. Tiny lamps from boats and ferries twinkled upon its waters as shouts and calls echoed across the wharf.

For a moment, Augustus was transfixed by the sight, until he came to his senses, muttering, "It's just a river, that's all."

He climbed over the edge of the roof and hung for a moment, swinging his legs back and forth through the empty window below. Once he'd built enough momentum, he swung through to land upon a blanket of broken glass.

Augustus crouched in the darkness, listening keenly, but all he could hear was his own ragged breathing. Sometimes he'd hear others moving in the warehouse below, desperate souls looking for a place to sleep and shelter from the harsh bite of winter. Thankfully, the staircase leading to the top of the building was rotten and broken, which left the snaking corridors above for Augustus and Augustus alone. He stole through the gloom until he reached the room at the end of the hall and closed the door softly behind. He delved into his coat and produced a book of matches, striking one and lighting the stump of candle he kept by the door.

The light threw his shadow against the wall. He nodded to it before stooping over the fireplace and lighting the twigs and coals he'd prepared on his previous visit.

Augustus reached for a book from the stack he'd left by the fireplace and tore a few pages loose, tossing them upon the flames until the kindling caught. Soon a lively blaze lit the room as he pulled his rickety old chair nearer to the fire, emptying his coat pockets and placing their contents upon a table.

Augustus took great care and patience as he stacked the coins from the wallets and purses into their various denominations and created a short pile of notes.

One of the purses had nothing but a bundle of letters, neatly folded and scented with perfume, their writing in a looped, curved hand.

"Love letters," Augustus said. He tossed them upon the fire, wondering if the love confessed within their pages would similarly burn out and turn to ash.

Finally, Augustus snatched up the satchel he'd liberated from the old man and pulled out the first of the boxes within, tearing off the wrapping. It was a small box filled with tin soldiers. Augustus threw them upon the fire and unwrapped the next package to discover a packet of chocolates. By the design on the box, they were expensive.

Augustus crammed the chocolates into his mouth, the delicate flavors of orange, cherry, and peppermint soon merging into one great sludge. He swallowed it and opened the next box, which contained soaps and lotions. He poured the lotions upon the floor and took a deep sniff, wrinkling his nose. "Disgusting!"

The satchel was now empty but for an old book. "Useless things," he sighed, but as he pulled it from the bag, he flinched as a charge of energy ran through his fingertips.

He dropped the book upon the table. Its cover was black with a large gold symbol, a rectangle within two circles. Carefully, he picked up the book once more, ignoring the tingling sensation as he read the title upon the timeworn black cover. *The Book of Kindly Deaths, Volume 23*.

As Augustus reached to open the book, he felt the merest flutter of trepidation. He ignored it and turned to the first page.

The Book of Kindly Deaths
February 12, 1724

Herein lie the tales of Flora Chambers, Michael Notwhich, Sally Cottle, Nancy Edmonton, & Simon Milton, all of whose lives have been blighted by the residents of Grimwytch. In their telling, these stories set them free from their fates, each tale a kindly death.

Ambrose Drabe

Augustus shook his head. "I hate fairy tales," he complained. "The only pot of gold is the one you steal, and who needs dragons when people are so horrible and vile? No one has a kindly death in this squalid old city."

He turned to the next page, gazing at the neat blue writing. Nothing interesting, just some stupid story, but as he tried to leaf through to the next page, it wouldn't turn.

Baffled, Augustus shook his head and turned the book on its side, expecting it to fall open.

The pages stayed firm.

Augustus dug his fingernails between them and pulled with all his might, but still they would not budge. "Damn you!" he growled, throwing the book to the ground and kicking it across the room. "Is this someone's idea of a joke?" He pulled a knife from his pocket, picked the book up, and set it on the table.

As he tried to force the knife between the pages, they stayed closed, as if sealed with glue.

"To hell with your stupid stories!" Augustus said, bringing his knife down upon the book. But before the blade could touch it, the book skipped to one side and his knife slammed into the table instead.

"Come here!" Augustus grabbed the book with one hand, holding it firmly as he stabbed his blade into its cover. As it struck, the book jolted with such force that Augustus was sent flying across the room, colliding with the wall.

He climbed to his feet and froze as from somewhere came the sound of tapping.

Like a gnarled old knuckle upon a door.

And as he looked around for its source, it seemed to be coming from within the book itself. "It can't be," he muttered.

Tap. Tap. Tap.

Augustus stepped away. "Who…who's there?"

He glanced to the door, but the tapping grew louder and he realized with terrible certainty that, as impossible as it was, the sound was indeed coming from within the book.

Tap. Tap. Tap. Tap.

And then the book opened, its cover slamming into the table as, one by one, its pages turned, flipping faster and faster. Augustus watched in hypnotic dread as finally the pages stopped turning and a thin column of black smoke wafted from the middle of the book. The smoke grew in size and filled the room with an abundance of scents—spices, blood, damp, rot, and the reek of something dredged from a river.

Augustus strained to hear the distant voices whispering from the pages, snatches of conversations in a strange, foreign language. He watched silently as the column of smoke gathered and hovered over the book. It formed a shape—a tall, thin man hanging in the air.

His heart began to pulse as the man continued to grow and the light of the fire dimmed. The shadows in the corners of the room swelled, snaking through the air, feeding the man, adding to his form.

Flesh began to wrap across the smoke, a cadaverous face turning towards Augustus with a thin mouth like a slit, the holes that formed his nostrils flaring as he sniffed. Finally, two embers flew from the fire, lending the man a pair of vivid red eyes, which narrowed as they bored into Augustus.

Clothes weaved across the figure as invisible tailors stitched together a dark, woolen suit that covered his vestigial form. The man reached up into the darkness above his head and pulled down a top hat, fixing it atop his long, wiry white hair.

Augustus was rooted to the spot as the man stepped from the air and held out a long, bony finger, saying, "You defiled the book, boy." Augustus stepped back, the fire behind him lending no heat as the room descended into an unholy chill. Icy wind swept from the middle of the book, and with it came a terrible sense of desolation. Augustus yearned to close the book but cringed away as the man stalked towards him. "Who are you?" he asked, his voice breaking.

"Grim Shivers, guardian of the book. I take the hearts and lights of thieves and defilers. You are both of those things, boy." He snatched a hand towards Augustus, who ducked away.

As Augustus's eyes glanced from the ghoul to the book behind him, an idea began to form. Maybe, if he could somehow find a way to destroy the book, it might take the guardian with it. Augustus walked towards the ghoul, waiting for him to reach for him before feigning a dash to his left and instead dodging right. He grabbed the satchel and book from the table and ran, flying through the door as he stuffed the book inside the bag.

The ghoul growled as he crashed after him. He was bearing down on Augustus, top hat brushing against the ceiling, his eyes shining in the gloom.

Augustus found the broken window, hoisted himself onto its ledge, and reached for the roof, pulling himself up.

As he clambered across the roof, he glanced at the web of lights twinkling in the city's thoroughfares. Where there were lights there would be people, and where there were people, there would be police.

For once in his life Augustus Pinch couldn't think of a more welcome sight.

And then two sets of bony, white fingers appeared on the edge of the roof, scuttling like a crab as they sought purchase. Augustus rushed forward to stamp on them, but the ghoul raised himself up to his shoulder and fixed him with its fiery eyes. As he spoke, his face broke with a look of sadistic hatred. "I'm going to enjoy taking your lights, little thief."

Augustus backed away as, with an insect-like leap, the ghoul landed on the roof, laughing without humor as he took in the terror on Augustus's face. Augustus ran. The edge of the roof loomed ahead and far below, a second roof.

There was no choice.

He threw himself across the edge, soaring through the air, the tips of his fingers barely finding the edge of the roof below, his arms wrenching his shoulders as he held on with all his might.

He howled as he pulled himself up and stood for a moment, gazing up at the ghoul on the roof above. "You won't make the jump without snapping your rancid old bones. But I wouldn't mind watching you try. Go on, then. Jump and fall, Grim Shivers, and get yourself back to Hell!"

The ghoul gave no reply, but watched Augustus for a moment before stepping over the edge of the roof, his feet finding the wall below.

Augustus stared in horrified amazement as the creature walked down the side of the warehouse, just as simply as if he were strolling on solid ground. The ghoul stepped into the alley below, crossed it, and began to walk up the side of the building Augustus stood upon.

Augustus pulled the book from the bag. Its pages were sealed once more. He thought about throwing it from the roof, but what good would it do? That wouldn't destroy it.

Nothing, it seemed, could halt the ghoul.

He needed time to think. As his mind ran through his list of hideouts, his heart sank. There was only one place he knew of that might slow the ghoul's advance. But it wasn't a place he liked to go to, at least not if he could help it. As the tap of the creature's feet drew nearer, Augustus ran. He reached the far edge of the roof as the ghoul appeared, a thin smile on his chalk-white face. "Give me your lights, thief!"

Augustus glanced below to the windowsills and saw a shop sign far below them. He climbed over the building, clinging to its edge for a moment, trying to ignore his growing panic as the creature stalked towards him.

And then he let go and fell.

His fingers found the first windowsill, but it gave way, its rotten wood dissolving in his hands. Augustus fell farther, missing the second windowsill, brickwork flashing by his eyes. The next windowsill slowed his descent for a moment before it, too, gave way.

As the ground hurtled towards him, Augustus threw his hands out, grasping a shop sign hanging over the alley. The sign creaked and swung. He let go, falling the last few feet to the cobblestones below, and rolled over. Augustus looked up to see the ghoul walking down the building, his red eyes blazing in the mist.

Augustus climbed to his feet, wincing from the ache in his arms and legs, his hands a mass of cuts and tears. He hobbled away, melting into the gloom, his heart racing as the *tap-tap* of feet grew ever closer.

He turned a corner in the alley, bumping into a large figure. He caught a glimpse of the man's swarthy face and grimaced at the stench of cheap, sour wine. "What's all this, you little bastard?" The man seized Augustus around the throat. "If you're looking for trouble, you've found it. What's in your bag?"

"Please," Augustus begged. "Let go. There's a ghoul coming!"

The man barked with laughter, his rancid breath blowing against Augustus's face. "I'm the only ghoul round here, boy. Now hand over your bag or I'll bleed you dry!" His eyes narrowed further as he squeezed Augustus's throat. He gasped, pulling at the man's fingers, but they held him firm in their vise like grip.

The world began to dim, and soon all Augustus could hear was the sound of blood thumping in his head. Until from somewhere in the gloom came a muffled cry, and the fingers let go of Augustus's throat. He leaned over, taking lungfuls of air, each one searing his chest.

"Get back, demon!" the man screamed, holding up a hand, his other bunched into a fist. "This is my manor!" the man warned. "I run these streets!"

The ghoul walked past the man and pointed to Augustus. "Come, thief. Give me your lights." As the ghoul stepped closer, the man pulled a knife from under his coat, stabbing at the creature, the handle of his blade sticking into the back of his neck.

The ghoul reached round, snatched out the knife, and dropped it to the ground. Then he turned and seized the man around the top of his head. The man froze, his eyes widening. "What…"

The man gurgled something, his words gibberish, as still the creature squeezed. Augustus watched dumbly as the skin on the man's face blackened like paper held before a flame. Lines and wrinkles spread across his flesh as he aged at a hideous pace, his eyes sinking into his skull, his teeth receding into shriveled gums.

As the ghoul continued to squeeze, his form seemed to grow, as if feeding and absorbing his victim's essence. And then he released the man, now nothing more than a charred corpse, and raised his head, releasing a keening wail that echoed across the alley.

Augustus backed away as the ghoul turned and regarded him. "It hurts when I take the lights, thief, for I'm forbidden to take pleasure. But despite the agony I shall incur, I will find much gratification when I snatch your lights."

Augustus inched away, the wall at his back. As the ghoul sprang forward, he ducked aside, leaping over the charred corpse and hurtling away as fast as his feet would take him.

He didn't look back as he fled.

Augustus sprinted down alley after alley until eventually he emerged in a dingy street. He threw a hurried glance at the bedraggled row of houses and the small graveyard beyond them before realizing he knew exactly where he was. He crossed the street and entered the graveyard, his chest and legs aching with exertion. Augustus staggered across the narrow path between the headstones and statues. From somewhere far behind came a scream.

It seemed the ghoul had found another victim.

Augustus sat on a gravestone, drawing in breaths and rubbing his ankles. He listened keenly as he recovered his breath, starting as something skittered in the dark. Augustus tensed and reached into his pocket for his blade. It was gone, no doubt on the floor of the warehouse. As he thought of his lair, he wondered why he'd stabbed the book, and why he had bothered trying to open the damn thing in the first place. He hated books.

The sound came again and Augustus crouched, preparing to flee once more when a shape broke through the murk, rushing towards him.

A fox, its teeth bared, its eyes wide with panic. Augustus was about to curse the stupid animal when he looked behind it and saw the two pinpricks of red.

The ghoul broke through the night as if it were black waters, his hands outstretched, his fingers *tap-tapping* one against another. Augustus jumped to his feet and ran, the tread of the ghoul so close he could almost feel the hand that was surely reaching for him.

He fled the graveyard and crossed a road, his mind whirring as he ran. Nearby was an entrance to a series of tunnels running below the city. He'd discovered them after hearing rumor of a stash of brandy hidden within its maze. He'd never found the brandy, but instead discovered a perfect hiding place, an old bank vault with a huge, heavy steel door.

A door that was still, hopefully, open as he had left it.

It was thick enough to halt the ghoul's advance and could even lend Augustus enough time to destroy the book—and perhaps its guardian along with it.

As he thought of the tunnels, Augustus felt a shiver of dread, for they wound their way through an abysmal place. One he rarely frequented. Could he dare enter the labyrinth with the monster behind him? He had to, for where else would he find a place to halt that thing's advance?

Augustus glanced back to see the creature's glowing eyes as it stalked along the street. The few people wandering in the cold winter's night slunk back into the shadows, leaving him alone with his demonic stalker. Augustus turned a street corner and ran, picking up his pace. The tunnel entrance was within a short passage nearby. If he could reach it before the creature saw him, then he might evade the monster once and for all.

And yet somehow he doubted it, for it seemed there was nothing that could stop his pursuit. He was like an automaton from Hell.

Augustus looked back to the empty street as he jogged down the passage. A foul stench rose from the tunnels below. He felt a flush of gratitude as he saw the heavy lid that sealed the tunnels was in place. It seemed no one else had entered the tunnels since his last visit, but, given their putrid air and desolate passageways, he wasn't surprised.

He reached into the debris where he stashed his lantern and metal bar and fed the bar's edge below the cover, pushing down with all his might.

Slowly, the lid began to rise. He nearly dropped it as he heard the *click* of footsteps in the street beyond. Augustus ignored it, using his terror to lend him strength. Finally, the lid slid free. He threw the metal bar into the shadows, grabbed the lantern, and stepped onto the ladder below.

Augustus pulled the cover over the entrance. It fell into place with a satisfying *clang*, but the last thing he saw was the red, blazing eyes of the creature as he turned into the passage. Augustus hurried down the ladder, gagging at the stench from below. As he descended, the air grew colder and he began to have second thoughts. Of all the places to be trapped with a creature like that... "Shut up and keep going," he muttered to himself. "I can outsmart that creepy bastard Grim Shivers still."

Somewhere below, a howl echoed along the tunnels.

Augustus shivered. The last time he'd come here he'd heard the same din. He'd told himself it was simply a pack of wild dogs and not the fabled beasts rumored to scavenge through these forgotten tunnels. But after seeing the ghoul that had billowed like a black plague from the book, Augustus was not so sure that there weren't monsters in the tunnels, too.

The scrape of metal upon stone came from above, and a semicircle of light appeared. The ghoul was coming.

Augustus fumbled in his pocket for his box of matches. He sparked one to life and lit the lantern. It cast an eerie light upon the high brick ceiling. He ran then, his feet splashing through rancid water, the lantern throwing his shadow upon the walls.

Whatever purpose these tunnels had once had was long forgotten. Even though they were known among the city's criminal underbelly, none would set foot inside. And as the piercing howl erupted once more ahead, Augustus knew why.

He flinched at the sound of clattering on the ladder as the ghoul descended. He turned a bend, ducking into a short passage that led to another tunnel. The vault was close now, but as Augustus emerged from the passage, someone ran towards him. He screamed, dropping the lantern.

It was a woman. If she could be considered such a thing.

Her face was covered in scales, her eyes bright green orbs. She hissed, raising her scaled hands as she pushed Augustus aside and staggered into the darkness. Augustus recovered his lantern, and from behind, the ghoul's footsteps drew closer, two glowing red eyes approaching in the gloom.

Ahead lay the vault door, ajar, just as he'd hoped. Augustus made for it but stopped when a new noise filled the tunnel.

The sound of scratching.

Another figure shuffled into the light, tall and wide. At first glance, Augustus thought it was a man with long hair and a thick beard. Only the beard and hair were formed of thick vines, the skin on his face as gnarled as an old oak's. The man's hands were outstretched, but as he shuffled closer, Augustus saw they weren't hands, but what looked like twigs issuing from the sleeves of his long grey coat. The man's full black eyes ignored Augustus as they stared off into the distance.

And then his twig-like fingers curled and twisted and as they met, the air shimmered darkly and the sound of scratching seemed to tear through the world itself.

Augustus stepped away, screaming as another figure appeared and then another, each reaching out with twig-like appendages. As he heard the splash of water behind him, Augustus knew he was surrounded. He began to crawl on hands and knees through the water, turning this way and that. He held up the lantern, searching for a way past the cluster of figures, their twig-like fingers scraping the air, their tendrils reaching towards him. As they reached, a scratching sound filled the tunnel, and it seemed to Augustus as if the very universe itself were coming apart.

The figures began to hum, their low chorus filling the tunnel.

"Get away from the boy."

Augustus turned to find the ghoul emerging from the passage, his bright red eyes fixed on the creatures.

"Leave him be, scrapers. He's mine."

The figures turned as one and shuffled closer to the ghoul as he strode towards them, his lips curled in a tight smile. "How long have you been here?" he asked. "How many moons have you hidden beneath these dank streets? How did you get into this world? And where did you breach the Grimwytch?"

The creatures he had called "scrapers" stepped closer to the ghoul, their tendrils curling as they scratched the air before them, causing it to shimmer like a road beneath a summer sun.

The ghoul backed away, but another figure shuffled towards him, its twig-like tendrils snaking towards the ghoul's neck.

As its twigs curled around Grim Shivers's throat, the others moved in, one wrapping its tendrils around the ghoul's hands as another yanked off the rings that were beginning to glow upon his fingers. As they fell dully to the floor, the ghoul screamed, a sound of outrage rather than pain, his face contorted. "You dare attack me?"

The scrapers began to scratch at him, and as their limbs touched him, he shimmered, his form twisting and thinning. "Stop!" he demanded, reaching into his suit and withdrawing a long blue-white blade. But it was swiftly yanked away by a scraper and sent clattering against the wall.

As the ghoul howled, Augustus was jolted from the spectacle. He ran for the vault door, his lamp swinging wildly as the tunnel filled with the din of scratching and cries of rage. He shoved the vault door closed behind him and waited for the sound of its slam.

But it never came.

Augustus flinched at the sight of the tendrils trapped in the steel door. They snaked through the air, scratching and causing it to shimmer.

Augustus stepped back as the scraper pushed the door open, its tendrils whipping before it. He stumbled through the ancient vault. At the end of the room, a stairway led to a trapdoor. Augustus flew up the steps as the scraper followed. He threw the door open, emerging into the old bank above, empty save for charred walls and the smell of smoky decay.

Augustus reached the door that led to the street and turned to see the scraper emerge from the trapdoor.

As its tendrils reached into the air, they sizzled. The creature withdrew with a low, despairing moan before descending back into the vault.

Augustus ran through the streets until, finally, he could run no more. He slumped against a wall and sat down, fighting to catch his breath and ease the pain in his side.

The road was empty, and he hadn't seen a sign of the ghoul since emerging from the vault. Perhaps the scrapers had killed it.

He hoped so.

Augustus opened the satchel. The book was still there, its cover scored by the slash of his blade. He closed the bag and peered at the signpost across the way. Kettleton Street. He was only a mile or so from one of his hideouts, a long-abandoned vicarage.

What better place to hide from a Devil than the former house of a holy man?

Augustus stood wearily, sighing as he walked. Soon he found himself approaching the old church. The derelict street surrounding it was empty, thanks in part to its terrible reputation. Legend told that the church's priest had turned from God to Lucifer, and following his conversion were evil tales of black rituals to his new satanic lord.

But despite the hideous stories of dark tidings, Augustus found the place strangely calming, and if the priest had ever existed, he was long gone.

Augustus skirted by the church, making his way through the hole in the side of the vicarage. He stepped over the traps he'd lain across the floor and ducked below the razor-sharp wire that crisscrossed the room. He entered the study and made his way across a floor littered with the books he'd flung from the shelves. Augustus slumped upon the threadbare chair he occasionally slept in, pulled the old woolen blanket across himself, and turned from the stars shining through the window.

Soon, he fell into a deep sleep.

He awoke to the sound of footsteps.

Augustus opened his eyes and wiped away his sleep before gazing at the room beyond. It was empty. But the footsteps still came, ever closer.

"Hello?" Augustus called. "Who's there? Show yourself!" He threw the blanket off, standing and reaching into his pocket for his knife.

It wasn't there.

Augustus opened the nearby desk and grabbed the meat cleaver he'd hidden inside, hefting it before him. "You'd better leave right now. If you don't, I'll take your head off!"

The footsteps drew closer still. Augustus swung the cleaver before him but there was nothing to strike out at, invisible or not.

And then the footsteps stopped and all at once he knew, with a terrible certainty, where the ghoul was.

For how could it be anything but the ghoul?

The hairs on the nape of his neck stood on end as he looked up.

The ghoul stood above with his feet firmly planted on the ceiling, one hand clasping his top hat, the other reaching for him. Augustus screamed as freezing fingers seized him and those fiery eyes glared into his.

"How...how did you find me?" Augustus cried.

The creature, whose pallid face now bore a series of slashes and scars, smiled. "The book sings to me, little thief."

Augustus reached for the satchel and held it out. "Take it. Please, just take it and leave me alone!"

"I told you, I protect the book. And you defiled it and dragged it across your city like a common trinket. You tainted it with your blade and now you must pay the price. *I am that price.*" The ghoul dropped from the ceiling, turning in midair and landing squarely on the floor, his hand still around Augustus's neck.

"Listen," Augustus begged. "Listen to me. I know I've done wrong. But I can put it right, you'll see. I'll find every last person I've robbed and pay them back. Just give me a chance and you'll see I'll make good."

"Far too late." The ghoul shook his head. "Ancient laws protect the book. Those laws are upheld by me."

Augustus gazed into the ghoul's eyes. There was no pity in those smoldering embers, only desolation and hatred. "Whose laws? I never knew about them."

"The laws of the Grimwytch. All transgressions against the midnight rule will be punished. Crimes against the sacred books are punishable by their guardian. I am the guardian, boy, and you have trespassed against our world. Now I shall take your lights."

The ghoul began to reach for Augustus's eyes.

"Please, don't kill me. Please! I don't want to die!"

The ghoul stopped. "You want to live?"

"Yes! Yes!" Augustus cried.

The ghoul smiled. It was an empty expression. "Do you want to serve your punishment alive? In the Grimwytch?"

"I'll go anywhere you want. Just don't hurt me!"

"Then so be it," the ghoul said as he reached out with one hand on the book, the other on Augustus Pinch.

The Book of Kindly Deaths
Addendum

I was resting at home in my study, gazing into the fire and hoping it would soothe my aching bones, when a knock at the window jarred me from my reverie. I knew at once, given the hour and the force of the knock, that the visitor brought bad news. I called for Sarah and opened the door to find one of my informants, a wizened old crone who perpetually reeked of gin, standing upon the doorstep.

"Come in." I ushered her inside, closing the door against the dreary winter night. Sarah joined us in my study as the old crone held out a hand and waited, like a fortuneteller, for it to be crossed with silver. I found money for her at once, for I could see by her look that her news was urgent; urgency in my business usually meant a soul, or souls, in mortal danger.

"I was surprised to see you sitting all cozy by the fire," she slurred, "when there's a ghoul running amok through our streets."

I was in no mood for games. "What does this ghoul look like? And where was it last seen?" I crossed the study, grabbing my map and glancing for nearby blots as the lady continued her tale.

"A tall thing with spindly arms, an old suit and hat, and red, glowing eyes. It was seen chasing a boy. Last I heard, it was out east, near Tidesworth."

I traced my fingers across the city. Several dark spots revealed recent intrusions from the Grimwytch, but they were minor compared with the dark blots that had revealed the hive of Gallowdim I'd dispatched the previous day. That encounter had taken much from me, and I still smarted from their wounds.

But now I saw a new spot upon the map. It was growing ever darker. I pulled my coat from the stand and grasped my walking cane. "Fetch my gun, Sarah. Indeed, fetch my rifle and handgun. And the sword. And arm yourself. We shall leave at once."

Thankfully, the street situated before my house was a busy one, and in little time I found a carriage and driver.

As we sped towards Tidesworth, I lit my lantern and examined the map. The dark spot had remained where it was, flickering beside a church that had risen to some notoriety after its priest had found a taste for darker forces.

While the map frequently led me to denizens of the Grimwytch, and even though all of my encounters were deeply sinister by nature, there was something about the black spot that made me wince.

I pulled my coat tighter around me, calling for the driver to hurry. Beyond the window lay the river and a black mass of warehouses. This was not a district I would usually choose to frequent. As we trundled through a series of disheveled streets, the horses slowed. We passed a dilapidated church, and the carriage came to a halt. I climbed out, seizing my rifle.

Sarah joined me, holding the map and lantern as we made our way to a once-grand structure now strangled with ivy. From within a hole in the side of the place came the sound of someone crying.

A child's voice.

As I entered the building, I caught the gleam of moonlight against a thin wire. Below, the floor was scattered with heavy iron traps. "Careful, Sarah," I whispered as I pointed to them.

Another cry set me hurrying. I ducked below the wires and along a dimly lit hallway, flinching as I entered the room at the end.

"You!" I cried. "What on earth possessed you to come here?"

Grim Shivers—for who else could that emaciated, ghoulish figure be?—turned and fixed me with a malignant stare, the embers of his eyes blazing. "Why are you here, writer?"

"I'm here because you're here," I replied. "You showed on my map. You know you're forbidden from visiting this realm without my consent." I took *The Book of Kindly Deaths* from Sarah. "Which means I have every right to set your story within this tome."

Grim Shivers held up another book. "You have no rights. This book, left in your care, was defiled by this miscreant." He stood aside, revealing a boy cowering before him. I recognized the child's curiously aged face at once. It was the boy who had stolen my book in the marketplace. He looked back at me with terror in his wide blue eyes.

"I'm sorry," the boy said to me. "Sorry I stole from you. I never meant to."

"I'm sure you didn't. Even more so now you've met the guardian." I sighed. "I tried to warn you."

"I didn't hear you," the boy said. Clearly no stranger to lies.

"Now, writer, take your book and leave." Grim Shivers handed me my book, its cover slashed. "And I shall settle my business with the boy."

"Let him go, Shivers. And get back to the Grimwytch at once. The guild will hear of this," I told him.

Grim Shivers laughed. "I shall visit the guild." He pointed at me with his long, bony finger. "And they will learn how you let the book fall into this child's hands. And that your city festers with denizens of the Grimwytch. And how I found scrapers in your tunnels."

I unfolded my map. "Can you see the marks, Shivers? How many are there? Fifty? A hundred? How does the guild expect me to cope with this? At my age? Why are there no more writers? I've appealed for assistance more times than I care to remember."

Grim Shivers sneered. "Wasting time here. Go and do your job. Leave the boy with me." He flapped his hand for me to leave and turned back to the sniveling boy.

I held up my rifle and jabbed it in the creature's back. He spun round, his teeth bared. "You threaten me?" he growled.

"It's no threat. Release the boy, and be on your way."

Grim Shivers held up his hands, the six rings upon his fingers beginning to shine, each with a different glow. Their colors were amber, the white of bone, sapphire blue, emerald green, black onyx, and blood-red ruby. "You should know better than to threaten me."

"Don't be ridiculous. Call them off," I demanded. "Now!"

But it was too late. The room darkened, and six figures appeared in a haze.

Sarah squeezed my hand. It was only the second time I'd known her to show fear. "It will be all right," I promised. Although as I saw the faces of the Grims appearing around Shivers, I wasn't so sure.

The first to emerge was a tall lady, her eyes huge, round, honey-colored orbs, her nose a pair of slits, her mouth a slash of red. As her eyes fell upon me, I looked away from her terrible gaze.

The second was younger, his hair ablaze, his eyes vivid blue. His face was so thin that his cheekbones looked as if they might tear through his paper-thin flesh. His smile had no trace of mirth.

The third, another man, had a face as raw as a side of beef. His eyes were as red as his face, with two tiny black pinpricks for pupils. He opened his mouth and hissed, revealing a serpent's tongue.

I stepped back.

A fourth Grim appeared next to the red man. A lady, taller than the others, her face pallid white below the tresses of her long black hair. Her face might have been considered fetching if it wasn't for the slashes and scars running down it. Something glinted at her hands; her nails were silver blades. She clicked them together, smiling mockingly.

The next Grim was the tallest, his legs thin and gangly, his head horribly elongated. His lantern-like eyes cast a piercing red light as he tottered forward, producing a small crossbow and aiming it at my head.

The final Grim to appear was another woman, of sorts. Her skull-like face turned to me, her black eyes wide as she held up a serrated blade. "Chop chop," she teased, striding towards me.

"Get away!" I turned to Grim Shivers. "I've already told you, I'm not threatening you."

"So he says," the man with the raw face said, "as he points his weapon at us."

I lowered my rifle and fixed Grim Shivers with a withering look. "Perhaps my assistant was chilled by your show of strength, but I'm not. Get back to the Grimwytch at once."

"We will return to the Grimwytch, writer. And take the boy with us," Grim Shivers said, snatching the boy by the back of his neck. "And you will get back to your work. Your city needs cleaning. I caught sight of more than just scrapers."

As difficult as it was, I met the eyes of each of the Grims, doing my best not to show fear, for to do otherwise would invite a massacre. They were hounds on the trail of a fox, keen to spill fresh blood.

Grim Shivers stared at me as his arms encircled the boy. By the law of the Grimwytch, he had jurisdiction and knew it.

I may as well have tried to snatch the moon from the sky than appeal for pity in that creature. I glanced at the boy, whose tearful eyes were on mine as I said, "I'm sorry. I really am. I tried to warn you."

"No!" the boy cried, trying to wrench himself free of Grim Shivers. "Make it let me go!"

"I have no choice. There's nothing I can do, at least for now. But I will try to help you. I promise."

I held out my book to Grim Shivers. "Before you take him, let me write him in. Let his story be told."

Grim Shivers paused for a moment before turning to his fellow Grims. "Return to the Midnight City. I have no need of you."

They nodded as one by one they began to shimmer, their forms becoming more and more indistinct until finally there was nothing left of them.

Grim Shivers stared at me for a moment. "I shall let the boy tell his story, writer. Because I know that is law. Were it not, I'd pluck the lights from him where he stands." He pushed the boy towards me.

Augustus made to run, but I blocked his way. "He'll hunt you down no matter where you try to hide," I told him, placing a hand on his shoulder. "You must go with him. If you resist, he will kill you."

"Can't you stop him?" the boy asked with a sob.

"Not presently. Which is why you must obey him. He will place you in a prison within the Grimwytch. But I shall appeal, I promise you. There may be a chance to free you yet, but before I can do this, you must tell us your story. That way I will have a record of events for your appeal."

The boy wiped his tears with the back of his hand. "What's it like? The place he's taking me to?"

"It's forever night. Or at least, it has been for as long as I've known it. And it's the place where...where they come from." I nodded towards the ghoul.

"Monsters?" the boy asked.

"We call them that. But they're not all monsters. There are many great beings in the Grimwytch. And not all of them are like him," I said, fixing Grim Shivers with a look of hatred. "I shall find someone to listen to me and do everything I can to free you. No matter how long it takes."

The boy nodded, his eyes straying to my rifle. I set it out of his reach. "Anything you do to harm him will be met with force. Don't. That's what he wants. Now, boy, what is your name?"

"Augustus Pinch."

I nodded for Sarah to produce my pen. "I need to hear your story, Augustus Pinch. Will you tell it?"

Augustus nodded. "I'll tell you everything. For what it's worth."

CHAPTER FOURTEEN

Over the Threshold

*E*liza sat up as she spotted the handwriting below the story. The words were written in fresh blue ink, and she recognized the writing at once.

It was her grandfather's.

Tom's.

Additional Addendum

Thomas Drabe 1943–November 4, 2012

The Guardian of Edwin Drabe's Edition of *The Book of Kindly Deaths, Volume 23*, otherwise known as Grim Shivers, today falls into a deep sleep. Grim Shivers leaves the Grimwytch and crosses to our world, transported to a cave on a remote isle in Scotland, the coordinates of which are marked on my map.

I, the writer Thomas Drabe, pass from my realm into the back room of the Malady Inn in Eastern Blackwood, unhindered.

Eliza reread the passage. "But it can't... It's just a story," she whispered, climbing from her bed and gazing through the window. It was light. Another day, another gray sky. Eliza glanced at the tangle of garden below, wondering where Tom had really gone, and why he'd abandoned the house without so much as a letter or phone call. And then there were the elaborate stories set out in a book rigged to only turn one page at a time. Why? Perhaps the stories had infected him with their strangeness. As she looked at the book, she held it up and read the last paragraph again.

It wasn't possible. He couldn't have traveled into a book.

"Of course it's not possible," she whispered. And yet, deep inside, Eliza knew that not only was it possible, but it had happened. That her grandfather really had gone to a world of monsters, and somewhere within, he was trapped.

Eliza was about to head to the hidden study to find more evidence when someone slammed a door. As she thought of her parents, she realized that now was the time to tell them. They had to know the truth about Tom, as difficult as they would find it. She could show them the book and how it only turned one page at a time, and the hidden room with the stained glass window. They would find it impossible to believe, but she had to try to make them understand. And if they didn't, what then? Perhaps there were other *writers*. If she could find them, they could help her. Tom couldn't be the only one, surely?

Eliza jumped out of the bed and pulled on her sweater, jeans, and trainers, determined now to tell her mother the truth. Even if she had to force her to listen. As Eliza passed the window overlooking the street, she froze. A figure walked towards the house. The man who called himself Mr. Eustace Fallow. The man who wasn't a man, but a monster.

As Eliza watched him, she thought of Tom's paragraph:

Grim Shivers leaves the Grimwytch and crosses to our world, transported to a cave on a remote isle in Scotland.

And now the realization made Eliza retch, her stomach rolling as if filled with curdled milk. "That's why his suit was wet. And why he stunk of the sea."

He looked up, his face battered and bruised, and Eliza recoiled. "What happened to him?" she whispered.

Grim Shivers, disguised as Eustace Fallow, vanished from her sight and, seconds later, a frantic knocking rang against the door below. "Don't answer it!" Eliza yelled, hurtling along the hall, but as she reached the top of the stairs, she stopped.

Too late.

Ice-cold air swept through the house as Grim Shivers, limping and hunched, was led into the hall by her father. "Get him out!" Eliza cried.

"Hurt," Grim Shivers moaned. "Accident. Need help."

"He's not real!" Eliza screamed. Her mother appeared from the kitchen with a distressed look. "Mum, he's not who he says he is!"

"What happened to you?" Eliza's mum ran to Grim Shivers, placing a hand on his shoulder.

He winced, repeating, "Accident. Need help." He glanced at Eliza and gave her a slight smile.

"I think he's concussed," Eliza's father said as he shouted to Eliza, "Call an ambulance."

"No!" she replied. "He's not hurt and he's not whoever he says he is. He's a monster!"

"Eliza!" her mother shouted. "What's wrong with you? Call an ambulance at once! Mark, get the poor man into the kitchen while I fetch the first aid kit."

Eliza stomped down the remaining stairs, snatching up the phone. She'd call the emergency services, all right. But it wouldn't be for an ambulance. It would be for a police car. She dialed, placing the phone to her ear.

The line was dead.

He's cut the line. "Well, he can't cut my cell phone off!" she shouted as loudly as she could, hoping he'd hear as she ran defiantly up the stairs. Her cell phone showed one flickering bar of reception. Eliza walked around her room, holding it up in the air.

Still, one bar.

She dialed emergency services and was met with a sea of crackles and static and distant snatches of conversation. Conversations in voices that she didn't want to hear. Eliza opened the window, gazing frantically to the gardens below. They were deserted.

She ran from her room, determined to make her parents listen to her, to make them get the creature out of the house. But as she descended the stairs, she stopped.

The house below was silent, aside from the *tick* and *tock* of the large grandfather clock in the hall.

"Mum? Dad?"

Nothing.

CHAPTER FIFTEEN

Trapped

*A*s Eliza passed the front door, she wanted more than anything to throw it open and flee. To keep running until this nightmare ended. But she couldn't leave her parents. They had no idea what they were dealing with. Eliza took a deep breath and walked towards the kitchen as something clattered in the front room, making her jump. She pushed the door ajar, flinching as Grim Shivers, in human guise, strode before the bookcases, scanning the books.

Eliza left him to it and tiptoed to the kitchen.

"No!" Her parents were slumped over the kitchen table, their hands outstretched, their faces contorted with horror. "No!" She ran to them, flinching at the sight of their eyes staring back at her.

Lifeless.

"Mum…" Eliza shook her mother. She flopped in her chair like a doll. "Please!" Eliza begged, her eyes filling with tears. "Please, wake up!"

A crash came from the living room. The sound of books tumbling to the floor.

Eliza ran to the back door, yanking the handle. It was locked, the key missing from the keyhole.

And then she noticed the items scattered below the kitchen table. Her father's glasses case, her mother's phone.

The ghoul had gone through their pockets. "He's got the keys." Eliza ignored the panic welling inside as she picked up a chair and swung it at the kitchen window. The glass shattered, leaving a mosaic of jagged shards. Eliza climbed upon the kitchen counter, sweeping the broken glass aside with a tea towel.

"Stop."

She flinched.

Grim Shivers stood in the kitchen door, watching her. "You'll cut yourself," he said. His voice was different now from how it had been when he had first turned up on the doorstep. As if he had grown into his body. Now he sounded just as Eliza had imagined the ghoul would have when it had spoken with Augustus in that horrible tale from *The Book of Kindly Deaths*. "I need you whole and in good working order, so you can tell me where the book is."

Eliza climbed down, seizing a carving knife from the block. Fury engulfed her as she stepped towards him. "Stay away! If you come near me," she gazed towards her parents' lifeless bodies, "I'll stick this knife in your heart."

Grim Shivers nodded. "I believe you would, Miss Drabe. But it won't hurt me. However, if you don't tell me where the book is, I *will* hurt you."

"I don't know what book you're talking about. There are thousands of books in this house. And my name is Miss Winter."

"But you're a Drabe, too," the ghoul said. "And I can see quite clearly from the look in your eyes that you know exactly which book I want. It's the one your grandfather used to take me from my world. The book he used as a bridge to mine. I *will* find him, Miss Drabe."

Eliza glanced towards the door behind the creature. "Okay, I'll give you your book. Just don't hurt me."

Grim Shivers nodded, placing a hand on his chest. "You have my word."

As Eliza passed her parents' bodies, she gripped the knife even tighter, walking into the front room and stepping aside as the ghoul entered. The floor was littered with books, the bookcases empty. "There's a safe behind that picture of the tower," Eliza said.

"Safe?" Grim Shivers asked, striding across the room.

"A hidden door. I asked my dad to put the book in there for me."

As the ghoul picked up the painting to find a blank wall, Eliza turned and ran.

She seized the front door. It was locked. She looked for the key on the shelf, but it was gone.

"Liar!" Grim Shivers growled from the front room. Eliza ran up the stairs as he emerged into the hall, his hands bunched into fists. She ignored him and flew down the hall, making for the study and its hidden room.

If she could reach the room in time, she'd be safe.

But as she passed her bedroom, Eliza remembered *The Book of Kindly Deaths*. She backtracked, her arms and legs shaking as she grabbed the book with numb fingers. Eliza screamed as she emerged into the hall to find Grim Shivers storming towards her, his long face contorted with fury. "Liar!"

Eliza ran, throwing the study door open and slamming it shut. She yanked the black book on the bottom shelf and dashed into the hidden room just as the study door smashed open. The last thing she saw, as the secret door swung shut, were the ghoul's smoldering eyes and the glowing blue-white blade at his side. Her head swam now, panic and nausea flooding through her. She closed her eyes as she tried to calm herself, but all she could see was her parents slumped across the kitchen table.

And then he began to kick at the door, howling, the sound low and terrible in its woeful rage. Eliza remembered the bookcases he'd emptied downstairs. If he did that now, which seemed likely in his rage… "He's going to open the door!" She looked around the room. There were no exits.

She was trapped.

Her eyes fell on the stained glass window. Eliza threw the book on the desk, clambering up and pulling the handle. It opened a fraction, admitting a cool air bearing rich, exotic fragrances, spices, blossoms and perfumes. But below the fragrances, a coppery, blood-like scent and the stench of rot.

Something slammed into the hidden door. Eliza pulled the window handle with all her might. It opened. She recognized the room on the other side at once. She'd seen it the night before. In her nightmare.

Despite trying to tell herself that *The Book of Kindly Deaths* was just a book and the happenings or the hallucinations of her awakened imagination, she'd known it to be real. Knew that her *nightmare* of the city was nothing of the sort, that it was not just a dream. And here before her was the proof. For beyond the window was the room with the whispering books and the slug-like creature in the glass tank.

Grim Shivers let forth another cry of rage, the hidden door shaking in its frame.

Eliza froze on the window ledge as the sound of heavy feet marched towards the room. Two guards entered. Eliza averted her eyes as she ducked back into the secret room, sealing the window.

A clank of feet rang out as the guards approached the window. Behind Eliza, the din of books being hurled around came as the ghoul bellowed.

"He's going to find the switch," Eliza whispered, her voice trembling. She glanced around the room, searching for another way out.

But there was none.

Her eyes fell to the desk and *The Book of Kindly Deaths*, and the pen beside it.

Eliza snatched the book, letting it fall open to the last page, and forced her thoughts to clear as she reread her grandfather's entry. He had written himself into the book. If he could, why couldn't she?

She picked the pen up, flinching as a charge of power exploded in her fingertips, running through her arm and shooting deep into her chest. Eliza gasped for air as her body began to flood and swell with energy. She let it guide her as she wrote, following Tom's words with her own:

Additional Addendum

Eliza Winter 2001—13 January 2013

I, the writer Eliza Winter, pass from my world into the back room of the Malady Inn in Eastern Blackwood unhindered.

And as she added the full stop, the room flickered, darkening as the book below her crackled with energy.

Then the study began to flicker and smolder like a heat haze. Dimly she saw the ghostly outline of Grim Shivers pouncing through the door, his skeletal fingers outstretched...

Eliza looked away, down to the desk, and the last thing she saw was *The Book of Kindly Deaths* closing.

And then it was gone.

And so was she.

CHAPTER SIXTEEN

The Malady Inn

*D*arkness surrounded Eliza. It was as if every source of light in the universe—every light bulb, star, moon, and sun—had gone out. She held her hand out but found nothing. Eliza took a deep breath, almost choking with surprise. The air was different, so intensely clean and fresh that it almost hurt her lungs.

She gulped another breath and exhaled, pushing out the old, stale air she'd brought with her. As she continued to take deeper breaths, her senses came to life, clearer and sharper, her energy and strength keener than ever.

And now she could smell something else, something musty and damp. "Where am I?" she asked.

Silence. And then, far away, a clamor of voices.

"Am I dead?" she asked, her voice louder than usual. She wondered if something catastrophic had happened, if somehow she was trapped in some strange limbo.

"Maybe I'm stuck inside the book?" Eliza held out her hands, almost expecting to feel paper pages or the hard cover of *The Book of Kindly Deaths*, but instead, her fingers brushed against cold stone.

"A wall?"

Eliza ran her fingers up and down across the stone. As she moved towards it, something jutted into her side. She cried out and reached down, finding the edge of a surface up against the stone. She knocked against it, producing a hollow sound, then her hands collided with something else. Eliza reached for it. It was cold and smooth, and on one side, she found a lid. She flipped it open, and as the smell of fuel filled the air, Eliza knew exactly what she was holding.

Her father had had one when he used to smoke. "A Zippo lighter." She flicked the flint wheel and a vivid spark lit the gloom as the wick burst into life, creating a flame.

Eliza found herself beside a desk. At its center was a candle. She lit it, flicking the lighter shut and placing it in her pocket. The room was small; in its corner were a neatly made bed and a tall wardrobe. The wallpaper was of dark flowers set against a light-grey background, just like the damask wallpaper she'd once seen in a Victorian museum. As Eliza looked around, she saw that there were no windows or doors.

"How do I get out?"

She turned to the desk and found another candle. As she lit it, she saw the photographs piled upon the desk.

Her own face grinned toothily back, six years younger. Behind her younger self, her grandfather beamed with a soft, generous smile.

Eliza remembered her grandmother taking the photograph while they were at the zoo. It had been blazing hot, the place filled with vibrantly colored birds and tired, lazy animals. She'd dropped her ice cream on the sweltering pavement just before the picture had been taken. Eliza recalled how instead of crying, as she usually would have, she'd accepted her loss. She'd felt a swell of pride moments later when Tom had handed her his ice cream, thanking her for being brave and adding, "Bravery should always be rewarded."

Eliza glanced through the other photographs. One was of her parents on their wedding day, a wary look on her mum's face as she stood with her own mother on one side, Eliza's dad on the other.

Tom must have taken that photograph. Which explained, perhaps, the look on her mother's face.

The other pictures were of her grandparents alone, except they were much younger. Tom smiled brightly in each of the photographs but, as Eliza looked closer, she could see the shadow in his smile. It was the face of a man who believed in being brave, no matter what, and in smiling and making the best of things. Behind his smile, however, his eyes told a different story. They were haunted. They were the eyes of a man who had lived with terrible things.

A man who had seen monsters.

Eliza searched the desk drawer. She found a box of matches and a few books, thrillers, their modern covers strangely out of place. Books by bestselling authors stashed in a room in another world.

The next drawer revealed two identical necklaces. Each long silver chain held a heavy jade amulet. Eliza remembered Tom wearing one when they'd gone to the beach. She recalled the addendum from the story about Victoria Stapleton and how the writer had mentioned a necklace made of Solaarock. She took one of the necklaces and put it on. It felt curiously reassuring and heavy as she walked towards the wardrobe. The clothes inside were unlike anything she'd seen outside of a museum. There were old-fashioned suits and rough woolen trousers and hooded jerkins, and each smelled of sweat, dampness, and blood.

A tiny crack allowed a glint of light to show through the back of the wardrobe. Eliza knocked against it. It was hollow. She pushed the clothes aside, scouring through the interior until she found a small brass lever, which she pulled. All at once, the back of the wardrobe folded in on itself, and Eliza found herself standing before a corridor, voices filling the passage beyond.

She stepped through, jumping as the back of the wardrobe folded back up with a clatter, leaving in its place a pitted brick wall. As she examined the wall for a way to return through the wardrobe, a peal of raucous laughter rang down the hall. Slowly and cautiously, Eliza made her way along it. The room at the end was illuminated with candles. It looked and smelled like a pub. A very old pub. But as Eliza saw the figures drinking at the tables, she gasped.

The room was full of monsters.

Three tiny men sat at the nearest table. They had claws for hands and hooves for feet and glanced at Eliza with tiny black eyes, opening their mouths to reveal rows of shark-like teeth. They began to laugh once more, their voices loud and grating.

Next to them sat an immense lady with one large eye where her mouth should have been and two mouths where her eyes should have been. She frowned at Eliza before shaking her head and taking a deep draught from her pewter tankard.

Behind the woman, a hooded figure sat gazing off into the distance. A bow and a sheathed sword rested against his table. As Eliza watched, the figure turned to her, two flashes of intense green light glowing within its hood.

Eliza looked away to the group of men and women that sat behind the hooded figure in a melancholy huddle. They would have looked normal if it wasn't for their waxy yellow skin and large, mournful eyes. And as Eliza glanced at their lank black hair and tattered clothes, she realized who they were. "The Wrong People…"

Before she could finish her sentence, a creature with a long putrid-green face and deep, sunken eyes slammed its tankard upon the table and shouted, "Human!"

It vanished for a split second, reappearing before Eliza, its claws outstretched as they swiped towards her.

CHAPTER SEVENTEEN

Shard

*E*liza flinched as the creature slashed the air and whimpered as her head struck the wall behind. The creature laughed and tensed as if about to lunge, when all of a sudden a bolt thudded into the wall.

The creature shot a furious glance to the bar, where a lofty man with a shock of white hair and two pure-black eyes quickly reloaded a small crossbow. "Step away," he called, aiming it at them. "And if you so much as look at the girl again, your head will hang on my trophy wall. Do you understand?"

"*Jaxma!*" the creature hissed.

"I'm no turncoat," the man thundered. "I served at Oakspell. Don't you dare call me a *jaxma*!" He strode over, jabbing the crossbow against the creature's head. "Is our business concluded?"

The creature nodded and scowled at Eliza, before crossing the room and vanishing into the shadows.

"Welcome to the Malady Inn, Eliza." The man lowered his crossbow. "You may call me Mr. Barrow, if it pleases you."

"How do you know my name?"

Mr. Barrow smiled. "Tom has told me all about you. And seeing as you managed to find your way from your world to ours, I'd say you'd have to be a Drabe. Am I right?"

"Apparently."

Eliza looked across the room. All eyes seemed to be on them as a deathly hush settled over the bar. It was like a dream.

Or perhaps nightmare was a better word.

Mr. Barrow turned and addressed the room. "All incidents of gawping and eavesdropping will be met with a lifetime ban from the Malady Inn. Back to your drinks, ladies, gentlemen, and those who are neither."

Gradually, their audience looked away, whispering to one another, and slowly their whispers became murmurs and the murmurs built until the room was once more filled with raucous conversation.

As Mr. Barrow led Eliza to the bar, she peered at the dozens of dusty bottles lined up behind it. Every color of the rainbow seemed to be represented, and more still. She wondered what the drinks inside tasted like, before deciding it was probably better not to know.

Mr. Barrow pulled a large pint of what looked like frothing green beer and pushed it towards Eliza. "Old Catwhist, your grandfather's favorite."

"I'm probably too young to drink it," Eliza said. She'd had a sip of her father's beer once and found it the most wretched thing she'd ever tasted. Even worse than liver.

"Then I'll sup it. It would be a shame to see it go to waste. How about some spiritberry juice? It'll keep your head where it needs to be."

"I...I'll try a sip, maybe."

Mr. Barrow reached for a bottle of plum-colored juice and poured it into a small glass. The juice was thick and gloopy, but he looked so happy as he offered it that Eliza took a sip. Despite its appearance, it was deliciously fragrant, reminding her of vanilla, blossoms, and coffee.

"Do you like it?"

"I like it," she said and swallowed the rest. Soon, her surroundings seemed slightly less threatening. Mr. Barrow placed a hand upon her arm. "You shouldn't be here, girl. This is not a place for you. It's not even a place for Tom, and he's an old hand with our people. As soon as my shift is done, I'll take you to a crossing place and you can go home."

"I can't go home," Eliza said and, as she thought of the hidden study in Tom's house, the warm, dizzy feeling from the spiritberry juice vanished. "I can't go back. There's a creature...Grim Shivers. He did something to my parents. And he wants to kill me."

A dark look crossed Mr. Barrow's face. "I...I'm surprised to hear that. The Grims are ruthless, but they've never spilled innocent blood. Only because they can't, mind you. I told Tom sending Shivers to your realm was an act of great folly. I warned him!"

"I need to find Tom." She looked around the room. "Why did he come here? And why did he send that...creature to us?"

"He said he came to right two wrongs. Things that have bothered him for years. There's much wrong in the Grimwytch, Eliza, much wrong. But to try and right it is like spitting to douse an inferno. I told him those things were none of his business, that he should leave the past where it belongs."

"What wrongs did he come to right?"

"Something about a boy whose mouth was stolen by a malefactrix. And another who was arrested by Grim Shivers himself. Said he could fix two wrongs and make them both right at the same time. He's old, Eliza. And tired. He thinks he's coming to the end of his days. Sadly, I'm inclined to agree. When...when your mother refused her calling and denied you yours, it changed him. He's not been right since, and that was years ago."

"What calling?"

"To serve as Tom's apprentice. To write down the wrongs. To send back those who seek to cross to places they don't belong. And there are plenty of them. But your mother wouldn't have anything to do with it, or with Tom. He felt her rejection keener than any blade. I'm sorry to have to tell you this, but you *did* ask."

Mr. Barrow looked as if he was about to say more, but he stopped as a figure rose from a nearby table and joined them at the bar.

At first glance Eliza thought he looked quite normal. A teenager, maybe two or three years older than she. He wore a dark-blue hood above his long black coat, the darkness of his garments in stark contrast to his chalk-white face.

As he glanced at Eliza, she tried to avoid the glare from his eyes, which were so green that she thought it had to be a trick of the light. Nut-brown sparks danced at their centers, hypnotizing her until he opened his mouth and displayed two long fangs nestling amongst his teeth.

Eliza stepped away.

"What can I get you?" Mr. Barrow asked. If he felt any sense of danger from the boy, he didn't show it.

"I need something to take for the road. Food, no drink. What do you have?"

"How about dirge dust? I have a couple of bags. Not the tastiest of things, but remarkably filling."

"I'll take it." The boy turned to Eliza. "You don't need to cower, girl. I won't bite you. Humans aren't to my taste."

Eliza shook her head. "I'm not frightened of you."

The boy smiled, a hollow gesture. "Of course you're not."

She turned away from him and gazed across the bar. Anywhere but at those piercing green eyes.

Eliza watched as a curious figure stepped away from the boy's table, slipping a small bottle into its coat. The figure was thin, but not in terms of weight. Thin in a way that meant it wasn't quite there.

Like a ghost. Not one of the other drinkers seemed to notice it.

"Do you know the man who just poured something in your drink?" Eliza asked the boy. He growled, shooting across the bar as the figure melted into the background and became one with the shadows upon the wall. Eliza strained to see a further sign of the figure, but there was nothing.

It was as if it had never existed.

The boy seized his tankard and flung its contents across the table, causing smoke to rise as the wood beneath blackened. Then he pulled off his hood, his dark hair whipping around his head like snakes, the two small horns buried within shining in the candlelight. "Who did this?" the boy demanded, unsheathing the sword by his table. He held it up, gazing defiantly at the monsters before him.

Not one met his gaze.

"He's gone," Eliza called. "He vanished into the wall over there." She pointed to the shadows.

The boy stalked over, running his hand along the wall and shaking his head. He sheathed his sword before joining her at the bar. "What did he look like?"

"I...I don't know. I remember he looked like a man. At least, I think he did. He wore a long coat and hood, like yours. And...I can't seem to remember anything else now. It's almost like...like it never happened. Like he was never there."

"It sounds like a darkwight," Mr. Barrow said to the boy. "You must have powerful enemies."

The boy shook his head. "I only have one enemy." He grimaced, playing with a chain around his neck. "That is, until I reach the Midnight City. "

CHAPTER EIGHTEEN

Bound by Wyrd

*T*he boy approached Eliza and held out his hand. She wondered what he was doing. The gesture seemed so *human* that she took his hand and shook it.

"I'm bound to you," he said. "For now."

"Bound?" Eliza asked.

"To protect you from meeting your end, as you protected me from meeting mine. Is this your first visit to the Grimwytch?"

"Yes."

"Then it won't be long until my duty is met. And once it is, I shall resume my task. Will you wander our roads?"

"I...I suppose. I'm looking for my grandfather. Tom."

The boy shrugged. "I don't know any humans. At least, I didn't until this evening. Where is your grandfather?"

Eliza shook her head. "I don't know."

"Well, I can tell you where he was going," Mr. Barrow said. "Although it was some time ago, and he could be anywhere by now. He was headed for the Midnight City. first, and from there, I don't know. He said he was going to 'free an asset,' whatever that meant. And then he was going to hunt for a malefactrix, although he didn't know where she was. He mentioned righting two wrongs, and maybe he managed to, but I doubt it." Mr. Barrow looked downcast as he added, "He'd have been back by now if he had. And I've heard no word from him."

"Well, this is interesting," the boy said. "It seems we're bound not just by duty, but wyrd also."

"'Wyrd'?" Eliza asked.

"Fate, destiny," Mr. Barrow said.

"So how come we're bound?"

The boy gazed at Eliza as if seeing her for the first time. "The Midnight City is also my destination. And I, too, have wrongs to right, girl."

"My name isn't 'girl,'" Eliza said. "It's Eliza Winter."

The boy nodded. "Then I shall call you Eliza Winter."

"Just Eliza will do."

"Make up your mind, will you?" He grimaced, but his eyes showed a slight flicker of warmth.

"And you are?" Eliza asked.

"You wouldn't be able to pronounce my name even if I could offer it to you. And I can't. But you may call me by the name my brother gave me. Shard."

"Shard?"

"A fragment." He held up his fingers, showing a tiny space. "My brother used to say I was a mere fragment of the cosmos compared to him."

"So, what does your brother say now?"

"Nothing," Shard said. "He's dead. Along with my parents. They were slaughtered." His eyes flashed. "Which is why I have business in the city. And why that darkwight, if that's what it was, tried to poison my drink. But enough talk—word will have spread of your arrival. We should leave at once."

"When I find my grandfather I'll tell him you were asking after him," Eliza told Mr. Barrow.

"Please, do that." The landlord smiled. "And tell him there's a pint of Old Catwhist waiting. Good luck, Eliza Winter. Or maybe I should say Eliza Drabe."

Shard walked to his scorched table and picked up his bag, a large black bow, and a quiver of arrows. He led Eliza from the inn, opening the door for her. Eliza found herself curiously touched by the gesture. It seemed strangely polite and antiquated.

The air in the countryside outside the Malady Inn was even cleaner. Eliza took a deep breath, filling her lungs. She realized she'd never really thought about pollution before. Now she was in a place with none, she realized how poor the air was on Earth.

As she stepped from the porch, she stopped, her mouth falling open as she took in the sight before her.

Beyond the inn, a muddy road led into a great black forest, and above, the moon hung low. But somehow, it was different. Larger, redder, and...just different. Maybe it was the stars surrounding it, for they seemed brighter...and although she'd never studied the constellations, Eliza could see these stars were arranged in unfamiliar ways.

"It's not the same," she said.

Shard looked up. "What isn't?"

"The moon. It's different. But I don't know why."

"Is it larger? Smaller? The same color?" Shard asked, and Eliza detected a tone of fascination below his gruffness.

" It's just...not the same as ours. I wonder if it tastes the same..."

"Tastes?" Shard looked at Eliza as if she were insane. "Humans eat their moon? How?"

Eliza laughed. "We don't. It's an old tale. People tell their children the moon is made of cheese."

Shard looked bemused as he shook his head, beginning to laugh; within moments he was doubled over.

"Do you know what cheese is?" Eliza asked. "Do you have cheese here?"

This seemed to amuse Shard even more as he held up a hand. "Stop. Stop it, please! No more."

Eliza tutted. It wasn't that funny, surely? And it did seem strange that monsters would eat cheese. At least to her. As they began walking, she continued to fix her eyes on the stars. "I've seen your sky before."

"You said you hadn't travelled to the Grimwytch before?"

"Well, I have. Sort of. I dreamt of it last night."

"If you dreamt the Grimwytch, then it must be in your blood."

"Maybe," Eliza said. "It's definitely in my granddad's blood. He's got these special books about this place. I've read about the Grimwytch. It seems odd to think that only last night I was reading of a girl who was brought here by those people in the inn. The ones with the yellow faces and greasy hair. *The Wrong People*."

"The Eiderstaark?" Shard asked.

"That's them. Anyway, when the girl came, your moon turned her. And she became…disfigured."

Shard placed a finger on the pendant around Eliza's neck. "Your necklace is made of Solaarock. It will stop the moon from turning you."

"How do you know so much about my people?" Eliza asked.

"When I was younger, before I'd go to sleep, my parents would tell tales about humans."

Eliza smiled. "That's funny. We tell stories about monsters."

"Do you consider me a *monster*?"

Eliza thought about it. "No. Not like some of the ones I've read about."

"I don't think we're much different from you," Shard said. "While you'll find *monsters* in the Grimwytch who are pitiless, selfish, and evil, you'll also find those who are good and kind. And there are those who are completely indifferent."

"It's like that where I come from," Eliza said. "People are just the same."

As the road cut through the forest, the grave demeanor Shard had worn in the Malady Inn returned once more.

Eliza looked at the trees. Their trunks were thick like oaks, but their branches were longer and barer, like tendrils reaching out and connecting with one another. "Is it winter here? Or are your trees always bare?"

"It's winter. In spring they'll blossom."

"It's the same where I come from," Eliza said. "I thought everything would be completely different. But you even use the same words as us. Well, for the most part."

Shard tutted. "Why do you assume we use the same words as you?" he asked irritably. "Perhaps you got your language from us. Did that ever occur to you?"

"I don't think so!" Eliza said. "Humans have been on Earth for a long time, you know."

"And so have we."

"On Earth?" Eliza asked.

"Well, where else do you think we are? What..." Shard stopped in his tracks, holding his hand up. "Shut up!"

"That's just plain rude—" Eliza began. Shard clasped a hand over her mouth.

Something approached in the distance, some sort of vehicle, its headlights on full beam. One of the lights struck Shard, but before the other could find Eliza, he pushed her aside.

She stumbled off the road and into the trees.

"Hide!" Shard whispered, throwing out his hands as if to hurry her along. "Quickly!"

CHAPTER NINETEEN

Malumdell

*E*liza ran, struggling through roots and brambles that slyly seemed to wrap themselves around her feet. After the bright shine of the moon, the forest was a wall of black. She wondered what kinds of creatures might be lurking within the trees as she stopped, turning to make sure she could still find the road.

Shard stood where he was, shielding his eyes with a hand as the light bore down on him.

Hooves clattered against the path, and a large dark carriage appeared, drawn by four horses. It reminded Eliza of a giant beetle. It stopped before Shard and four figures jumped from its roof. They towered over Shard, who was still caught in the beam of the huge lamps mounted to the top of the carriage. Within the lamps, mirrors surrounded gaslights, boosting their glare.

As the figures stepped into the light, Eliza gasped, for their heads looked like those of monstrously large bees grafted onto human bodies.

"What are you doing on the road, boy?" boomed a voice from within the carriage.

"What does it look like I'm doing?" Shard asked. "Aside from trying to walk along this road."

"What insolence!" the voice replied. "Take me to him."

The four bee-headed figures returned to the carriage, sliding out a stretcher from beneath. They helped a huge woman as she emerged from the carriage and placed her on the stretcher before carrying her to Shard. Her head shone in the moonlight, smooth and bald. As she neared Shard, Eliza noticed a series of six mouths opening above the folds of fat obscuring her neck.

The woman held her head up, sending her jowls quivering as she sniffed the air. "I can smell drearspawn!" she announced, her voice booming through each mouth, the tone of each just a little different, producing an unsettling, discordant sound. The guards around her tensed, their bee-like heads turning to the forest.

Eliza's heart thumped as she stooped towards the ground.

"I don't smell drearspawn," Shard said. "All I smell is the stench of your sweating flesh. You might consider a bath."

"Who are you," the woman demanded, "to talk to me like that? I shall have you flogged. I shall have you cleaved in two. And your remains shall be a feast for my workers. Seize him!"

Shard pulled his sword from his sheath, reversed it in his hand and held the pommel so it shone in the light. "Tell me," he sneered, "do you recognize this mark?"

The woman glanced closer, and all at once, her tiny hands flapped in the air. "My mistake. Take me back to the carriage." She gave a shrill cry. "At once!" The guards carried her to the carriage, locking its doors as they nervously glanced at Shard before climbing upon the roof.

Shard smiled as the carriage trundled past, and the moment it disappeared from view, he turned to the trees. "Where are you, Eliza?"

Eliza called to him; his bright green eyes fixed on her as he threaded his way through the trees. "We'll have to make our way through the forest to reach the city," Shard told her. "The road is too dangerous. At least, too dangerous for you."

"Do you know the way?" Eliza asked as they weaved through the colossal tree trunks.

"Yes. I've spent countless moons roaming Blackwood. There's a lot to find in the forest if you know where to look. Beautiful places. And terrible ones, too."

"What did that woman mean when she said she smelled '*drearspawn*'?" Eliza asked.

"She meant she smelled a human. You."

"What does it mean?"

"It's not a very nice word. Some inhabitants here feel humans are...limited. They call you drearspawn. I don't."

"Good," Eliza said. She thought back to the story of the Wrong People. How the creatures had laughed at Katherine's normality, in just the way humans might if a member of the Grimwytch were to be placed in a circus.

"Don't let it worry you," Shard said as they stepped into a large clearing. He gestured towards a tree stump. "Sit a moment." He began to pace around the edge of the clearing, his head lowered. "My situation has become complicated," he said. "Before, I knew what I was doing. But then..."

"But then I came along?"

"Yes. You saved my life, and for that I am eternally grateful. We both have purposes in the city. Mine is a matter of great urgency, and yet, I cannot attend to it while I have to protect you."

Eliza shrugged. "So, take me to the city and then go about your business."

"I can't. We're bound. I *have* to protect you. There is simply no other option."

"So what is this urgent business?"

"I cannot tell you," Shard replied with an uncomfortable look.

"Why not?"

"Because..." he looked away. "Because when we part, I don't want you to think ill of me."

Eliza was about to probe further but stopped as she saw his discomfort.

He looked so sad and angry. Like a boy struggling to grasp a situation out of his control. Far removed from the cold and assured warrior he seemed to want to project.

Shard met her gaze. "This is a dangerous place. Sooner or later, you're going to be attacked," he said. "And once I've defended you, I can go on my way. So, the sooner something threatens your life, the better for me. But," he paused, "I quite like you and your tales of moons made of cheese. And I'd like to hear more about your strange world, so I don't really want you to be murdered."

"That's very kind of you," Eliza replied.

"Indeed," Shard agreed. And then he gave a slight smile. "So, in order to stop you from being slaughtered, we need to find a way to stop you drawing attention to yourself."

"I don't try to draw attention to myself."

"Maybe not. But the reason our people notice you is because you stink."

"What?"

"Of human. Your scent is...not unpleasant. But it invites danger to you."

"Which is why you're here," Eliza reminded him. "That woman with the guards seemed pretty scared of you. And the monst...people in the inn."

"They were only frightened because of my family. Once word travels that they're dead, they won't be frightened for much longer."

"So, what can I do about my *stink*, as you put it?"

Shard laughed. "We can't really get rid of it, but we might be able to hide it. The only way I can think of is to find a scent powerful enough to mask yours. And you need a change of clothes; those garments you're wearing look ridiculous. Their reek would give you away to a cobblefoot."

"Cobblefoot?" Eliza asked.

The Book of Kindly Deaths

"Tiny, strange things with five legs which wobble all over the place. And they don't have any noses, which is a good thing for them because they smell like decaying goats."

"You have goats here?" Eliza said. "Silly me, of course you do. They were probably invented here. So, where am I supposed to get perfume and a change of clothes? Are there any all-night shops around here? Assuming this is night?"

"Of course there aren't any shops!" Shard tutted. "But…" he glanced to the stars. "I know somewhere that we can find a change of clothes. And they'll smell as vile as a cheesedung fly at the height of summer."

"I don't need to know what a cheesedung fly is," Eliza told Shard as they set off. "But I've got a perfectly hideous image in my mind."

They walked, passing through the woods as Shard asked Eliza questions about her world, greatly amused by most of her answers. And she asked him of his world.

"Remind me to keep away from the sheep if we see them!" Eliza said, worried now about the species of lambs that Shard had explained were savagely carnivorous. A part of her was sure he was joking, but if he was, he hid it well.

"How is it that you don't know of our beings?" Shard asked. "Your grandfather's a writer. You must be one too."

"I write, but not in the way you mean. I didn't know this world even existed until two days ago."

"How could that be?"

Eliza slowed now, gazing off into the trees. "My mother kept it from me. She's kept me in a safe little bubble for as long as I can remember. Anything even remotely weird or imaginative is a big no-no in our house. She told me stories were just made-up and a waste of time. Perhaps she was trying to protect me from all of this. If she was, I guess she meant well."

"You don't sound so sure," Shard said.

"I could see why she would do it, I suppose, but whatever the case, I resent her for not trusting me to make up my own

197

mind about things. This is all so…huge. She should have told me."

"And if she had, would you have wanted to come here? Would you have become a writer and battled the bad seeds in our realms?"

Eliza laughed, her face reddening. "I don't think I can battle anything. Even my cello lessons defeat me. I'm not like you."

"What am I like?" Shard asked.

"Well, you're a warrior, aren't you? You've probably bested loads of foes."

Shard ran a hand through his writhing hair and patted his horns. "Don't let appearances deceive you. I can fight; I've been trained to fight. That's what my family does…or should I say *did*. Fought for justice for those who choose to live in our fiefdom. But I haven't spilled blood yet. That will change soon enough, though." His face was grave now.

"I hope you catch whoever hurt your family," Eliza said, unsure of what else to say.

"I will," Shard replied, fingering a necklace about his neck. "It's only a matter of when."

He pulled his hood back up then, and Eliza was glad. For while Shard was perfectly friendly and she knew she could trust him, the sight of his horns and his hair, which seemed to move of its own accord, unsettled her. She looked forward to the time where she'd no longer notice it, praying he hadn't picked up on her awkwardness.

"So," Shard said, "what do you make of our land, then?"

Eliza shrugged. How could she put it without causing offence? "Well, it's very interesting. I mean, there are so many weird and wonderful things here. And the air is *really* clean. And, well, it's very dark. I don't know if I would want to live somewhere where there's no sun."

"There will be light one day. Or so legend says. But legends say a lot of things, and some of them never come to pass. "Anyway"—he gestured up at the moon—"she won't affect you. She won't make you change into one of us, not while you wear that Solaarock around your neck. So, does everyone look like you where you come from?"

"What do you mean?"

"I don't know, a lack of wings, horns, tails, things like that. And your eyes are very mild. They don't seem to shine much. Do they ever?"

"Not really. I suppose we do look pretty plain compared to you. Although some people try to look different. They spike their hair up and wear colored contact lenses—those are things that can make your eyes look really weird. And some people wear strange clothes and have bits of metal in their face. Mum says they're idiots, mostly, but I don't see why everyone should look the same all the time. If we lived in my mum's world, it would be as interesting as cardboard. Which is not very interesting at all. I know she doesn't really mean most of what she says. She's just scared."

"Of what?"

"This." Eliza swept her hands before her. "I don't know what happened between her and my grandfather, Tom, but I have a pretty good idea. I think he tried to teach her about the Grimwytch and something must have gone wrong. Perhaps she got really frightened. Which is probably why she's spent her whole life trying to keep all of this from me."

Suddenly Shard stopped, grabbing Eliza's arm. "Don't speak," he whispered.

Ahead, squat figures stood as still as statues amongst the trees. Until something moved in the forest beyond them, and the figures turned their elongated, canine heads as one.

The sound of movement came once again as something crashed through the foliage, and then the figures were off, leaping and tumbling through the brush. They vanished into the gloom and, moments later, a terrible, agonized scream rang through the trees.

"Hackthins," Shard said with a note of disgust. "Vile beasts. It's the first time I've seen them in this part of the forest. Usually you find them near marshes and foggy places. They appear from nowhere and pounce upon their victims as a pack. They like to skin their prey alive."

"That's horrible!" Eliza said, shivering as she strained to hear the creatures, but the forest was once again silent.

"As I said, there's much evil in our world, and good, and plenty in between. Come, we should be near Malumdell."

"Malumdell?"

"It's a village. Or was a village. My parents used to go there for the festival of windfall. The villagers made the most delicious wine from their fruit. I wasn't allowed to drink it, but my brother and I used to borrow the odd bottle or two."

"You said it *was* a village. What's it now?"

"A dead place. Fireghasts razed it to the ground. And apparently it has a new occupant who might have clothes for you somewhere within its collection."

They stepped from the forest onto a narrow, ancient trail as black as the stunted trees rising like spikes on either side of it. Eliza looked ahead to what must have been the village—mounds of stone, bricks, and the charred remains of roofs and timbers rested in a sea of ash.

At the end of the blackened, leveled village stood a solitary house. Its walls were darkened with soot and smoke, but its sloping roof had been seemingly untouched by the blaze. Its windows were smashed, jagged shards of glass reflecting the moonlight in a toothy red display. As they drew closer, Shard stopped. "Stand still and do not move. The wind is at our backs. It will raise our scent and bring it out."

"Bring out what?" Eliza said as something burst through the broken window.

At first she thought it was a stag beetle, until she saw its tatty black wings and the hundreds of legs kicking the air below, each covered with spikes. As the creature neared them, its maw wide open, Eliza realized with a thrill of horror exactly what it was.

"Repulsive fetcher!" Shard growled. As the creature soared towards his face, he snatched it from the air. Eliza stepped back as the creature's pincers frantically snapped.

The fetcher flipped in on itself, its pincers slashing the back of Shard's hand, its tiny feet reaching for him but missing, their bright green venom dripping in the moonlight. Shard cried out as the fetcher slashed him again.

"What should I do?" Eliza screamed as his face darkened with agony.

"Get back!" Shard threw the fetcher down and, before it could spring up, caught it by the back of its neck, holding it at arm's length, blood dripping from the gash on his hand.

The fetcher gave a shrill scream. Seconds later, its cry was answered from the building by a wrathful roar of outrage.

Eliza's heart pounded as she glanced at the dark, ancient house.

CHAPTER TWENTY

The House at the End

A crash came from the house, followed by a scream. And then the door exploded open as a huge creature emerged.

She was taller than anyone Eliza had ever seen, at least eight foot. Her face, below her straggles of nicotine-yellow hair, was a mass of pus-engorged boils but for two narrowed eyes and a great, yawning mouth. She reached into her ragged, grime-encrusted smock, removed a claw hammer, and howled, her voice as loud as a thunderclap, "Give me back my fetcher!"

Shard gripped the fetcher as he drew his sword, resting the blade against the creature's head. "How many pieces would you like your familiar in? Because for every step you take towards us, I'm going to cut it. And when I've finished slicing it, I'll smite your woefully ugly head from your neck."

The hoardspike stopped, holding out a gnarled hand. "Don't hurt my baby," she begged, absently rubbing her chest. As Eliza remembered the story of Victoria Stapleton, she was glad for the smock covering the hoardspike and the wound in its chest that nurtured the fetcher.

"I'll spare your fetcher," Shard said. "And you with it, even though the idea revolts me. But only if you keep your end of the bargain."

"What bargain?" the hoardspike asked.

"My friend here needs a change of clothes."

As the hoardspike glanced at Eliza, her eyes widened and she licked her lips. "Drearspawn! So *that* was the delicious scent…"

"She needs to mask her *delicious scent*," Shard said. "Which is why you're going to let her enter your dwelling to find clothes. Either that, or I'll slay you and your servant and we'll take what we want."

"What a cruel boy you are," the hoardspike said with a look of admiration on her gnarled face.

"I have no pity or forgiveness for darklings."

"Let's hope you don't become a *darkling* yourself, boy. You have slaughter and revenge in your eyes. And who knows what direction you might take on your life's path?" The hoardspike spat, then nodded to Eliza. "You realize the drearspawn sees us all as darklings. Why are you helping her?"

"That's none of your concern," Shard answered. "Just tell me if you'll allow the girl to search through your hoard unharmed. Or if I must shed blood."

The hoardspike swallowed, glancing to her house. "What will she take?"

"Only what she needs. Clothes, so she can pass through the Grimwytch unhindered."

Thinking again of Victoria Stapleton and the hoardspike, Eliza understood the Collector's anguish. "Once I find something suitable, I'll leave these behind," she reassured the hoardspike, pointing to her dark-red sweater and her favorite jeans. "It's like a trade. So you're not really losing anything."

The hoardspike smiled. "Drearspawn clothes for Grimwytch clothes. Doesn't seem like such a loss. And who knows, perhaps the girl and I will have dealings further along the road, and I'll find something else for my collection."

A shrill wail filled the air as Shard pressed his blade against the fetcher. "Enough threats, hoardspike. Eliza, go into the house and find whatever you can. And be quick."

Eliza ran, giving the hoardspike a wide berth.

She stepped through the shattered door into a large room heaped from floor to ceiling with towers of junk. Beyond the debris, most of which was charred and covered with ash, was a half-flight of blackened steps. The walls and ceilings of the house were scorched, yet somehow the building stood. Although judging by the creaks coming from its timbers, it was surely only a matter of time before it collapsed altogether.

Eliza clamped a hand over her nose as the stench from the hoardspike's collection wafted over her.

It was the reek of dead and rotting things. A cloud of red, bloated flies swarmed in the air, buzzing around the decaying bounty.

The floor was a narrow maze winding between mounds of objects. Eliza navigated her way through columns of charred, mismatched bricks and heaps of soot-encrusted furniture. She moved aside the broken chairs and drawers barring her way as she searched for a change of clothes. The thought of actually wearing anything from this revolting trove made her retch, but she pushed on, stepping carefully over a huge collection of bones.

She picked through a nearby pile, finding a large bowl. Eliza looked away from its bloody contents to a small, tattered box, which appeared to hold a collection of eyes. She tried not to think about who, or what, the eyes may have belonged to.

Something squawked. A large cage housed what appeared to be a crow with a dark, rat-like head. It gnawed at the cage bars, hissing as she drew closer.

Eliza moved on, her shoes slipping over a jumble of cutlery, each of which was bent out of shape.

Ahead, she found what she was looking for, a pile of clothes heaped in a tangle. Eliza picked through them, tossing them down and stepping away, lest anything crawl out of their jumble. Most of them appeared to have belonged to a woman three times her size and weight. There were lots of old hats, dresses, and shawls, each of which was coated in mold.

Below the clothes, she found a filthy, black-hooded cloak, mercifully free of fungus. She set it aside and picked up a dark, midnight-blue dress. Slightly large, but it would fit.

Eliza changed into her new outfit, holding her breath against the stench, frowning as she dropped her favorite jeans amongst the pile.

They looked strange lying there, amongst the hoardspike's pile of rubbish. Literally out of this world.

Dozens of shoes hung by twine from the ceiling. Eliza sorted through them until she found a suitable pair. They were slightly large, but she could make them work. She reached for an old book, tore out some pages, and stuffed them into the toes of the shoes.

"Now I'm almost perfectly uncomfortable," she said, rolling her eyes and praying her journey to the Midnight City. would be a brief one. The ceiling creaked, as if in answer. Eliza made her way back through the mountains of rot and squalor.

But as she reached the door, she stopped.

Something was humming. It was a strange, low sound. One that seemed to call to her. As Eliza wound her way through piles of book covers, their pages torn out, the sound grew louder. And then she found its source. The hum seemed to be coming from a small dagger with a navy-blue blade, its pommel a dirty gold, inscribed with a series of symbols.

As she reached for the blade, it sang even louder, and a distant part of Eliza begged her to tip over the tower of book covers and bury the thing. But she didn't. Instead, she picked up the blade, gasping as a charge of energy ran along her arm and it seemed to come alive, hacking the air before her.

Eliza tried to set it down, but the blade continued to cut and slash, inscribing dark-blue patterns in the air. "Stop!" she said. But it wouldn't. She glanced around, spotting a sheath attached to a belt.

As Eliza reached for it, the blade slowed, its energy dissipating. As she slid it into its sheath, the humming stopped, the house silent once more but for the creak of rafters and drone of flies.

Eliza disregarded the voice in her head yelling at her to throw the blade as far into the debris as possible. She thought of the hoardspike waiting outside and the other creatures she'd encountered since leaving her world for this dark, insane place. Eliza fastened the belt over her dress, the sheath heavy and reassuring against her thigh, and concealed it below her cloak.

"You look…interesting," Shard said as she stepped from the house.

As the hoardspike regarded Eliza, her eyes narrowed. She sniffed the air. "What did you take?"

Eliza met her gaze, swallowing. "Just these clothes. I left my *old* ones behind. So you haven't lost anything; you've done well with this trade."

"Liar," the hoardspike growled. "Drearspawn liar!"

Shard tightened his grip on the fetcher, making it squeal. "Enough. Or I'll carry out my promise. You call the girl 'drearspawn' as if you come from a place of superiority. To my kind, you're less than vermin."

"She's stolen something from me. I can smell it!"

Eliza held her hands up. "Why would I want to steal anything from you? These clothes are disgusting! And now you've got my clean clothes. Hardly a bargain, is it?"

Eliza stepped past the hoardspike, avoiding her accusing eyes as she joined Shard.

"Give me my fetcher!" the hoardspike demanded.

"In a moment," Shard said as he and Eliza began to walk along the path. They passed the hoardspike's house, the path snaking between the forest trees.

When they were thirty or so feet away, Shard turned and released the fetcher. It flew, slicing through the air as it returned to its mistress. The hoardspike tore open her smock, revealing a bloody hole in her chest. The fetcher squirmed inside, and she clasped a gnarled hand across her chest, her expression like that of a mother reunited with her newborn.

"That's hideous," Eliza said. "And creepy."

"The parasite finds its host. Though I'm never sure which is which," Shard replied. "Either way, now would be a good time to run."

They sprinted through the trees, Eliza's shoes hampering her as she ran. The hoardspike pursued, a look of malicious hatred on her putrid face. Eliza ran harder, but as she glanced at Shard, she found him grinning. "What on earth are you smiling for?" she cried, her words labored as her feet pounded the stony road.

"Twenty, nineteen, eighteen, seventeen…" Shard counted.

Eliza looked back; the hoardspike was feet away now, her great hands reaching for them, a snarl of fury on her spittle-flecked lips.

"Sixteen, fifteen, fourteen, thirteen…" Shard ground to a halt and seized Eliza's cloak.

"What are you doing?" Eliza cried.

But the hoardspike had also stopped, her hands on her knees as she leaned over.

"Why's she stopped?" Eliza fought to catch her breath.

"I thought she'd stop at fifteen." Shard laughed and then shouted to the creature, "I admire you. You almost made it!"

The hoardspike shot them a look of unadulterated venom as she turned away, clomping back along the path to the burnt village. She let forth a furious scream, causing Eliza to flinch and a swarm of crows to fly from the trees. "What happened?" Eliza asked. "Why did she let us go?"

"Greed," Shard said. "Absolute, all-consuming greed. She cannot bear to be away from her collection. It's as much a part of her as that disgusting creature festering in her chest." He smiled at Eliza. "You see, that's the trick to surviving in this place. You don't need to match an opponent's strength, you only need to know their weakness."

CHAPTER TWENTY-ONE

Grim Shadows

*A*s they traveled along the path, Shard told Eliza all about the Grimwytch's many monsters and answered her questions as to how to defeat them. Eliza's head swam with the information and the descriptions of all the myriad, strange species.

"So, you're all set now. I can probably leave you to it," Shard teased. "You'll do your grandfather proud. And your father, too. You do have a father, don't you?"

"Yes, why do you ask?"

"Because you haven't mentioned him. Is he a writer, too?"

"No, he's a dentist."

"What's that?" Shard asked. "Does he knock holes in things?"

Eliza laughed. "No, he *fixes* holes in things. Dents, too, if that's what you meant. He fixes people's teeth."

Shard opened his mouth and ran his fingers over his fangs. "How about my teeth? Could he fix these?"

"What's wrong with them?"

"They ache sometimes. Mother said it's because they're growing. I hope they'll stop soon."

Me, too, Eliza thought. Try as she might, she couldn't help but think of a vampire when she looked at him. She'd seen one on a movie poster once, before her mother had hurried her away. "If my dad did come here, he would find your teeth fascinating, and I'm sure he would be only too keen to look them over."

Shard grinned. "I might well take him up on that if he ever ventures to our land."

Suddenly, a noise filled the sky.

At first, Eliza thought it was some great helicopter, its blades slicing the air, until she spotted two huge creatures soaring through the sky. Their forms were silhouettes, but she could make out enough to see what looked like giant bats with the round, furry heads of spiders. Figures sat on the backs of the beasts, peering down.

"We need to get under the trees." Shard grabbed Eliza's hand and led her into the woods. "If those riders set down in Malumdell and happen upon the hoardspike, they'll hear of us. And I'm sure she will take great pleasure in setting hunters upon our trail."

"Who are they?" Eliza asked.

"They could be anyone. The guards of the Midnight Guild use aranachiros to fly above the city, looking for criminals. Perhaps something has escaped."

"Aranachiros?"

"They come from the Foggypeake Mountains. Besides the Guild guards, they're commonly used by hunters."

"Would they hunt us?" Eliza asked as the creatures soared overhead.

"Yes. Especially you. There are underground markets in the Midnight City. that trade in rare and unusual goods. Your head would fetch quite a decent price. Whether attached to your body or not."

"Nice," Eliza said. "And that's where we're going, right?"

"To the city, yes. But now that you smell like a dead cat left below the fullest moon, you shouldn't have any problems."

"You have cats here?" Eliza asked. Somehow the concept seemed even stranger than the Grimwytch containing cheese.

"By that, I take it you have cats, too. It seems there's a lot our two worlds share. Tell me, in your world, are cats as lazy and imperious as they are here?"

"Yes. They're totally arrogant and quite useless. But I like them."

"So do I," Shard said. "Especially with applenut."

Eliza shook her head. "Tell me you're joking."

"I may be," Shard offered. "Stop!"

He pointed to the mossy ground, where a large, bloated lilac mushroom nestled in the gloom of a tree root. "Don't get near it. If it smells us it will explode, releasing spores. And if you breathe them, you'll feel like you swallowed a thousand tiny razors. It's then a question of whether the poison kills you before your heart stops."

Eliza stepped away from the fungus, glancing at the trail to see if there were any more. "Does this mean you just saved my life and your debt is paid?"

"In a manner of speaking," Shard said. "But I also saved you on the road just after we left the Malady Inn. And I saved you from the hackthins and the hoardspike."

"But you made me go to the hoardspike."

"Perhaps. But either way I'd…" Shard stopped, cocking his head to the left. "Can you hear that?"

She could. It sounded like a great river was pouring through the forest.

Coming right towards them.

The ground began to shake. "Do you have earthquakes?" Eliza shouted over the din.

"I don't know what an earthquake is. But I *do* know that that noise is a bad thing!" Shard pointed to the base of a giant fallen tree. "Get up!" As Eliza clomped after him, struggling to climb, the sound grew to an almost deafening pitch.

Shard reached for her, taking her hand and swinging her up onto the fallen tree.

Ahead, through the forest, came a swarm of beasts.

Hundreds.

As they came closer, they shimmered in the moonlight, black-and-white striped, deer-like creatures galloping, panic in their wide, glowing eyes.

They stampeded past Eliza, causing the tree to shake with the sound of their hooves.

And then they were gone.

"They were harmless enough, weren't they?" Eliza said.

"Perfectly harmless," Shard agreed. "But the question is, what are they running from?"

And then came the din of someone running towards them, as branches snapped and the forest was filled with the sound of a labored, panicked gasping. A man appeared in the clearing. At least, he looked like a man, until Eliza spotted the tiny iridescent scales covering his skin. He was so intent on escape that he didn't notice them until he neared the fallen tree. He screamed as something thudded against him, causing him to falter and drop to his knees with a look of agony.

Eliza threw a hand over her mouth as she saw the arrowhead glinting in his chest.

The scaled man reached towards her before falling face-down upon the ground.

"We need to..." Shard stopped as something wove through the trees towards them.

Eliza's first thought was of a suited man on stilts.

He had to be over nine foot, surely?

But as she looked again she saw that he wasn't wearing stilts. His legs were immensely long and thin. Just like a stork.

His pale, elongated head was emaciated, his eyes huge. They projected bright red beams of light that sliced across the forest floor. As his eyes swept over Eliza and Shard, he fitted a bolt to the small crossbow cradled in his gloved hands.

A pang of dread hit Eliza in the stomach as she realized that she had read of him in *The Book of Kindly Deaths*.

He was one of the Grims.

Eliza winced as his eyes passed over the corpse at his feet. He kicked the scaled man over before turning back to them. He bared his teeth as he stalked towards them.

"Human," the Grim said, his voice strangely mechanical. "I smell human."

"I thought…" Eliza began.

"Nothing could smell you." Shard grasped her hand, leading her from the fallen tree. "Except a Grim. And this one is said to have a particularly keen sense of smell. His name is Grim Shadows."

The Grim's eyes followed them. "Humans are not allowed in the Grimwytch without permission. It's against the law. Prison or execution, my choice." The Grim smiled, raising his crossbow. "And I choose execution."

CHAPTER TWENTY-TWO

Endings

*E*liza," Shard whispered. "I'm going to stall him. And when I do, run. As fast as you can."

"Will he hurt you?"

"He'll try. But it's you he's focused on. We need to use that to our advantage."

"Speak up!" Grim Shadows aimed his crossbow at Shard. "Or carry on whispering, if you want to be executed with the human."

Shard stepped away from Eliza. "The drearspawn has nothing to do with me, Grim Shadows. Do what you see fit."

The Grim nodded. "And so I shall."

Eliza reached out as if to ward off the crossbow as the Grim raised it towards her chest. The last thing she saw as she closed her eyes was its finger curling around the trigger.

And then a piercing cry split the air.

Eliza opened her eyes to find the Grim raising his head towards the stars, agony on his long white face.

Shard pulled his sword from the Grim's leg and cried, "Run!"

Then he took off into the trees.

Eliza skirted the Grim as he began to limp after Shard. She ducked through the trees, her eyes on Shard as he ran, leaping over the ground and throwing panicked glances behind.

The Grim's eyes followed Shard, sweeping across him as it illuminated him in its beam. The lights of its eyes had changed color now, from red to deepest crimson. Shard screamed, clasping his back as smoke rose from his cloak. He rolled across the forest floor, sweeping left and losing the beams as the Grim followed, limping and howling, his lights searing tree trunks.

They continued their flight until Shard suddenly came to a halt, throwing his arms out to steady himself, crying out for Eliza to stop.

Eliza found herself inches from where the trees and ground came to a sudden end.

She peered down to find herself on the edge of a cliff, and below, pitch-black darkness.

The Grim thundered towards them, its red beams on Shard, making him wince.

Shard offered Eliza a brief smile before raising his sword. "Be safe, Eliza Winter."

The Grim loped across the ground, arms outstretched. As he reached for Shard, he sidestepped the arc of Shard's sword and grasped him, pushing him back.

"No!" Eliza screamed as they plunged into the abyss.

The last she saw of them was a flash of red light far below. And then it flickered out.

CHAPTER TWENTY-THREE

Monsters

*E*liza stared into the darkness below.

She listened for the sound of Shard fighting the ghoul, but there was only silence, and as she thought of her companion, a tear ran down her face. She let it fall unhindered. She'd only known him for a short while, and yet she still felt an overwhelming sense of loss. He'd made this strange, dark world a lighter place. Or at least, a safer one.

And now he was gone. Joining his slaughtered family, their deaths unavenged. And it was her fault. Because if she hadn't turned up in the Malady Inn, he'd still be alive.

Something howled behind her.

Eliza backed away from the cliff edge, gazing across the chasm to a series of twinkling lights in the distance.

The Midnight City.

As the howl came again, closer now, she turned and made her way back into the forest.

It didn't take long for Eliza to realize that she was utterly lost and that the likelihood of finding anyone to give her directions was probably zero. "At least anyone who doesn't want to drink my blood or steal my immortal soul," she whispered.

She began to walk in what she hoped was a straight line, directly away from the cliff. Perhaps she could find the road that led to the Malady Inn. Mr. Barrow would help her.

Maybe he could even find some sort of transport to take her to the Midnight City.

As she recalled the inn, her introduction to this alien world, she thought of the place she had left behind and her parents slumped at the kitchen table. She prayed that they were okay, that Grim Shivers hadn't vented his fury at her escape on them.

Eliza shuddered at the thought of the ghoul and his sibling, Grim Shadows. There were more of them still. The story of Augustus Pinch had told of Grim Shivers summoning six others. And the thought of them crossing over to Tom's house, surrounding her sleeping parents, made Eliza dizzy with fear and nausea.

She started as two vivid green lights zipped past her head. They shot into the air, one chasing the other, and for a moment Eliza was entranced by their giddy display as they illuminated the branches and trunks of the nearby trees.

Until one stopped dead, trapped in a talon that clamped down upon it.

The claw of an owl. A giant bird, at least half Eliza's height. Although she'd seen many owls and always found their faces and eyes unsettling, this one was far worse. For it was bone-white, its head like a skull.

It called to her, hooting, the sound almost metallic.

And then she heard the word within its call.

Drearspawn.

The owl raised the squirming light to its beak, swallowing it whole, a dim glow lighting its throat before fading. The other light blazed furiously about the owl, but the bird paid it no heed, instead swooping and landing on the branch above Eliza's head.

"Drearspawn," it hooted once more.

Eliza ran, her eyes scouring the ground for the mushrooms Shard had warned her of, her ears straining for the bird's approach.

The eerie silence of its wings filled her with foreboding as it beat towards her. It swooped over her head, landing on a branch before her, its pitiless black eyes boring into hers as it hooted its insult once more.

Eliza ran past it, expecting it to tear into the back of her neck. But it didn't, and as it flew past her again, she realized it was toying with her. Frightening her.

It had its desired effect.

As Eliza staggered from the trees onto a road, the owl wheeled over her head, hooted, and swept back into the forest. She watched as it disappeared into the gloom, looking from left to right. The road stretched for as far as she could see. "Which way do I go?" If she'd had a coin she would have flipped it, but instead she glanced at the sky. To her right was a bright star. Eliza decided to follow it.

She walked with aching feet for what seemed like hours, until a distant sound caught her attention.

A horse-drawn cart approached from behind, trundling slowly towards her. The horses were tall, gaunt creatures with long legs, their hair muddy brown, their eyes large, melancholy black orbs.

Eliza considered leaving the road and hiding, but the cart was slow and the driver would have seen her already. Surely if they meant harm they'd have picked up their pace?

So she stood her ground, deciding to ask for directions; if the driver became a threat, she'd take her chances in the forest.

As she waited for the cart, something long and grey swept through the branches across the road, vanishing from sight.

It seemed that wherever she looked in this world, there was something unusual or unpleasant to see. But, she supposed, it would be the same if someone from this world visited hers. They'd be completely overwhelmed by the sheer abundance of people, technology, and nature. Eliza imagined Shard looking up at her sky filled with airplanes, sunlight gleaming off their wings. He'd probably be as terrified as she was in his world.

And then the cart stopped a few feet away. The driver, an old lady in a hooded shawl, regarded Eliza with caution. She would have passed for human were it not for her eyes, which shone like silver-white pearls.

"Need a ride?" the lady asked, patting the seat beside her.

"I'm lost," Eliza said, pulling her own hood lower over her face. "I was looking for the Midnight City. "

"Then you're not lost, are you, dear?"

"How do you mean?"

"Well, you can't be lost if you know where you're going, can you? Hop on, we share a destination."

"Thank you." Eliza clambered onto the cart. The seat next to the old lady was hard, but the idea of resting her aching feet more than made up for the discomfort.

A terrible stench wafted over her, and Eliza glanced over her shoulder to see taut, grimy sheets thrown over the back of the cart. It appeared that the reek was issuing from below them, reminding her of a butcher's shop on a sweltering summer day. She was about to ask what the source of the stink was, but she thought better of it.

"Where are you from, dear?" the old lady asked as they cantered along the road.

"I...Blackwood."

"Which village?"

"London!" Eliza blurted, feeling her cheeks reddening. Why had she said London?

"I don't know London, dear. Still, there are plenty of places I don't know. What takes you to the Midnight City.?"

"An errand," Eliza replied. "I need to find the Midnight Prison."

"Which one?"

"Um, the one where I can find Grim Shivers."

The old lady quivered, pulling her shawl tighter. "In that case, tell me no more. Your business is your own."

They continued in silence, and Eliza yawned, closing her eyes for a moment.

She was jolted awake as the cart came to a halt, to find a man standing beside the road, aiming a hand-held crossbow with a bolt that dripped something green and viscous. His face was yellow and set like a fresh yolk, his eyes hidden by the brim of his hat. He licked his lips with a forked tongue, rasping, "I'll take your cart. And your passenger."

"If you value your life," the old lady said, "you'll put your weapon down."

Eliza glanced about. The road was wide, cutting between two huge hills. She swallowed as she looked at their peaks, wondering if the robber had accomplices.

"Step down." The man stepped closer, crossbow still on Eliza. Adrenaline coursed through her as the old lady jumped down and stood before the man. He whipped round, training his crossbow on the woman.

She smiled. "Put your weapon down and get back to the hills. Because if you don't, I'll be selling various parts of you in the market before the hour is through."

The man's finger tensed on the trigger. But before Eliza could shout a warning to her, the old lady screamed, her head ballooning to five times its size. Her mouth opened, revealing layer after layer of needle-like teeth.

The man tried to back away, but it was too late. The old lady leaped upon him, her mouth engulfing his head.

As she bit down, her eyes shone with such intensity that they lit up the road.

Eliza clamped her hands over her ears, blocking out the sickening sound of crunching as something fell to the ground.

"You're a squeamish one, aren't you?" the old lady said.

Eliza nodded, gazing at the hills, trying to clear her mind of the hideous event.

"Well, I *did* warn him, didn't I, dear?" The old lady removed what looked like a hacksaw from her shawl. "Given your sensitivities, I'd advise you look away as I prepare what's left for the market."

Eliza didn't need telling twice. She winced at the sound of chopping and sawing. She heard the old lady walk to the back of the cart, whipping back the filthy sheets and unleashing a terrible stench as she dumped the remains upon the cart.

She joined Eliza, taking up the reins. "Fortune smiles today, dear. You have your ride, and I have even more to sell at market. We should become partners, you and I. I think you're a lucky charm!"

Eliza nodded, not knowing what else to do.

As the cart rolled on, she looked away from the reflection of the moon in the dark pool of blood spreading across the edge of the road.

CHAPTER TWENTY-FOUR

Into The Midnight City

"So, you sell...um, meat?" Eliza asked, feigning an air of nonchalance.

The old lady cackled as the cart turned a bend. "That's not all I sell. And I only take the meat of those who have wronged me. That's my code, dear. Everyone should have a code. The meat fetches quite a price down by the docks. You should try the Kishspik stew on the Vashhaal wharf; it's out of this world."

Eliza remained silent as the cart went around a bend in the road, revealing the vista below. The city was colossal, far bigger than anything she'd ever seen. A huge, dark mass upon the land. Everywhere she looked there were buildings and houses, countless chimneys pouring gray curls of smoke into the sky. And between the houses, immense buildings, reminding her of palaces and churches.

Darkly foreboding palaces and churches.

Across the city, like shards of jagged glass, rose seven black towers, tall and thin, pointing to the sky like witches' fingers. And enclosing everything, a great wall, its stone as black as flint. To the left of the city, a huge sea stretched for as far as she could see, the moon shining down upon its glass-like surface.

"It's...beautiful," Eliza muttered. "Beautiful and nightmarish."

"It's both those things and more, dear," the old lady said, cracking the reins and sending the horses trotting. "But I'll be glad when I'm on my way back up the hill. I never spend too long in the city. It's not a good place to be."

They rode through a pair of enormous curved gates that opened like bat wings, admitting the damned to hell, and as the cart rolled into the city, Eliza swallowed.

A long road stretched beyond the tall, grimy buildings. Their soot-smeared walls reminded Eliza of a film she'd once seen, set in Dickensian London. And in the street below, rotting things festered in thick, oozing mud. Here and there figures walked, stooped, and shuffled, silently making their way along the thoroughfare and ducking into darkened alleys.

The old lady lowered her voice. "Listen, dear, I'd take you to the docks for stew, but I don't think you'd like it there. It's not a nice area and you're very green."

"What do you mean?"

The old lady rested a hand on Eliza's arm and smiled. "You smell of Grimwytch, but you're not of Grimwytch, are you?"

"How long have you known I'm…"

The old lady shook her head. "Don't say it. Not here. Not if you want to keep your pretty little head where it should be. Pull your hood down low, my love, and tread carefully and with purpose as you go."

Eliza nodded, her heart thumping wildly as she realized the old lady must have known she was human from the moment she climbed upon her cart. "Do you know where I can find Grim…"

"The prison is a fair walk. Keep to this street, and when it reaches a large square of white buildings, take a left. Mortignue Street will lead you to his prison." The old lady nodded briskly as Eliza stepped away. She turned her cart down a small lane between two rows of crooked houses.

Eliza walked, stepping through the mud. Here and there came snatches of chatter, some in English, some not, none particularly conversational. Two tall, eyeless figures whose faces looked like freshly peeled onions leaned against the wall before her, smoking stumps of cigars. As Eliza passed, one blew a stream of smoke. It snaked towards Eliza as if alive and formed a giant, smoky eye, which winked at her. The smoke curled towards her face, probing beneath her hood. She batted it away, ignoring the dark mutters from behind.

Show no fear, she reminded herself, *for fear will make you stand out.*

She walked on, lifting her head a little as she kept her eyes on the road, ignoring the myriad strange sights that seemed to grab her attention wherever she looked.

The other pedestrians paid no attention as Eliza wove her way through them, until she encountered a group of small creatures that looked like children.

Monstrous children.

They were playing a game of chase, their faces an almost impossibly red color over their muted woolen suits. Eliza noticed the tiny stumps of horns upon their heads; she wondered if they were Devils. If they were, it seemed they bore her no malice. Then the smallest turned to regard her, poking out its fat black tongue.

Eliza grinned, poking her tongue back, instantly regretting her mistake as the creature gasped in amazement. It whistled to the others and pointed at Eliza, grunting and barking as it leaped up and down in the mud. And now other passersby were staring at her, the impish child's curiosity seemingly contagious. Eliza stopped, glancing around and spotting an opening in the street.

A dark stretch of alleyway.

She stepped inside, eager to escape the monstrous children's excited attention as they jabbered behind, pointing and howling and shaking their heads. Eliza ignored them, following the curve of the alley, glad to leave their din behind.

The alley opened, and as she turned another bend, she found a long, straight passage leading to a distant street.

A sense of unease began to creep over her.

Eliza glanced behind.

The alley was empty.

So why could she feel eyes upon her? She looked up to the large stone walkway connecting two roofs. Empty.

Or was it?

Because for a second, she thought she glimpsed a pair of eyes watching from the brickwork at the bottom of the walkway.

Directly above where she had to pass.

And now, as she looked closer, the shadows below the walkway seemed darker than they should be. Perhaps she should return to the street and brave the attention of the impish children. Surely they'd get bored and leave her alone?

Eliza glanced over her shoulder.

A figure turned the corner and came down the alley, thin and ragged and only slightly taller than she, the claws by its sides splayed. Eliza turned to run but stood rooted to the spot as beyond the shadows of the walkway another figure approached, almost a mirror image of the one behind her.

She was trapped.

Eliza shivered as she caught the flash of eyes from the bottom of the walkway. She screamed. Then another set of eyes opened beside them. And then another, until there were eyes everywhere, opening on the walls, opening on the rooftops, and opening on the ground. From the shadows, more ragged figures emerged, hunched and clawed like the ones stalking towards her.

A hiss filled the air as the figure that had been watching from the bottom of the walkway fell from the shadows onto the ground. This one was taller than the others. They moved aside as it stepped into a patch of moonlight.

It was like a wolf formed of shadows.

Eliza tried to focus on it, but it was difficult, because aside from its metallic claws, it was perfectly indistinct. She got a sense of fur, fur somehow made from shadows and night. And roving eyes, and a snarl of teeth.

"What do you want?" Eliza pulled her hood lower. "I need to be somewhere. It's really important."

The figure cackled, and soon the others joined it.

"I'm late for an appointment," Eliza said. "With Grim Shivers!"

The creature snickered before throwing back its head and howling. The others joined it as it stepped forward, reaching for Eliza's hood and pulling it down. Eliza screamed as she clutched her hands over her face, but it was too late.

"*Drearspawn!*"

"No!"

"*Yes!*" The creature slashed the air, a claw raking across Eliza's face.

Eliza flinched, clamping a hand to the cut, her fingers wet with blood.

The other creatures began to bay, a primal, savage sound, as the smell of her blood seemed to lend fuel to their excitement.

"Leave me alone!" As Eliza stepped towards the wall, a figure detached itself from the shadows, pushing her back towards the tallest creature.

"'*Leave me alone,*'" it mocked. "We'll leave you. When you're nothing but bone and entrails."

Now, as it loped towards her, its cruel playfulness was gone.

I'm going to die, Eliza thought. *I'm going to die here, and no one will ever know.*

She tried to sidestep the creature, but it brought its hand down on the top of her head, fixing her in place. And as it held up its other hand, its claws shining in the moonlight, Eliza was suddenly reminded of the blade in her belt.

As she yanked it free, it sang, taking control of her hand. The blade pulled Eliza across the path and plunged itself into the creature's chest.

The shadow creature howled.

It was beyond the sound of agony.

Something worse than pain.

The creature dropped to its knees, shaking and writhing. "Phasmatis!" it cried. "My phasmatis!"

The blade Eliza held twisted inside the creature and produced a sickening sound of tearing. She tried to pull the blade free, but it resisted her, coating her hands in blood.

And now the blade's song filled the alley, sending the other creatures running, their cruelty and excitement replaced with horror. They leaped upon the walls, bounding up them and vaulting over the rooftops.

The slain creature slumped to the ground, taking Eliza's blade with it. She pulled with all her might, finally wresting it free. It shone in the moonlight, somehow larger as it glistened with an iridescent sheen. But as she plunged it into the sheath at her side, its song slowed, until finally it vanished altogether.

Eliza walked away from the corpse, her hands and legs shaking.

Numb.

Hollow.

Then sickness swept over her, her stomach roiling as if filled with bugs as she released the flood of hot bile searing her throat. Eliza leaned over and vomited, clutching the wall as a tide of nausea threatened to engulf her.

Finally, when there was nothing left, she stopped and stood, taking a deep breath and gazing at the stars. "It was going to kill me," she heard herself say. "It was going to kill me. So I killed it first."

But she hadn't just slain the creature. Something else had happened, something even worse. For while the idea of taking a life was almost more than Eliza could bear, she knew the blade had taken more than the monster's life.

Leaving it writhing in something far worse than mere agony or terror.

CHAPTER TWENTY-FIVE

The Tower

*E*liza walked, the walls seeming to blur around her as her thoughts turned in ever-tighter circles.

But as she emerged into a wide street, her senses flooded back. Carts and carriages clattered by, and figures shuffled past in the gloom. She forced herself to think of anything but the hideous event that had just taken place. "Can't think about it now," she whispered. "Focus."

Eliza pulled her hood down, joining the throng, her eyes on the jagged black tower rearing up before her.

She'd seen the tower before, in her dream. Or perhaps *nightmare* was a more fitting word. It had looked as real as it did now, filling her with the same sense of dread. The malice exuding from its black stones was so thick she could almost feel it.

It was almost as if whoever had built the place had gone out of their way to create a ghastly spectacle. But perhaps that was the intention.

After all, it was a prison built for monsters.

A few windows ran along its side, issuing weak, flickering yellow lights. Eliza wondered if anyone was watching her approach. If so, was one of them her grandfather? Would she find him inside? And if she did, would she be able to take his hand, as she had all those years ago when she'd fallen off her bicycle and he'd made everything better?

But as Eliza climbed a set of steps leading from the road to the tower, her hopes crumbled, for below the tower whirled a hive of activity.

Four figures stood positioned before the tower's door, moonlight gleaming on their polished black armor. Eliza recognized them at once. She'd seen them in her dream. The guards with the hidden faces.

Faces she never, ever wanted to see.

Before the tower and the guards, figures hurried to and fro as an audience gaped at the building, among them vendors selling squirming things on trays, books, and spyglasses. Eliza walked towards a man so huge and obese that his pasty white belly rested on the ground, covering his lower half. A reptilian man stood on a stool, painting words upon the man's great stomach in thick blue paint, but as Eliza drew nearer he stopped, flicking his head towards her and hissing.

Eliza held her hands up as the reptilian man leaped from his stool, brandishing his paintbrush. "You didn't pay to read! Fifteen coins or no show."

"Don't pay," a voice insisted from behind Eliza. "It's old news."

She turned to find a gaunt man with a mane of curly red hair and full, black eyes. He was dressed in finery, a walking cane by his side.

"What's he painting?" Eliza asked, pulling her hood down over her face.

The man stared for a moment before smiling. "This morning's news, of course. Why, I wonder, would such an everyday thing mystify you?"

"I…I live in the woods. We don't get news there."

"Don't you?" the man asked. "Well, as I said, don't pay a single coin. It's a rehash of the same old story, the tower, the disappearing guardian, the breach." He feigned yawning.

"The breach?" Eliza asked, gazing up at the tower.

"You really *are* green, aren't you?" the man said, and for some reason this seemed to please him as he licked his lips.

"The tower's guardian, Grim Shivers, has gone. Following his disappearance, a drearspawn breached the tower and freed a prisoner. And the freed prisoner was another drearspawn. And now the pair of them are trapped."

"Trapped where?" Eliza asked.

"In the light house. But this is not half as interesting as the news my publication will paint this very afternoon." The man gazed around before licking his lips again and fixing Eliza with a perfectly insincere smile. "I could share my news if you like. Give you an exclusive. But not here. Let us find a quieter place."

Eliza shook her head. "I need to be on my way. But thank you anyway."

The man stared at Eliza, trying to gaze below her hood. "What are you hiding under there?"

"I...I'm diseased." Eliza moved away from him.

"Diseased with what?"

Eliza struggled to think of a word and blurted, "Porridge."

"Porridge?" the man asked. "Never heard of it."

"It's awful. My face is covered in oats. And when they burst, the pus is boiling hot." She stepped towards the man as he backed away. "Would you like to see?"

"Get away from me." He raised his cane. "If you take another step, you'll make today's obituaries."

Eliza hurried down the steps, casting a quick glance behind her, but the man had vanished. At the edge of the street, two ladies sat upon the ground, chatting and laughing as they combed each other's towering white beehive hair. Like the man, their eyes were pure black. "Excuse me," Eliza said as she approached them.

The ladies stopped chattering, snapping their heads towards her. "What have you done that needs excusing?" asked one.

"I'm looking for a place called the light house. It's where..."

"We know what the light house is, you dullard." The other lady rolled her eyes. "Listen, if I tell you how to get there, do you promise to leave immediately and take your stench with you?"

"I do," Eliza agreed.

"Take the alley over there. In the next street turn left. At the end turn left again, and then take the first right past the Twisty Entrails."

"The twisty entrails?" Eliza asked.

"The inn, you buffoon," the other lady said.

"And now that you have your directions, you must go," said the other. "Before we're forced to do something rash with our knives."

Eliza didn't need to be told twice. She hurried across the street, peering down the alley.

While it was perfectly unwelcoming, it was mercifully short.

She looked back to make sure the ladies weren't following before jogging along a narrow stretch, holding her breath against the reek. Eliza followed the ladies' directions, walking with purpose as she made her way down ever-darker streets.

The figures Eliza passed seemed lost in their own worlds and, judging by their furtive glances, equally as paranoid as she was.

Finally, she spotted the inn. A large sign hung above the door with a gaudy picture of dripping red innards, the name "The Twisty Entrails" written in hacks and slashes.

Light spilled from inside as the sound of a broken piano drifted towards her.

CHAPTER TWENTY-SIX

The Light House

As Eliza passed the inn, she tried to peer inside, but a blind covered the window and all she could see were misshapen silhouettes.

And then someone inside screamed.

Eliza hurried on, taking a right turn at the corner of the inn and stopping. "Oh…"

Halfway along a wide street was a light so bright, she was forced to clamp her hand over her eyes. She waited for her eyes to adjust before peeping through the cracks in her fingers.

It looked like daylight. Daylight shining upon a tall, crooked building in the middle of the night. "The light house." As Eliza walked towards it, her eyes grew accustomed to its glare and, suddenly, she realized she'd seen it before.

In her dream.

A crowd of figures gathered at the edge of the light, their voices rising as they chattered and shrieked. There were hundreds of them, clamoring in the street and gawping at the house.

Eliza took a deep breath and set off, winding her way through the horde, trying her best to ignore them as she squeezed by all manner of hideous things, scales, fur, clammy skin, and dead, cold flesh. Here and there, bodies lay strewn about, smaller figures crushed in the heaving throng.

Eliza stepped on something. It was a foot. Its owner produced a deafening roar. She looked up to see a large, muscular man with the head of a bull. "A minotaur..." she said stupidly, wincing as it bellowed once more and swung its fist towards her.

Eliza ducked, stepping aside as the minotaur's fist connected with the head of a tusked lady. The lady yelled, reaching into her coat and producing a hammer.

And then they began to fight.

Eliza pushed her way through the crowd as the fight began to spread, the street full of crunching sounds and cries of rage and pain. She was almost at the edge of the light when a child, just like the imps she'd seen earlier, reached from its carrier's shoulders and pulled Eliza's hood back.

"Get off!" she cried, but it was too late as the child emitted a high-pitched squeal.

And then, it seemed, all eyes were upon her.

"Drearspawn!" a man with a skeletal face declared. "Drearspawn!"

The crowd reached for her, nails and claws scraping against her face as they fought to catch her. Eliza pushed them aside but there were too many, and now they were closing in.

She reached into her cloak, unsheathed her blade, and pulled it forth. "Get back!"

As the sound of the blade's song rose, several creatures stepped away, pushing the crowd back behind them. Eliza let the blade do its work, hacking and slicing through the air, clearing a perfect circle around her. She winced as she stepped through the parted crowd, the light from the house smarting her eyes.

As Eliza set foot into the circle of light, a great wrenching sound ricocheted across the street.

Eliza stopped, glancing back to find the creatures mesmerized as they gazed at the house, an air of expectation rising. And then a long, skeletal finger issued from the crowd, pointing at the ground.

Eliza followed its path.

The light was flickering, slowly shifting towards the house, its circle of protection diminishing.

Eliza ran, hammering on the front door as the light flickered once more and a triumphant cheer rose behind.

The door opened. A filthy hand reached through and snatched Eliza by the scruff of her neck, pulling her inside.

The first thing she noticed was the club the boy held as he glared at her. And then she looked at him again. Was he a boy? For his face was haggard and etched with lines and wrinkles. "How did you get through?" he demanded.

"Enough, Augustus!" a voice called from a room at the end of the hall. A silhouette appeared in the door beyond.

Augustus?

"Augustus Pinch?" Eliza asked, straining to see the figure in the door. "Tom? Is that you?"

As the man walked towards her, his step was slow and uncertain. "Who's asking? And how did you reach the house?" he asked, placing a hand on Augustus's arm so he lowered the club.

"It *is* you!" Eliza cried, pulling back her hood.

"Eliza?" Tom leaned closer, his eyes narrowing. "My, you've grown!" He raised a trembling hand to her cheek, his eyes misting over. "I never thought I would see you again."

"Me neither." She was sure she had grown since he had last seen her, and while she'd grown, he'd shrunk, just a little. And aged. His body more stooped than she remembered, the skin on his face a little thinner. He looked frail, nothing like the confident, authoritative figure she remembered. She smiled, hoping he hadn't noticed her shock.

"But what are you doing here, and how…?"

"I followed you," Eliza replied. "I found *The Book of Kindly Deaths* and your pen. I wrote myself in, like you did. I had to. That…ghoul, Grim Shivers, attacked us."

"Attacked?" Tom's face was stricken with horror. "Is anyone hurt?"

"I don't know." Eliza's eyes welled up. "Mum and Dad looked like they were sleeping. But they wouldn't wake."

"They're asleep. In a sense," Tom said. "But they will be fine. The ghoul cannot shed blood on our side unless his blood is shed first. And I can't see either of your parents doing that. So how did Shivers come to attack you, and why?"

"We were at your house…"

"My house?" Tom looked confused. "What were you doing there? Your mum told me she never wanted to see me again."

Eliza glanced at Augustus Pinch before turning back to her grandfather.

"You can talk openly in front of Augustus. He's on our side." Tom guided Eliza to a window and glanced out. "But you must tell me quickly. The light shadow I cast broke when you entered. It allows our kind to pass, but not the Grimwytch. However, it was only meant for Augustus and myself. So please, Eliza, be quick. What were you doing at my house?"

Eliza took a deep breath. "Mum tried to contact you in the summer. A friend of hers lost their mother, and I think it made Mum think about…time. And family. She's changed. A bit. I'd been asking to see you for years, and she finally gave in. When she couldn't reach you by phone, she went to your house and found it empty. So she called the police and they searched for you. But after a few months they seemed to give up. We were at your house, and Grim Shivers turned up, pretending to be a book collector."

Tom laughed, waving his hand. "A book collector! He's inventive, I'll give him that. The spell I used to strand him was only supposed to be temporary; I knew nothing could contain him for the long term. And besides, he has his uses; he has a function here, no matter how distasteful. I just needed him gone from the Grimwytch for a time while I made amends for some of the injustices that have been meted out to our kind. I wonder how he found my house? Perhaps the book called to him. But anyway, please continue."

"So, I found the hidden room. I remembered it from before."

"How could you forget?" Tom gave her a sad smile. "I never meant for you to encounter the Grimwytch. At least, not at your age."

"Well, I had forgotten it, sort of. But when I came to the house it brought it all back. I found *The Book of Kindly Deaths* and began to read. I realized who Grim Shivers was, but before I could stop him, he tricked Dad into letting him into the house."

"And then he cast his sleeping dust over your parents," Tom finished.

"Will they be alright?"

"They will. But *we* won't be if we don't find a way out," Tom said. "We've been holed up here for ages. I liberated Augustus from the prison. He went on a little job to liberate a stolen mouth from a malefactrix. Unfortunately, we got caught. We were chased to this house and have been stuck here ever since."

"But what about the guild?" Eliza asked. "Can't they help?"

"Their guards are in the crowd right now, waiting for us. I've tried to reason with them, but they've made it clear we'll be arrested as soon as we set foot outside," Tom said.

"But you're a writer. Why would they arrest you?" Eliza watched in terror as the darkness swept towards the house like a tide, the crowd following close behind.

"I've committed several crimes. If you read the book, then you read of Robert Chandler...the boy whose mouth was stolen."

Eliza nodded. "It was the first story."

"That tale has always bothered me. The poor child should never have been written into the Grimwytch. James Maybury, the man who removed Robert's mouth, should have been forced to return it. The malefactrix should have been hunted down and forced to return what she'd taken, too. But instead, she got away and our forefather, for whatever reason, let the matter pass."

"But what does that have to do with anything?" Eliza asked, her heart thumping as she watched the crowd approaching in the darkness. "That was years ago!"

"There were two wrongs that I felt needed to be corrected," Tom said. "Augustus being the second. Yes, he stole the book, but to allow Grim Shivers to pass judgment on him was a monstrous error. One that was never resolved."

"So you came back to fix it?" Eliza asked.

"Yes, I did," Tom said. "After your mother refused my final plea to become my apprentice, I realized our family's work was over. So I decided to fix these loose ends before retiring to whatever fate awaits me."

Eliza pulled the tattered curtain aside. The darkness was almost at the door and now, through the crowd, she could see the guards who had stood before the Midnight Prison. "What will happen when they arrest us?"

Tom swallowed. "I don't know. When I first arrived at the Malady Inn, I heard of changes within the guild. Its chief justice, Lord Styxsturm, is said to have become a tyrant, the majority of his judgments resulting in execution. But I hope I can persuade the guild to be lenient."

"The darkness is here," Augustus cried. "What are we going to do?"

"Hand ourselves over to the guild," Tom said. "We can't fight them. There are too many."

CHAPTER TWENTY-SEVEN

The Ghoul Triumphant

"*N*o," Eliza said. "You can't just hand us over! What about Mum and Dad? What about me?"

She noticed the tremble in Tom's hand as he pointed at the window. "I've faced these creatures most of my adult life. But never like this, Eliza. I'd give anything for you not to be here. All we can do now is give ourselves over to the guild. At least they'll stop the crowd from devouring us."

"And then they'll lock us up? Even though I've done nothing wrong?" Anger blazed through Eliza. "This is your fault. You've let this happen. Instead of hiding in this house, you should have found a way out. You told me *bravery should always be rewarded*. Where's your bravery? And what about Mum and Dad? Anything could happen to them. No." Eliza pulled her cloak aside, unsheathing her blade. "I'm not going to let that happen."

The blade filled the air with its dark song.

"What's that?" Tom cried, stepping away and taking Augustus with him. "Where did you get it?"

"I found it," Eliza said. "And I killed a creature with it. And I know it terrifies them."

"You killed something *here* with that blade?" Tom shook his head, his face turning pale in the dim light.

The door shook as thumps and fists rained down upon it.

"You can't use that blade!" Tom yelled over the growing din. "It's darkling made. It's forbidden!"

The door juddered.

Eliza stepped towards the door, brandishing the dagger. "I'm not going to bury my head and hope this goes away, like you and Mum did."

She threw the door open.

A giant creature with two mouths squeezed into the house, a starved look in its malicious eyes. As Eliza swung the blade towards it, the creature howled, backing away and taking the crowd with it. Eliza followed, allowing the blade to sweep through the air. The tide of creatures stepped back, anger and frustration on their deformed, monstrous faces.

"How do we cross back to our world?" Eliza shouted to Tom.

There was no answer.

She turned.

Two armored guards held Tom and Augustus, their arms around their throats, their hands resting on the visors of their helmets.

The crowd kept a respectful, fearful distance, watching in silence.

"Run!" Tom cried as the guard holding him began to open its visor.

"I'm not leaving you!" Eliza held up a hand to the guard holding Tom. It stopped opening its visor, and as she lowered her blade and sheathed it, it took its hand down from its helmet. Eliza watched numbly as a guard stepped forward and squeezed her neck until there was only darkness.

Eliza woke to find herself in a comfortable chair in a brightly lit, book-filled room. Tom sat beside her, staring into a fire as

Augustus Pinch knelt on the floor, regarding Eliza with his vivid blue eyes.

"What happened?" Eliza asked.

"After they knocked you out," Augustus replied curtly, "they brought us to the guild."

Eliza looked around the room. The door in the corner was ajar. "The door's open; we can leave?"

Augustus shook his head. "They don't need to lock us in. There are two guards outside, and if we so much as set a foot beyond the door, it's all over. I'd rather go back to the Midnight Prison than see their faces."

"What do they look like?" Eliza asked. "Under those visors?"

"No one knows," Tom replied. "Because anybody who's seen them has gone mad and killed themselves in a most horrific way."

Eliza felt for her dagger. It was still in its sheath. "I have my dagger!"

Tom nodded. "I know. It's not good, Eliza."

"Why?"

"They've only allowed you to keep it so it can be used as evidence against you. I've broken several laws in writing Grim Shivers out of the Grimwytch and myself inside. But the law you've broken is much more severe than any of my crimes."

"Why?" Eliza asked, a twitch of panic building inside her.

"You journeyed to the Grimwytch without leave to enter," Tom said. "And then..." he sighed. "Then you spilled blood. It happens here almost every other moment and usually goes unpunished. But in your case, you're human."

"I had to!" Eliza said. "Those things were going to kill me!"

"I believe you," Tom said. "But you used a darkling blade. It's completely forbidden to use such a thing. Those weapons don't just take lives; they take phasmatis, as well. That is, the soul. There's nothing crueler."

Eliza flinched as she recalled the creature's agony and how the blade had forced itself ever deeper inside. "But I didn't know."

Augustus Pinch shook his head. "That won't matter to this lot. They don't like humans at the best of times."

"But they like you," Eliza said to Tom. "You work for them, don't you?"

"I did. But my work over the last few years has been... I've struggled. I was supposed to hand my duties on to your mother and...well, I'm not getting any younger. When she refused to take over, refused to even acknowledge that any of this existed, everything fell upon me. And I didn't cope very well. But I'm not blaming your mother, believe me. This is my personal failure." Tom sighed.

"So my mum *does* know about all of this," Eliza said.

"I told her when she was not much older than you. At first she thought I was making it up, so I showed her the Grimwytch. I opened the stained glass window, the window between worlds. I don't know what I expected from her, but it certainly wasn't the reaction I got. She took one look through the window and turned as white as a sheet. She fled from the study and from the house. I found her later, sitting at a bus stop, expressionless and silent. It took days to coax a word from her. When I tried to speak about the event, she shut down. She said she had no idea what I was talking about and wouldn't discuss the matter any further. I tried to engage with her over the years, tried to tell her how important her role was, but in the end she forbade me from ever seeing her or you again."

"What about my father?" Eliza asked. "Does he know?"

Tom shook his head. "I doubt it very much indeed. Your father was both polite and friendly, but I always got the impression he thought I was a bit soft in the head. Who knows what your mother told him. I don't blame her, though; fear does strange things to people. Still, it doesn't help our problems. My failure to do my job is coming home to roost now. I don't know how many breaches have been made between our worlds over the last few years. I dread to think…"

"Breaches?" Eliza asked.

"The places where the denizens of Grimwytch cross to our world. There are locations where the space between our worlds is narrow. So narrow that sometimes the Grimwytch can just step across. Other times, where the rift is less narrow, they need to be invited."

"Like the Wrong People?" Eliza asked.

"Yes, that was an unfortunate accident. However, there are people in our world who know perfectly well that the tales of monsters are not tales at all. That they're real. And a few have found ways to invite the peoples of Grimwytch over for their own selfish, sickening purposes."

"And you send them back," Eliza said.

"I try. As do the other writers. But it seems there are not enough of us. You see, when the guild first approached our family, hundreds of years ago, things were different. There were fewer creatures. Fewer humans, too. But as our population has grown, so has theirs."

"So they need you more than ever!" Eliza said. "They'll need both of us. I'll be your apprentice!"

Tom smiled. "If only, Eliza, if only. I don't know what's going to happen, and I pray they'll show mercy. But I'll be honest with you, as honesty is the one thing which has been wholly absent in our family of late—I'm frightened."

"Of what?" Eliza asked.

"Of the judge. I've heard dark things about Lord Styxsturm, how he's changed from being moderate to brutally merciless. It's Styxsturm who has the final say in our fates."

Eliza stood, removing the sheath around her waist. She was about to throw the blade upon the fire when the door swung open and Grim Shivers, last seen masquerading as Eustace Fallow, swept in, followed by two guards. All pretense at humanity was gone from the ghoul as he stood before her, long black robes covering most of the dark suit below. He tipped his top hat to Eliza, a humorless grimace on his pale, cadaverous face. "We have the body of the nightblind you killed. Its corpse is evidence enough; nonetheless, if you throw the darkling blade upon the fire, I shall make you retrieve it."

"What did you do to my parents?" Eliza asked as the blade in her hand lashed out, seemingly desperate to hack into the ghoul.

"Your parents are safe. Asleep. Asleep for a very long time," Grim Shivers replied. "Or they will be if I don't return to the house and cut their throats. Sheathe the blade and hand it to me."

Eliza stared at him, her eyes burning with hatred.

"Do as he asks, Eliza," Tom said as he stood, Augustus joining him.

Eliza swallowed, returning the blade to the sheath. She held it out, flinching as Grim Shivers snatched the blade and handed it to a guard.

"How did you get back to the Grimwytch?" Tom asked the ghoul.

"Through the window," Grim Shivers said, fixing Eliza with a look of contempt. "But I didn't find you on the other side. Where did you go, girl?"

"Don't answer," Tom said. "We don't have to answer any of his questions. You're not the judge, Grim Shivers."

"Maybe not," the ghoul conceded. "But we shall soon see how Lord Justice Styxsturm passes judgment. And after, I shall ask for time alone with you. For repayment."

"Repayment?" Tom shook his head.

"For writing me from my domain. For leaving me on an island. You wronged me, Mr. Drabe. There *will* be consequences. But now, it's time for justice. Follow me, and do not falter."

CHAPTER TWENTY-EIGHT

Styxsturm

*G*rim Shivers led them along a wide corridor lined with dark wooden panels and polished floorboards. Eliza found Tom's hand and gripped it. "We'll be all right. Won't we?"

"We won't be here within the hour," Augustus Pinch said. "At least, not in one piece. You should have left me in the prison, old man."

"I'm sorry," Tom said, his eyes welling. "Sorry to both of you. I've made a terrible mess. I'll tell Lord Styxsturm this is all my doing, I promise."

"For all the good it will do," Augustus muttered darkly.

Grim Shivers threw open a set of double doors and turned, blocking the room beyond. "You will be silent in this chamber. Not a word until it's asked of you."

He strode through, admitting them into an immense courtroom. Eliza gazed at the ceiling. Above the rafters, which looked like huge bleached bones, there was a colossal stained glass window. Moonlight filtered down to the cold, hard flagstones below. On the walls, the arched stained glass windows showed images of towers and palaces and pious-looking figures writing in huge books.

It reminded her of a church. A church for monsters.

Polished benches stretched before them; at the end, a desk towered upon a platform. Two guards stood to either side, their hands on the hilts of their swords and visors.

Grim Shivers led them along the aisle, motioning for them to sit on the bench facing the desk. Eliza glanced at Tom, but he shook his head. Beside him, Augustus Pinch stared down at his hobnailed shoes like a boy condemned.

A door at the side of the room burst open and a man bustled through.

He looked like a judge, wearing the same long black robes as Grim Shivers, with a white wig above his pale blue face. As he crossed the chamber his eyes found them, oversized and white with slits for pupils, an expression of mild disgust on his angular face.

Behind the man, two more figures followed.

Eliza recognized them at once. Mr. Bumbleton and Mrs. Sallow, who she'd dreamt of the night before.

Or was it the night before? The memory of reading *The Book of Kindly Deaths* in that comfortable bed seemed so distant now. As if from another life altogether.

Mrs. Sallow glanced at Tom with resignation, Augustus with disgust, and Eliza with a fleeting glimpse of curiosity.

The man with the blue face brought down a wooden gavel upon the bench. "We're gathered here today to pass sentence on the accused. As my time is limited and evidence has already been collected, I shall dispense with needless formalities. The accused stand guilty. The boy, *Master Pinch*, is hereby accused of theft from the home of a frail malefactrix. The penalty for which is hanging."

Mr. Bumbleton held up his hand. "Lord Styxsturm, I may be mistaken, but I thought the penalty for theft was incarceration?"

"It was," Lord Styxsturm replied, "but I've been busy these last few weeks rewriting the *old* laws. These changes will soon become apparent to you." Lord Styxsturm smiled, glancing at Tom. "The writer, Thomas Drabe, shall also be hanged, his crimes being treason to the Grimwytch, dereliction of duty, the kidnapping of the guardian Grim Shivers, and the breaching of the Midnight Prison. He has no doubt committed further crimes, but these are sufficient enough for him to hang."

"But my lord"—Mrs. Sallow held up her hand—"without the writer or his heir we will lose a valuable agent in the other world. This could have serious repercussions."

"I do not find it an issue," Lord Styxsturm said.

"But sir," Mrs. Sallow continued, "you, as Lord Justice, are a custodian for the guild, and therefore…"

"Do you wish to hang with them, Mrs. Sallow?" Lord Styxsturm asked.

Mrs. Sallow clamped a hand over her mouth.

"I thought not." Lord Styxsturm smiled. "As I have already explained, I have written *new* laws. They shall be served, and *anyone* who opposes them will be held in contempt of my Midnight Court."

Mr. Bumbleton looked as if he was about to ask something when he thought better of it, nodding briskly.

"And finally"—Lord Styxsturm pointed to Eliza—"we have Eliza Drabe, a girl who has shown complete and utter contempt for the laws of the Grimwytch. A girl who used a sacred book to transport herself into our realm and, while here, used a darkling blade to end the life of one of our citizens. This cruel and savage act will not result in hanging…"

Lord Styxsturm paused as he gave Eliza a cold, thin smile. "But instead, the darkling blade she used to commit murder will be used against her. And who better to carry out the severance of head from drearspawn neck than her grandfather?"

"I won't do it. This is an outrage!" As Tom stepped towards the platform, the guards turned towards him, drawing their swords. Tom stopped. "This is madness. The guild must overrule this. When I entered into contract with you these laws were never—"

Lord Styxsturm brought his gavel down with such force that Tom flinched. "Silence, writer. I'm tired of your words. As you can see, Mrs. Sallow and Mr. Bumbleton have held their tongues. Wisely. Which means there's nothing more to be said. And if you won't execute the girl, then I shall pass the honor to Grim Shivers. Would that please you?" he asked the ghoul.

Grim Shivers stood, turning to regard Eliza with a look of delight. "More than words can describe."

Eliza shrank away, but he snatched her by the hair, dragging her to her feet and pulling the blade from its sheath, its song buzzing in her ears.

Eliza tried to writhe free, but the ghoul held her firm.

As Augustus attempted to flee, a guard seized him, another holding the blade of its sword against Tom's neck.

There was no escape. Grim Shivers threw Eliza to the floor. Her head cracked against the cold, hard flagstones, and as she fought to right herself, she found the tip of the blade at her throat. She lay still, her heart pounding, her body shaking. "Please!" she cried. "Please, stop."

She glanced at the hem of Grim Shivers's robes, and the carpet below with its elaborate weaves of gold and red. "I shouldn't be here," Eliza said. "I don't belong here. I'm only twelve!"

She watched as Grim Shivers lifted the blade, gazing dumbly at its sharply honed edge.

Behind the ghoul, Tom sobbed, fighting to free himself, a gloved hand clamped over his mouth.

Eliza shut her eyes and waited.

CHAPTER TWENTY-NINE

Of Beast and Arrow

*A*n almighty explosion filled the chamber, and stained glass fell like a shower of colored rain.

A hooded figure soared down, a rope tied around its ankle.

The guards and Grim Shivers rushed towards it. Eliza stood, watching numbly as the figure hacked the end of the rope, falling and rolling across the floor, leaping up, an arrow nocked to its bow.

The guards stopped.

Everything stopped.

Eliza followed the path of the arrow. It was trained squarely at Lord Styxsturm.

And then the figure stepped closer to the platform. "Tell the guards to drop their weapons."

"Shard?" Eliza whispered.

"Stand down. And drop your swords." Lord Styxsturm nodded to the guards. "For now."

There was a clatter of steel on stone.

"What do you want?" Lord Styxsturm asked. "Are you here to free the condemned? I hope you realize the punishment for this outrage will be the severest this kingdom has seen."

"*You* are the condemned. I've come to execute you," Shard said, for now Eliza could see his face as he glanced towards her. "And to free my friend. Wyrd is with us once again, Eliza Winter."

"And why do you wish to execute me?" Lord Styxsturm asked. If he was afraid, he masked it well. "We've never met, *boy*."

"True," Shard replied. "And yet your hand set my world on its head and left it a black and hollow place." Shard stepped closer to Lord Styxsturm. "I was out hunting the day you entered my house and slaughtered my family, making me the last of the line. And by blood oath, I'm here to end *your* line."

Lord Styxsturm shook his head. "You're mistaken. I'm a supreme ward of the guild, not a common assassin. I haven't left these chambers for months. And I'd say your family's demise was a recent one by the tears gleaming in your eyes."

"It's true," Mrs. Sallow said. "Lord Styxsturm hasn't left this court for many, many weeks. This is a case of mistaken identity."

"Lord Styxsturm, is it?" Shard asked. "Well, I'm sure *Lord Styxsturm* hasn't left this place for weeks. But whoever Lord Styxsturm was, this isn't him."

"This is madness," Mr. Bumbleton said. "Utter madness."

"Is it?" Shard asked. "I see by your badges of office you're members of the Midnight Guild. So you should know what a shapecaster is. But in case you don't, a shapecaster is a creature that mimics the form of its last victim. In this case, Lord Styxsturm."

Lord Styxsturm shook his head. "The boy is grieving. And while I shall show him some mercy, delusional or not, he will need to hang."

"And," Shard continued, "previous to this incarnation, he wore my father's likeness as he travelled to the city. Can you imagine how I felt when I heard my slain father had been seen walking the city's streets? But your arrogance is your undoing. As was the theft of my father's locket, for it has a twin, which I wear. He gave me it when I was a child, so I could always find him. They call to each other."

Lord Styxsturm's hand strayed beneath his robe as he pulled out a necklace, holding it up. "This trinket was given to me by an admirer."

"No," Shard replied, "it was not. When you heard of my survival, you sent two assassins. The first I bested. The second, a darkwight, was foiled by my friend here, Eliza Winter. *Wyrd* once again. But not for you, shapecaster."

"Put down your toy," Lord Styxsturm said, but now Eliza could hear a flicker of fear in his voice.

"I will, but not before I kill you," Shard replied. "Tell me why you did it. Tell me why you murdered my family."

Lord Styxsturm shook his head. "There are machinations at play which, even if I tried to explain, you could never fathom." He glanced to Mr. Bumbleton and Mrs. Sallow. "None of you. But mark my words when I say there's a storm coming to the Grimwytch. One that will sweep you all away."

"But that's not an answer," Shard said, his fingers tensing on his bowstring. "So, once again, why did you kill my family?"

"And once again," the shapecaster cried, his voice quivering with rage, "I shall tell you nothing."

"Well, in that case, you have no further reason to live. These arrows are tipped with iron, as I know exactly how much torment iron causes your kind. Yet your pain will be little more than a splinter's worth compared to the agony you've brought me."

Before the shapecaster could reply, Shard released the arrow. It thudded into the monster's chest, causing it to stagger. It clutched the arrow as a terrible sizzling sound issued from its body. It flailed and gnashed its teeth, and a stench of burning flesh filled the chamber. It forced its gaping mouth into a malign grin. Its hide seemed to ripple, as if something below fought to be free. Eliza looked away as the creature's face began to tear apart

A terrible roar caused Eliza to look back. A towering creature stood in the place Lord Styxsturm had occupied. It was immense and covered with putrid-green flesh. Clawed hands reached from gangly limbs as it turned its long, horned head and stared at Shard through three spite-filled eyes. It opened its mouth to reveal two sets of spike-like teeth before roaring once more as two wings sprouted from its back, their unfurling clearly causing the shapecaster fresh agony.

It took off, soaring into the air, sweeping towards the hole in the ceiling.

Shard loosed another arrow. It pierced the creature's arm, bringing a new wail of pain.

And then the creature was gone.

CHAPTER THIRTY

Flight

*E*liza followed Shard as he pulled his bow across his shoulder and ran.

"Eliza!" Tom stumbled after her as Mrs. Sallow commanded the guards to stand down.

"I have to help Shard," Eliza called to Tom.

He'd saved her again. She couldn't let him face the shapecaster alone.

They ran from the hall.

"Where are we going?" Eliza shouted.

"To the aranachiros in the courtyard. If he gets away now, I'll never find him. Go back to your grandfather, Eliza," Shard said as he flew through the doors.

Eliza followed him. "No. I'm going to help you!"

Shard was silent as they ran into the night.

Eliza found herself in a large courtyard with stables at the far end. By the time the guards saw them, Shard had already untethered one of the aranachiros.

Eliza flinched as it turned its huge, furry round head and regarded her with six beady black eyes. "It's harmless!" Shard shouted as he climbed upon its saddle. Eliza took his hand and hiked up her skirt with one hand, swinging up behind him into the large saddle and trying her best to accept the horrific appearance of the creature below. That became almost impossible as her bare ankles brushed against its fuzzy fur. Eliza shivered.

"There!" Shard pointed. Eliza followed his finger to the distant speck of the shapecaster as it climbed into the sky.

He kicked his feet against the aranachiros; it howled and cantered across the courtyard, sending the pursuing guards scattering for cover.

It beat its wings and they were off, rising into the sky. Eliza looked back at the receding buildings, gripping Shard as tightly as she could.

"It's seen us!" Shard yelled, the air snatching his words.

The shapecaster hovered above them, treading the air, before sweeping down, its talons outstretched as it threw back its head and screamed. Shard unsheathed his sword, passing it back to Eliza. "Take this and strike when I say!"

The shapecaster was mere feet away when Shard yanked the reins, sending the aranachiros dipping down. "Now!" he cried.

Eliza swung the sword through the air as the shapecaster shot over their heads. The tip of the blade caught the creature's chest with such force it was almost wrenched from her hands. The shapecaster fell away, issuing a desolate howl.

It wheeled back towards them, its claws raking into the side of their aranachiros, and shot past, turning and rising back into the air.

The aranachiros let out a hideous squeal, rocking so hard that Shard and Eliza were nearly sent tumbling through the air. Shard leaned closer to the aranachiros. "Climb!" he yelled to the creature. It obeyed, taking them soaring into the sky.

Eliza looked down at the city lights, so far away now. She winced as the aranachiros howled, the force of its wings beating the air as it took them ever higher.

"The shapecaster's injured!" Shard cried. "But so is our steed. Look, it's making for the tower."

Eliza looked over his shoulder. They were close enough to the tower that she could see the silhouettes of its inhabitants. They watched from their windows, a din of cries and shouts rising from the prison as Eliza and Shard flew past, climbing up into the night.

And then the shapecaster flew over the tower's roof, vanishing.

As they coasted over the top of the tower, Shard snatched the reins, sending the aranachiros flying down. It landed heavily upon the roof, its breath labored as it slumped to a halt. Shard leaped off, throwing back his hood, his hair rippling around the two horns on his head like hissing serpents. He nocked an arrow in his bow.

The roof was empty.

"Where's it gone?" Eliza's heart thumped wildly as she glanced up at the moon. It was so much closer now.

Just like in her dream.

The wind battered her clothes and whistled in her ears as Shard shouted, "I don't know." Eliza followed him across the roof, searching for the creature as, far below, the sea glimmered like a sheet of black metal.

And then the shapecaster appeared, vaulting onto the roof and pirouetting through the air. Eliza screamed, too late as the creature smashed into Shard, slamming him down. It raised its claws, drops of liquid falling from their tips, smoke rising from the stone where they fell.

Eliza hefted up Shard's sword and swung it as hard as she could, the blade lopping off the monster's hand. It yelped, leaping off Shard, leaving him lying lifeless and still as it stalked towards Eliza, cradling its bleeding stump. Eliza backed away, the sword limp in her hand, hypnotized by the sight of the horror bearing down upon her. She was alone now. Utterly alone.

Just her and the beast.

"Cut, slash, tear the drearspawn," the shapecaster hissed as it threw back its head. "And when I'm done I'll cast your remains to the wind."

Eliza held out the sword. "Get back."

The shapecaster laughed. "*You* get back. Tumble over the roof. It will hurt less than what I'm going to do." It licked its lips. "My, your terror looks so exquisite. You won't touch me with that sword, *drearspawn*. No, you'll drop it and fall weeping to your knees and beg for mercy."

Eliza shook her head. "I won't beg you for anything." She fixed the vile creature with an even stare. "I've already taken a life tonight."

"It was not y*ou* who used the darkling blade. The blade used you. You're a weak, pathetic little girl, grown soft and useless in your sheltered world. Oh, but to pile up all you little writers on a great pyre."

"Why?" Eliza asked. "What have we done to you?"

"Interfered with *my* kind. Dared to tell us where we can and cannot go. But that's going to change. I said a storm is coming, and it is. And when it hits, the Grimwytch will overrun your realm." The shapecaster smiled. "And the best part is your kind assisted me in sowing the seeds of their own destruction"

"I don't believe you. Why would anyone help a monster like you?"

"Greed. Lust for power. The only true desires your kind know. Both will be sated, but at a price. We're growing tired of our kingdom, girl. It's time to find another. Yours."

"And you think *my kind* will just stand around and let you? You think they won't notice you clomping around?" Eliza laughed, her voice shaking. "You'll be shot dead before you know what's hit you."

The shapecaster nodded. "Maybe. But I am but one head on a beast of such magnitude that you couldn't even fathom its immensity. But none of this concerns you, little writer. For you're not going to live to see your revolting kind wiped away. You're not going to live to see anything. Take one last breath, little girl, and savor it."

The shapecaster loped towards her, arms outstretched, claws flexed, beads of venom dripping as it came.

Eliza gripped the sword with both hands and swallowed, taking a step towards the creature.

It matched her, stepping closer still.

I can't do this, she thought, her hands trembling as she looked at the sword in her hand, remembering the nightblind's hideous howl of agony.

"You have no appetite for murder," the shapecaster said. "It's not in your blood."

Eliza looked to Shard's lifeless body and back to the creature's mocking, vicious grin. "I told you to leave me alone!" Eliza swung the sword in a circle of steel. As it wheeled towards the shapecaster she lunged forward, thrusting it into the beast's chest, closing her eyes against the sight of its agony.

It screamed. Eliza held still, her eyes clamped shut. The sword jolted in her hand as the beast slumped against the roof. Only when the scream became a gurgle and then a dying gasp did Eliza look down.

The shapecaster stared blankly, eyes wide, its head lolling as its blood, black as night and thick as oil, poured from its chest.

Eliza glanced away to the pommel of the sword—Shard's family crest. She wrenched the sword free and ran to where he lay.

Voices rang from behind as Mrs. Sallow and a handful of guards landed their aranachiros on the rooftop. Eliza turned away, placing a hand over Shard's mouth, desperate to feel his breath and know he was alive.

But if he still drew breath, any sign of it was snatched away by the wind.

CHAPTER THIRTY-ONE

The Deal

The moment her aranachiros landed on the ground before the Midnight Court, Eliza ran to the winged beast that carried Shard's slumped body. Mrs. Sallow ordered the guards to take him to the hall.

"Will he be alright?" Eliza demanded.

"The shapecaster has a venom in its claws that renders its victims unconscious. It's the same venom used to create sleep dust," Mrs. Sallow said.

"The same sleep dust your ghoul used on my parents?"

"Grim Shivers is very much his own *ghoul*, Miss Winter," Mrs. Sallow said as they walked to the hall. "Now, did the shapecaster tell you anything?"

"Yes," Eliza began to reply and then stopped. "I want to see my grandfather first, before I tell you anything."

Mrs. Sallow sighed. "Very well."

Tom sat in the chamber beside Augustus, the guards and Grim Shivers mercifully gone. As soon as Tom saw Eliza, he jumped up. "Are you hurt?"

Eliza shook her head. "I killed it." She swallowed. "That's the second thing I've killed tonight. Two things that were alive before I came to this horrible place."

Tom gave her a sad smile. "It's what we do, Eliza, if we must. But you didn't invite that. You defended yourself. Do you understand?"

Eliza understood. But it didn't make her feel any better.

"Is your friend okay?" Tom asked.

Eliza watched as the guards laid Shard out on a bench. "Mrs. Sallow said the shapecaster's venom put him to sleep. That it's the same stuff Grim Shivers used on my parents."

Tom nodded. "It is. And they will wake. All of them. It's over, Eliza. We can go home."

Someone coughed behind them.

Eliza glanced past her grandfather to Mr. Bumbleton. As he watched them, he offered a faultlessly hollow smile. "I hear you've slain the beast." He extended his hand.

Eliza thrust her hands into her pockets. "You were going to let the *beast* slay us, Mr. Bumbleton. Weren't you?"

A flush of red colored Mr. Bumbleton's pale face as he stuttered. "And what would you have had me do, girl? Why would I endanger myself to save a..."

"Human? Was that what you were going to say?" Eliza asked. "Or were you going to call me a *drearspawn?*"

"Listen to me," Mr. Bumbleton said. "Slaying those who have wronged our worlds is *your* job. Not mine."

"It's not my job," Eliza replied. "I don't have a job. I'm twelve years old."

Eliza flinched as a hand rested on her shoulder. Shard gazed at her. He looked ill, his green eyes dim now. "I owe you my life, Eliza. Once again."

"No, you don't. But if you're keeping a tally, I think we're about even. Are you okay?"

"I feel as if someone has filled my blood with liquid fire. But aside from that, I'm fine. So, you killed it?"

"I used your sword. So, in a sense, *you* killed it," Eliza replied.

Shard smiled. "Thank you, Eliza Winter."

"All very touching," Mrs. Sallow said as she joined them. "But now we need to know what the shapecaster told you before it was slain."

"What will happen to us?" Eliza asked. "Me, Tom, and Shard?"

"*You've* been pardoned. Shard, as he has chosen to call himself, will be sentenced at a later date."

"For what?" Eliza demanded.

Mrs. Sallow gestured to the roof. "He's defiled the Midnight Court. Do you know how old that window…"

"What would you have had me do?" Shard asked. "Knock on the door and ask your guards to let me in? Styxsturm was going to kill all of you—you *do* realize that, don't you? He might have started with Eliza and her grandfather and me, but you would have been next."

"Pardon Shard, and I'll tell you what he said," Eliza replied. "And while you're at it, pardon Augustus as well. He was only trying to help my grandfather."

"I should never have been locked up in the first place," added Augustus.

"You stole a *Book of Kindly Deaths*, Master Pinch. And never was a name more fitting!" piped Mr. Bumbleton.

"If I'd known what the book was and where it would take me," Augustus said, "I'd have left it well alone."

"If you return to your world, you'll die," Mr. Bumbleton said. "While you haven't aged in our realm, you will in the other. Is that how you would go?"

Augustus shook his head. "No. But if I have to stay here, then I want to be free. No hassles from Shivers, either. Free to come and go as I please."

"You're asking me to allow this miscreant to wander our streets?" Mrs. Sallow asked Eliza.

"Yes, I am. Let's face it," Eliza said, "far worse things than him roam your streets."

Mrs. Sallow nodded briskly. "Agreed. Just tell me what the shapecaster said."

Eliza sighed. "It said my kind have sown the seeds of our own destruction. That there are people in my world who have helped it. And that it didn't matter if it died as it was just a single head on a giant beast. It said it regretted that I wouldn't live to see the coming storm."

"Working with your kind?" Mrs. Sallow said. "Then there *are* people in your realm conspiring against us."

"That's always been the case," Tom replied. "There have always been those who have sought to bring the denizens of Grimwytch over as slaves."

"But this sounds bigger than a single event," Mrs. Sallow said. "It sounds...bad."

"It does," Tom agreed.

"You're not getting any younger," Mrs. Sallow told Tom. "And you've made some abysmal decisions of late." She looked at Eliza. "We need young blood."

"Not Eliza," Tom said, shaking his head. "She's just..."

But Eliza held out her hand. "I've killed two monsters tonight, Granddad. And I'll kill more if I have to. If they're coming into our world, then we have to stop them. How can I sleep at night knowing what's out there?"

"And you're not alone," Shard added. "I'll help you."

"He can't go to your realm!" Mr. Bumbleton's face turned bright purple. "The very idea!"

"He can if you let him," Eliza said. "And he knows his prey better than I do."

"It's ridiculous," Mr. Bumbleton said, shaking his head as he repeated, "The very idea!"

"It's not ridiculous," Mrs. Sallow said. "It makes sense. And given how grave this news is, we shall need every resource we can find. Very well. The boy travels to and fro unhindered."

Shard nodded. "I will do all I can to right this. The shapecaster murdered my family for a reason, and helping Eliza and her grandfather may help me find out just what it was."

"So, now that's settled," Eliza said, "how do we get back and wake my parents up?"

CHAPTER THIRTY-TWO

Through the Window

*M*r. Bumbleton handed Eliza a vial filled with smoke. "Hold this under your parents' noses. It's concentrated essence of cheesedung fly, easily one of the most revolting scents in the Grimwytch. It could wake a corpse."

"You can use the window to return to your world, Miss Winter," Mrs. Sallow said. "But out of interest, where did you cross into the Grimwytch?"

Tom smiled. "We all need a secret or two, Mrs. Sallow."

Mrs. Sallow gave him a withering look. "You need to report to me daily. We shall use the window. Now, how are we going to find out who is behind this *coming storm*?"

"I shall use the map to find breaches, as usual," Tom said. "But this time I'll look for patterns."

"Higher incidents of breaches?" Mr. Bumbleton asked.

"No. Quite the opposite," Tom said. "Whoever's working with my kind is likely to be acting alone, or at least in a small group. They will not want attention. That's how I shall begin to conduct my search. It will mean a lot of travel. So I can't update you daily, but I will update you as often as I can. You have my word."

"And the girl and her friend will assist you," Mrs. Sallow added.

Tom shrugged. "We'll see. First we have to speak with Eliza's mother, and if you think the shapecaster was a menace…"

"She'll listen to me this time," Eliza said. "I'm going to make sure of it."

Mrs. Sallow nodded briskly and escorted them to the courtyard.

Five aranachiros awaited them, each mounted by a guard.

One by one they climbed upon the saddles, Eliza wrapping her arms around the guard's chest as their aranachiros took off, sweeping into the air.

As they soared over the Midnight City, Eliza peered down at the higgledy-piggledy buildings, crooked houses, pale white palaces, and the great black towers dividing them. It was a terrifying place, for sure, but one she felt curiously attached to.

And then the aranachiros landed before a lavish white building that Eliza recognized from her dream.

The Midnight Guild.

They hurried past the guards, Mrs. Sallow leading.

As they entered the small room with the slug and the stained glass window, they found Mr. Bumbleton standing before it, inscribing patterns in the air. A guard brought a small ladder into the room, setting it before the window, which opened as Mr. Bumbleton lowered his hand.

"What's it like?" Shard asked with a hint of nervousness. "In your world?"

Eliza thought for a moment. "It's different. Very different. There's a sun, which lights everything each day, and a moon at night. You're probably going to find that strange. And people don't dress in cloaks. Or carry swords, or bows and arrows. So we're going to have to sort that out."

Shard nodded, feigning nonchalance as Eliza hid her smile.

They climbed the ladder, Tom leading. As he clambered through the window, he offered Eliza his hand. She took it and climbed back into her world and onto the desk, leaving space for Shard.

It seemed strange to be back in the house again. To look back at a room she'd once seen in a dream.

Eliza took a deep breath, recoiling. The air seemed heavy, dirty, and laced with the scent of chemicals. It smelt old, stale, and almost heavy, as if weighted down with pollutants.

Shard wrinkled his nose, coughing as he gazed at the light on the ceiling. "This is the sun?"

Eliza laughed. "No, it's a light. There's a lot I'm going to have to explain to you. Maybe electricity should be a priority." She leaped from the desk, clutching the vial Mr. Bumbleton had given her.

The door to the hidden room was ajar, no doubt left open by Grim Shivers. She hurried through, Shard and Tom close behind.

The study was a mess, books strewn across the floor. Eliza stepped over them and out into the hall. She ran down the stairs and into the kitchen, where she found her parents still slumped across the table. Tom looked down at them with a wistful expression. "It's the first time I've seen your mother in six years. And your dad. They look well. Older, and maybe your father is a little pudgier…" He stopped, wiping away a tear from his cheek.

Shard looked around the kitchen, clearly uncomfortable as he held a hand over his eyes. "It's so bright," he mumbled.

Eliza uncapped the vial, recoiling from its stench of overripe cheese, rotting fish, and cow dung. She held the vial beneath her mother's nose first, watching as its black vapors snaked through the air.

And then her mother began to choke, her eyes wide with horror.

"It's okay, Mum," Eliza said. "Sit, while I wake Dad up."

She rushed to her father, holding the vial beneath his nose before the last of the vapors could escape.

Her dad flinched, blearily rising from table. "What the hell is that you've got, Eliza?" He stopped as he looked from Tom to Shard. "Oh."

"Dad?" Eliza's mum glanced uncertainly at Tom. "You're alive?"

Tom nodded. "I am. And may I say, seeing you is quite a tonic after all these years."

Eliza's mum stood, swaying as she crossed the kitchen and wrapped her arms around Tom. They held each other for a moment, until Eliza's mum's memory seemed to return and she pulled away. As she glanced at Shard, she swore, her eyes traveling from his face to the bow at his shoulder and the sword by his side.

"It's okay, Mum," Eliza said. "This is my friend, Shard, and he saved my life. And in a way, he saved yours, too. Now, I'm going to put the kettle on and we're all going to sit down, and then…then I'm going to tell you a story."

THE END

THE END

Acknowledgements

*T*here are so many people who have guided and helped me with this book, and I am eternally grateful to one and all.

I would especially like to thank Laurie McLean for not only finding this book a wonderful home, but for also being a true agent savant. As well as a constant source of optimism and energy.

I would also like to give a huge thank-you to everyone at Spencer Hill Press, with a special mention to Trish, Owen, and Rich "the Closer". You've all been immensely helpful in blowing the cobwebs away and providing shine to this book. It's been a pleasure working with you.

To Hanna, the wise and magical Mary Poppins of editing and writer's mentor extraordinaire.

I'm also exceptionally grateful to Lisa Amowitz for her amazing cover and for her almost superhuman powers in getting it so right in such short time. Thanks also to Steve and Neil for various feats of graphical magic and endless distractions of lunacy and amusement.

To Mum for your support, belief, and patience and for pushing me ever on. Aunty Strange, I thank you for your eagle-eyes and ever-ready editing-wand—I shall pay you back one day with a chin cast in solid gold. To Nanna, much love, wherever you are astrally traveling through space and time.

Finally, a huge thank-you to my wife Lora for eight years of support, patience, editing, even more patience, and for making those little black Books of Kindly Deaths, xo.

About the Author

*E*ldritch Black is a writer of tales of dark fantasy and dread. Originally from London, England, Eldritch has since moved to a small island in the Pacific Northwest of the United States. He now lives in the middle of a forest where he collects shadows, converses with crows, and documents the creatures that crawl from the trees and slither in the undergrowth. When he isn't writing stories of magical eeriness, Eldritch likes long walks on the beach in the rain at midnight, communing with cats and ghosts and the ghosts of cats, all things autumnal, photographing dreams, and attempting to play the Theremin.

*Y*ou can find out more at eldritchblack.com

CPSIA information can be obtained at www.ICGtesting.com
Printed in the USA
LVOW04s0258240814

400624LV00002B/2/P